"*Apocalypse Baby* is more than a compelling ～～～, ～ ～ n spin on the noir genre. It is a choral performance that tumbles its readers into the heart of violent spectacle, with all its attendant grief, unease, and unclarity."

—Maggie Nelson, author of *The Argonauts*

"Powerful and empowered." —*Kirkus*

"An addictive feminist thriller that reads like shameless gossip from your smartest friend."

—Johanna Fateman, writer and musician

Praise for *King Kong Theory*
by Virginie Despentes

"*King Kong Theory* is essential reading!"

—Dorothy Allison, author of *Bastard Out of California*

"Despentes argues compellingly about women's guilt, men's power, and the way that both are still abused three decades after the supposed triumph of feminism."

—Katy Guest, *Independent*

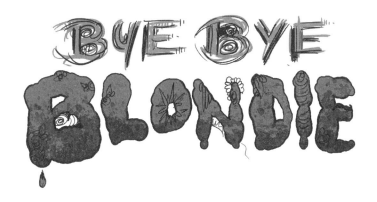

BYE BYE BLONDIE

VIRGINIE DESPENTES

TRANSLATED BY SIÂN REYNOLDS

THE FEMINIST PRESS
AT THE CITY UNIVERSITY OF NEW YORK
FEMINISTPRESS.ORG

Published in 2016 by the Feminist Press
at the City University of New York
The Graduate Center
365 Fifth Avenue, Suite 5406
New York, NY 10016
feministpress.org

First Feminist Press edition 2016

Text copyright © 2004 Éditions Grasset & Fasquelle
Translation copyright © 2016 by Siân Reynolds

Originally published in French as *Bye Bye Blondie* by Éditions Grasset & Fasquelle
in 2004.

 This book is supported in part by an award from the National
ART WORKS. Endowment for the Arts.

 This book was made possible thanks to a grant from New York State
Council on the Arts with the support of Governor Andrew Cuomo
NYSCA and the New York State Legislature.

First printing July 2016

Cover design by Molly Crabapple
Text design by Suki Boynton

Library of Congress Cataloging-in-Publication Data
Names: Despentes, Virginie, 1969- author. | Reynolds, Sian, translator.
Title: Bye bye blondie / Virginie Despentes ; English translation by Sian
    Reynolds.
Other titles: Bye bye blondie. English
Description: First Feminist Press edition. | New York : Feminist Press at the
    City University of New York, 2016.
Identifiers: LCCN 2015046360 | ISBN 9781558619272 (pbk.)
Subjects: LCSH: Man-woman relationships--Fiction. | GSAFD: Love stories
Classification: LCC PQ2664.E7895 B3913 2016 | DDC 843/.914--dc23
LC record available at http://lccn.loc.gov/2015046360

For Philippe and Manon

*Mental asylums are receptacles for black magic,
conscious and premeditated.*

Aliénation et magie noire, Antonin Artaud

SHE'S REALLY LOSING IT. IT'S NOT GETTING better, not even staying the same. She'd been sure, from experience, that every time she got too near the brink, she'd be able to swerve away. But this time, she's out of control: *Look, no hands.* All the warning lights are flashing in vain, and she senses that people are alarmed—they're actually moving out of the way when they see her coming. She's just had a fight with her boyfriend. She could have killed him. It came that close: a centimeter, a second! She'd diced with tragedy. What if he'd been just a bit slower and clumsier? And like after every explosion, she is particularly calm, lucid, and ashamed.

Gloria takes great strides up the rue Saint-Jean, under a pelting shower of rain. Soaked through, she feels stupid, grubby, and above all, back on the streets. She'd moved in with him, but something tells her that after the scene she's just made, she is—temporarily—homeless. She makes a mental list of the apartments of people she knows. Most of them have children, and no room anymore to put someone up. In the fight just now, she'd hurled her phone against the wall. When for once she had a bit of money left on it. She would've liked to call Véronique, the one person who might help her out for the next few days, but now she doesn't have her number, or even a euro left to call her with

. . . and anyway, at this time of day, she'll be at work. Gloria doesn't have a cent in her pocket. She decides to walk on up to the Royal, i.e., up by the railway station, i.e., at the other end of town. How often had she complained that Lucas lived too far away from her favorite bar?

Even when the sun's shining, the city of Nancy isn't a cheerful place, not in her eyes anyway. So in the rain, it stretches out in shades of gray and looks underwater, drenched, so depressing it becomes borderline interesting. A town in eastern France, low clouds, low buildings, just two floors, some of them with rather fine architecture, but you can't help but be aware that they don't belong to doctors. Because of the rain, the homeless and the young punks with dogs have taken shelter in the Saint Sébastien mall. Passersby are walking close to the shop windows, to protect themselves a little. Trolleybuses clang their bells, not unpleasant to the ear. Her route is lined with logos that could be found anywhere in Europe: Foot Locker, Pimkie, H&M, The Body Shop. The window displays are ugly, too brightly lit, clinical. Never anything odd, original, or surprising. The whole length of the street now, there isn't a single window that breaks the monotony—no room for that in modern-day towns. Morbid and frozen, it's like walking through a morgue decorated with bright colors.

The rain trickles down Gloria's back, dripping coldly to her waist. She feels inside her pockets, checking that she's got her ID papers. She's sobbing openly as she walks, making no attempt to be discreet. Too bad for the people who see her and look sympathetic or scornful, anxious or disapproving. What the fuck does she care about the reactions of people she doesn't know?

For a few years now, since things have gone downhill, she has often wept in the street, and she thinks she's noticed that other people get some kind of kick out of that. They come up to her at once, saying something, consoling her, wanting to talk. She'd like to be struck by lightning, but her number-one fantasy is that someone puts a bullet through the back of her neck, finishing her off like an animal.

On the rue Léopold Lallement, she looks at the posters outside the cinema. Even if she had any money on her, and even if a show was just starting, none of the advertised films would tempt her inside. One ad for a Japanese animation holds her attention: the globe suspended in blackness. She wonders if it's just for little kids or for everyone. She turns her head one last time, then crosses at the light without paying attention. A car screeches to a halt, just missing her. It had come up silently—shiny black bodywork—even if you know nothing about cars, you can't miss that this one's top of the line. Gloria stops dead, in the middle of the road. She's completely in the wrong. Well, so damn what? Anyone in that car want a fight? Here it comes again, same as ever, she's pumped up with rage. And she's well aware that not only is she being super tiresome, but her attitude is stupid. Whether you look at it from an ethical, pragmatic, or logical point of view, this urge to take on the rest of the world will never come to any good—on the contrary, it'll bring her nothing but grief. But as usual, knowing that doesn't change her reaction. Like junkies who know perfectly well they shouldn't do drugs, but carry on, day after day, Gloria is addicted to pointless anger. Hour after hour, she's burying herself in it.

So there she stands, in the middle of the pedestrian crossing, with the rain beating down on her head, as if heaven incarnate were trying to make her see reason. The lights change to green again, she stays where she is for a few seconds, staring in the direction of the driver. She can't see his features, given the veil of water between them. She contents herself with pulling a mean face. Jutting out her jaw, she swallows hard—her eyes are like molten lead. *If someone gets out of the car now, please God, let him be big enough to defend himself.* In the end, someone does get out, but from the backseat. She's drawing herself up, ready to call him everything under the sun, but the guy shouts, "Gloria!" which rather undercuts the adrenaline rush. Very tall, classy overcoat, automatically she glances at his shoes and can see at once they cost a lot. He's clean-shaven, with *very* white teeth.

"Gloria, is that you? I can't believe it, it *is* you!"

She stands transfixed, openmouthed, in a stupor. She clears her throat, says nothing, tries to smile. He takes her in his arms, she hasn't time to back off.

"How weird is this! Don't you recognize me? Get in, I'll drop you off. Where are you going?"

He's left the back door of the car ajar, other cars are waiting for him to get out of the way. She hears herself say feebly, "Eric? You've changed, oh, wow! A lot. But you don't look like you do on TV either . . ."

At the time, she is too surprised to realize what she's said. It's when she remembers it just afterward that she discovers what an utterly cringeworthy remark that was.

He insists: "Can I drop you somewhere?"

She points vaguely at the sky behind her, as if it were a precise place, and refuses.

"No, I'm nearly there, it's just here."

"What about a coffee, have you got time?"

"No. No, I'm, um, double-booked."

The guy at the wheel shuts the back door of the car and pulls over to the side of the road, parking a few meters away. Eric gazes at her intensely. Even soaked to the skin, he looks fantastic.

"Incredible isn't it, bumping into each other?"

"Oh, this isn't Paris, you know. We're all on top of each other here."

"You're joking? I *never* come back to Nancy, and no sooner do I arrive than . . . I'm here for work, we're recording a show for a few days. And I was thinking about you, wondering if we'd see each other. But, well, you don't look . . . um . . ."

He shakes his head from side to side, making a comical face, to indicate that she doesn't look in great form. She puts him right.

"Ah no, I'm not exactly top of my game right now, but these days, I'm always like this."

"Red in the face and soaking wet?"

"Yeah, you know, in the *provinces*, we never leave the house unless we're red in the face and soaking wet."

He bursts out laughing. He looks like a guy in fantastically good shape. Such good humor and health on display always makes Gloria want to throw up. Bubbling, and quite at ease, he insists: "Look, let's meet up tonight, I'll be free around ten. We could—"

"Oh, I'm a simple girl, I'll be at the Royal. Tonight, tomorrow, night after that, I'm at the Royal. It's my bar."

"Got the address?"

"You're getting really wet, aren't you?" remarks Gloria in

amusement, watching as he pulls out an electronic organizer from a pocket of the impeccable suit he's wearing under the fancy overcoat. He agrees.

"Yeah, that's what happens if it's raining. We could have been sitting inside the car to say all this, but you see, I haven't forgotten you. If you want to stand talking in the pouring rain, I'm not going to argue."

"Oh, put your electronic gadget away, you poor lost Parisian, and the little matchstick too. It's easy to find the Royal, rue Mondésert, by the station. Ask anyone, it's been there twenty years, everyone knows it."

"Tonight then?"

"Like I said, I'll be there."

He hesitates before leaving, tries to think of the right move, finally chances it, and grips her arm quickly and firmly. Then he runs to the car and gets in the back. It moves off, and Gloria carries on, cursing herself.

"Why didn't you punch him in the jaw, for God's sake? Fucking prick. Over twenty years you've waited for this moment, and all you find to say to him is that the Royal is a nice bar."

The Royal, a bar that's practically empty during the day. A big room with high ceilings, colored moldings, and pictures by a pal of the owner on the walls. It isn't really designed for broad daylight, what seems fabulous at night looks a bit tatty by day. Just pushing open the door to the bar is reassuring in itself, in spite of the combined smell of stale tobacco and cleaning products.

"Ooooh, old lady! In one of our moods are we?"

Jérémy, behind the bar, bursts out laughing when he sees her. She would like to stay looking furious, on her high horse, but it doesn't work. She smiles, and leans on the counter.

"Can you put it on my tab? Till Tuesday?"

"I'd like to say no, but I can see you'd smash the place up. A Jack?"

"Thankyouthankyouthankyou," she chants, twisting her head on her neck to make the vertebrae click. That very morning, leaning over the washbasin, vomiting up her guts, she had sworn not to have a drink at all today. Her liver's crying out for understanding, mercy, and respite. But seeing how the day's turning out, to remain clearheaded wouldn't be appropriate.

Gloria takes her glass and goes over to a seat. Slight head-ache, backache, she feels stiff. The warmth of the alcohol immediately unlocks her joints, her knees, the insides of her wrists and elbows. Something relaxes. But it's still not enough to let her draw breath without pain.

She's been here before, of course she has, she knows the score by heart. Pain doesn't lessen with age, on the contrary. But she knows there's nothing to be done, except wait, day after day, for it to get bearable. Another failure, par for the course, another breakup.

Gloria's not her real name. Her parents had her christened Stéphanie. But even in primary school she'd changed it, every new year she tried a different one. That wreaked havoc when the teachers realized what she was up to, and it made the other kids suspicious when they figured out she was lying. She'd almost given up when Gloria the "punk princess" became a media icon. She realized it was time to settle on something. It was the early eighties, and she'd just discovered that there was something out there that spoke to her: the Sex Pistols, Bérurier Noir, Sham 69, and Taxi Girl. Hair carefully dyed electric blue, one evening in town she'd met this young guy who'd shown her the three chords for "Gloria" on a guitar. He'd announced, with that confidence possessed only by kids under twenty, that "it's the most beautiful name in the world." He was wearing a white Perfecto leather jacket. A dark-haired boy with broad shoulders, fleshy lips, and a piercing gaze. Possibly it wasn't piercing at all, perhaps he was just nearsighted, but she had thought this was someone who could fathom the depths of your soul and caress its vice. Whatever, he'd blown her mind, and starting the next day she had told every new person she met: "Hi, I'm Gloria." And the name had stuck. Because twenty years later, that's still what people are calling her.

Jérémy sweeps by grandly, carries off her glass and brings it back full. He's humming, walking with shoulders a little bent, his low-slung, hyperbaggy jeans exposing a band of belly: smooth golden skin, young man's skin. With one hand, Gloria hoicks up his trousers, scolding: "Hey kid, get your ass back inside your pants."

Jérémy wanders off, delighted that someone in this place has protested yet again about his trousers.

Two men have just arrived, and now they're hardwired to the counter. Difficult to put an age on the older one, he's so destroyed by drink. A caricature of the wine-bibbing Frenchman: strawberry nose, puffy face, sepulchral voice, rotten yellow teeth. With him is a hulking, ruddy-faced youngster, head sunk into his shoulders, probably his son.

The old man is yelling, he's already plastered, and now he's furious: "I don't believe it! You got a brain or what? God should've given you another asshole, you're so full of shit."

Gloria exchanges a quick glance with Jérémy. They both roll their eyes and turn away to hide a smile.

Every day, these two come into the Royal, just to shout at each other all afternoon. Around aperitif time, off they go to the betting shop, the old one still yelling at the young one. Gloria predicts, as she watches them stagger away every night at about seven, that one day they won't be back: the young one will have chucked the old one out the window.

The young one blows his nose, making a hell of a noise. Gray-and-red tracksuit, picked up on sale, no doubt, and he has these enormous feet. Gloria can't get used to how big young boys' feet are, she wonders if there's some plan up there in the cosmos for the human race. Should it be planning to go and live underwater, growing long flippers? The kid's jaw drops when he sees her, he looks truly impressed.

Gloria gets up and goes to the washroom to check what it is about her appearance that seemed to strike the youth so much. Looking in the mirror, she realizes better why all the dumb idiots she'd met on her way there had stared at her, trying not to show it. She's been weeping her heart out so hard that there are broken blood vessels under her eyes and on her cheeks, and her face is tomato red. Makes her eyes look puffy. The cherry on the cake is that in her frenzy back at Lucas's place, she'd banged her head against the wall a few times, so it looks like she's wearing a red clown nose. The whole lot topped off with a wild-eyed expression. Yeah, she'd have stared at herself too.

She sings under her breath as she splashes water on her face: "*Qu'est-ce que j'en ai à foutre et je ne crois en rien / je peux vivre au coup par coup / en coups durs de plus en plus*" ("What the fuck do I care / Got nothin' to believe in / Live day to day / Take what's comin'"). She tugs several times on the roller towel to get a clean stretch. She plunges her face into the clean cotton fabric, it feels soft, like new. She stays like that for a bit.

Then she goes into a stall, and closes the slightly twisted bolt. A very clean hole, the size of an old five-franc coin, has been drilled in the door. At about knee height. More-or-less surrealist graffiti covers the walls from top to bottom. She's always liked one of them, a little palm tree up to the right of the door. Whoever drew it took some trouble, using different colored felt pens. Among all the death threats, revenge slogans, and drawings of private parts, somebody stood on tiptoe to draw a little palm tree.

Back in the bar, she looks around for *L'Est Républicain*, the local paper, and sees it clutched in the pink false fingernails of the woman sitting at the bar. Classic slut. Another regular. Always lots of makeup, come-hither eyes. She's fat, dark-haired, no great looker, but not letting on she knows that. Gloria has to make do with a TV listing lying around for no particular reason. She leafs through it as she sips her second whiskey. It falls open at a two-page spread: Eric Muyr, his life, his mad period, his achievements, and his shitty new show . . . someone has drawn spots on his nose and given him a little Hitler mustache. *He doesn't look like himself, either in real life or in the photo*, she thinks. At this point, a hand laden with heavy rings, pharaohs and skulls, bangs down on the table between the presenter's eyebrows.

"There's an article in *L'Est* as well, about that wuss you're looking at."

Looking up, she sees Michel and gives him a big smile—he pulls a face.

"I won't ask how you're doing . . ."

"No, don't bother. What article?"

"A whole two pages on the local hero, his amazing success, his fantastic pioneering new TV show . . . just a game show, as if that's anything to write home about."

"Actually I met him in town just now . . ."

"No!"

He takes off his leather jacket, pulls up a chair, and sits down. Leaning toward her, he listens to her story attentively, eager to pick up the scoop of the day.

"I was crossing the road and he nearly ran me over, well his driver did . . . then he got out of the car—yeah, *wuss* is the word for it, so pleased with himself, I didn't even shout at him, I was so stunned to see him. Mind-boggling."

Michel frowns and waits for her to go on. Gloria realizes that he's wrongly connecting her disheveled appearance with this chance encounter. She reassures him.

"Oh, no, that's not why I look like death warmed up. Nothing to do with it. Tell you what though, I surprised myself: it really did nothing for me, bumping into Mr. TV Celebrity . . . If he thinks he's going to impress us all . . ."

"So, the red eyes . . . that's because of Lucas?"

Even hearing his name hurts, and she knows from experience that the first days won't be the worst. The most intense perhaps—spectacularly so, in fact. But the worst will come later, when the sharp pain of a breakup recedes a little, leaving behind a sense of loss, a familiar ache, the lucid and unbearable consciousness of something irredeemably lost, gone . . . She repeats her mantra: *Change your ways, Gloria, stop suffering, you don't need this.* But it doesn't work. There are some people who torture themselves more than others. And in this category, she knows she's a world-beater.

Michel brings out his rolling kit, but Gloria flicks her packet of Russian cigarettes under his nose. He thanks her and takes one. He has rings on every finger, the same ones since last century, Egyptian scarabs, skulls, and precious stones. His nails are always black. She has no idea why. Perhaps he fixes cars on the sly? Dismantles engines when everyone's back is turned . . . whatever. He stands up, goes over to collect his beer, and exchanges a few jokes with Jérémy, then brings out a newly cut CD from the pocket of his leather coat. Since his pockets are full of holes, he has to contort himself, feeling around in the lining to get ahold of it. Jérémy yells, "Yay!!! Another garage punk compilation, eh?" with almost the same degree of enthusiasm as if he'd just scored in the World Cup.

Two young girls arrive, schoolbags on their shoulders. Given the time of day and their faces, they're cutting class. They whisper and giggle in turn. Baby Goths, black makeup and pierced lips, they're done up so they look almost like sisters. Baggy khaki trousers, skintight tops with pictures of improbably named groups. Black high-top Converse. Gloria knows what Michel is thinking, that's the advantage of knowing each other so well. No way can he get used to the way the kids look today, starting with their trainers. He was born a bit too early for all that. A girl in trainers has the same effect on him as if she turned up in army combats: a complete turnoff. *Sad for him, since that's where we are now.* Still, he goes over to say hi, and gives them a couple of pieces of solid advice about real life and how it is. They listen, heads to one side, taking it in. Tonight before going home, they'll be in Place Carnot, drinking beer with some punks and reporting what they've learned.

Michel does his cool act for a couple of minutes, then comes back to Gloria's table, and like a reliable friend, he asks questions.

"This time it's serious, is it? Want to tell me about it?"

"Hiroshima . . . I went ballistic."

"Ah."

He knows her history, so he needs to check: "But he's . . . I mean you didn't . . . ?"

His concern makes her smile, although she knows it isn't funny.

"No, no, I didn't hurt him, nothing like that. Didn't lay a finger on him. Anyway, he's very quick, damn his eyes. But I did some damage on the way. I trashed his place a bit. But that's not the worst. Well, maybe it is . . . Anyway, it's over. It's over, over, over, finished, I know. I swear, I'm so pissed off, every time I find a guy I really like, I drive him nuts and he chucks me out."

"I've heard this before from you. And if I was you, I'd be pissed off too."

"Yeah, but usually it's just me that's moaning in my corner. But it's him that's had enough this time. Totally, totally had it. You know the effect I have on guys: at first they love it that I'm in such a bad place, they always want to help. But if you overdo it, there's too much pain, bad news for the furniture."

"So where are you going to crash?"

"At your place?"

"Ah, no."

"Not to worry, I guessed you'd have had enough of putting me up. I'm going to ask Véro."

"No, it's not that, but Vanessa's coming tonight, so it's not really the moment . . ."

"Cool for you. She doesn't work during the week?"

"She just got the sack."

"Too bad."

"No, it's okay, she wanted out anyway. Records, you know, not really where it's at now."

"Well she's right, because before we go back to the shop and give them all our cash to buy their CDs, hell might've frozen over."

She likes saying this. But she doesn't like Vanessa, Michel's new girlfriend. Of course, there's a bit of basic jealousy in there. Why would Michel need another girl around when he's got her? But Gloria is old enough to know it's best that her friends are happy, have someone to sleep with. Otherwise they start complaining and get to be a pain.

But this Vanessa really is the pits. Pretty, yes, blondish, big boobs, wide blue eyes. She's got delicate features, a long neck and a rather nearsighted gaze, so she reminds you a bit of a giraffe. She looks down her nose at you, she's totally full of herself and really, really dumb, which would be quite funny if she wasn't around so much. Envious, super competitive, always ready to complain. Aggressive, but in a very feminine way, roundabout and insidious. The remarks she makes are usually wounding, but not openly so: the punch in the jaw that she seems to be asking for the whole time wouldn't look justified to a bystander.

In Gloria's view, this girl is only hanging around because she regards them all as provincial hicks, among whom she can easily shine. Reigning, even if it's only over pigs and chickens, is still reigning—the sad duty of a slightly shop-worn princess.

Gloria and Vanessa exchange smiles of overwhelming hypocrisy every time they meet. Broad, murderous smiles.

For the moment though, everyone finds this bimbo *really nice*, interesting, and charming. With her determined little expression and her calculating ways. Gloria knows she just has to wait. The Vanessas of this world don't last long. You've got to have a bit more upstairs to be a girl that people really remember.

But in the twenty years she's known Michel, it's the first time things have taken this unwelcome turn. He's never stayed so long with a girlfriend without covertly starting to find fault with her. He falls in love often, quickly puts the girl on a pedestal—but it has an eject button.

You need to watch it, Gloria tells herself anxiously, *because people can change, when you least expect it. You know them so well, you're used to them, you don't spot when the day comes they can't take it anymore, you don't necessarily realize.* But now, apparently, Michel is fed up with being on his own. So he's closed down a section of his brain, the one that tells him what this girl is like: a château-bottled bitch.

Gloria, chin on hand, elbow on the table, is humming

a France Gall song: "*Laisse tomber les filles, laisse tomber les filles / un jour c'est toi qu'on laissera*" ("Give up on the chicks, give up on the chicks / Next time around you'll be in the fix").

Michel finishes his beer, elbow in the air, flexes his neck with ease, stands up, and takes Gloria's glass with his own.

"Same again?" She nods with a sniff, she's in no position to refuse.

Then he stops, saying nothing, gazing out at the street, and searches for words, before saying without looking her in the eye, "You're sure you don't want to try . . ."

"A shrink? Are you nuts?"

"You can't carry on like this."

"Yes I can."

She pretends to think it's funny, but her eyes are stinging and she'd like to put her head on the table and cry, or bash her forehead in. She swallows, forces herself to reject the thoughts that arise, and looks once more at the TV listing. She's choking with rage, her heart is pounding irregularly. Once more, that image, very clear in her head: someone puts a barrel of a gun to the back of her neck and pulls the trigger. A release.

She'd like to go back in time three months, to the days when Lucas used to follow her in the street after every fight, when he didn't want to let her go, when he loved her at whatever the cost. When she felt herself desired. She'd like to go back three months and sleep with him tonight, have him feel for her feet with his in his sleep, as he used to.

Michel sits down again and asks: "So what was it about this time?"

"He installed AOL on my computer."

"And?"

"I'd asked him not to."

"So?"

"I trashed the place."

"Really? I mean you just saw he'd installed AOL and you smashed everything up?"

"Exactly. I picked up the computer and I threw it on the floor."

"Ah, that would make an impression, yes."

"Yeah, well, I'd never done that before, makes a hell of a noise. And you know Lucas, he doesn't do conflict."

"Even if he was a macho guy, it would still come as a surprise."

"Hmm. He said I'd gone psycho. He was different than usual, this time he'd made up his mind. I think he's met someone else."

"Perhaps he just wants to stay alive."

"Well, we'll never know now, will we?"

She raises her drink and they clink glasses. The memory of the scene makes her feel bad, genuinely. But she can't stop herself from joking when she tells anyone about it. She concludes: "When the mood takes me, it takes me. Honestly, nothing I can do about it."

"Thing is, Gloria, the mood's taking you a heck of a lot these days. If you weren't sleeping with anyone, people might say find a guy. But you're never *not* sleeping with someone. Maybe it's the opposite, you should try giving up sex."

"Yeah, you're right. I'll be sober as a nun, that should calm me down, but that's not so much fun as being weird and killing everyone in the street, as many as possible in an afternoon."

Michel smiles and remains polite. But she knows he's thinking she really ought to get this sorted out. Only last week, she broke the pinball machine in another bar because it went "tilt" on her. She'd picked up a chair and smashed the machine with it. Michel's often there when she blows a fuse. Last month, they'd been standing in line at the town hall to get a passport, and this young guy had tried to push in front of them, pretending to be tough, when you could tell at a glance he was from the better end of town. In two minutes she was raging at him, with her madwoman-in-the-attic look. Michel had had to drag her outside, too bad about the passport. And then Michel had made the mistake of letting her have a coffee in the bar opposite, to calm down for a few minutes. As soon as she'd seen the same stupid boy come out, she'd run into the street, unthinking, and without even realizing it, she'd got him down and was banging his head on the ground. Luckily he was a strong kid, and he managed to get away without too much trouble. At least for the moment, she only picks fights with people stronger than herself—she likes to say she does it on purpose.

Gloria licks her lower lip. She's known Michel a long time, and he's the last real male friend she has. She'd be sorry to lose him. But she's out of control. Before, she might lose her temper now and then, and it made people laugh, it made her seem kind of a character, out of the ordinary. A girl you didn't mess with. But she's mutated from picturesque fury to dangerous madwoman. And now it isn't just a few times a year, it's practically every day. As if she never gets tired of it.

"See, I think I've gone from being manipulative to being aggressive. Dunno why . . ."

"*You* were manipulative?"

"Yeah, before, it depended who I was talking to. I could be passive, aggressive, or just normal, and I always got my way. But now, I'm just aggressive."

"And do you get your way now?"

"Nope. Don't want anything from anyone anymore, so I can't be bothered to manipulate them. I just prefer to bite their balls off."

That makes him laugh. She tells herself that he doesn't yet quite hate her, and that soothes her for a couple of minutes. What she doesn't tell him is how much of a kick she gets these days out of being aggressive. How much she loves the moment when everything tips over, when the other person is caught off-balance and you have to go on, attacking, screaming, and seeing his fear. That's the moment she likes. The pleasure she gets from it is dirty, degrading, and dangerous, filling her with shame—a filthy and super powerful pleasure. She doesn't tell him this because like most people with a serious problem, she's sure she can deal with it on her own, no way is she going to crawl and admit it to anyone else.

In Lucas's apartment block, where she'd gone to live less than six months ago, everyone looks at her sideways, with a half-pitying look. They're so used to hearing her yell, roll on the ground, break dishes, and slam doors. The tricky thing, in fact, after these tantrums is the next day: closing the door, meeting the neighbor in the elevator, greeting her cheerfully as if nothing had happened. *If I act normal, perhaps she'll think it wasn't me.*

Michel comments: "The funny thing is when you're *drunk*, you don't piss anyone off."

"No, not yet. I'm fun when I've had a few."

"Should drink more then."

"Should start earlier, you're right."

Gloria spots Véronique going past in her blue Clio. She's slowing down to see who's in the bar. She waves to them and stops. She reverse-parks neatly, one-handed, in a single go. Then the driver wriggles around for a couple of minutes inside the car, putting on her coat, finding her glasses, her handbag, checking the mirror in case she has lipstick on her teeth. She comes to join them. Gloria wonders how she's going to ask if she can stay with her, praying she'll say yes. Véro lives in this comfortable little apartment, and she's genuinely nice. A good person. And you eat very well there too. Truly the woman of choice, if you want a sleepover.

Véronique kisses them hello and asks Gloria, "What happened to *you*?"

"I made a fool of myself."

"Someone beat you up, you mean?"

Michel bursts out laughing.

Gloria protests, "You're out of order, she's right, it could happen."

Véronique raises one eyebrow. She's the kind of girl who can do that, raise just one eyebrow. Gloria reassures her, "No, nobody tried to attack me. All men ever want me to do is PISS OFF."

Véronique smiles, and takes off her coat, which she folds

carefully over the back of her chair. She's wearing a pink-and-black dress, close-fitting. She's slim and looks great, not just great for forty-five, which she is. That's the only reason Gloria wouldn't want to live with her. She doesn't want to see her in her nightie, or in a bra and panties. She feels too fat herself to be able to stand the sight of women with good figures.

Véronique sighs and slumps back in her chair. She tells them: "It was funny in school today, I tried to teach them the difference between a short *o* and a long *ô*—every year since I got back to Lorraine, this bit of the syllabus makes me laugh."

"Why?"

"In a Lorraine accent, do you think the long *ô* exists? The kids listen, they stare at me, they have no idea what I'm talking about . . . but anyway, you're not going to be interested in this . . ."

Both speaking together and with great sincerity, they say, "Yes, yes, we are."

And it's true that her stories of primary school are so exotic for Michel and Gloria that it's like being on holiday. But what they really like is when she gets started on the parents . . .

Véronique plunges into the TV listing for that evening. Gloria is shredding a cardboard beer coaster to pieces, and in her mind formulating her request in several ways: *I've got this little problem, I don't know where I'm sleeping tonight*, or, *Are you by any chance looking for a lodger?* Michel rolls himself a cigarette, the Sonics are singing, "*'Cause she's the Witch,*" and he beats time with his foot.

Véronique taps her finger on the two-page spread showing Eric smiling, with the drawn-on mustache.

"Apparently you used to know him when he lived in Nancy?"

"Yeah. I was a teenager, so was he. It was a long time ago, I have to say . . ."

"What was he like?"

"Oh, cool. We got on okay. But, ouf, he was fifteen. Not hard to be cool at fifteen."

Michel agrees and adds: "Yeah, after thirty it gets harder."

Many of their mutual friends have left the cool scene, as the years have gone by: they've changed drastically, often in surprising ways. How can a punk with a Mohawk, who listens to the right music, has the right attitude, the right leathers, who's good fun, a real amigo, mutate in a season into a solid respectable citizen, with buried dreams and a mortgage? With the pariah's meaningless excuse: "That's life, eh?" as if he'd had good reason for falling into line, conforming, putting up with things. It's a subject she's often thought about: in Nancy, it's true, you can often bump into your old school friends. Beautiful teenagers who've turned into fat slobs. Bitter, freaked out, wounded egos, losers, or victims of their pathetic successes.

Michel sits up. "Oh, yeah, you didn't finish telling me. You saw him again?"

"Yes I did, I just told you everything, it lasted all of two minutes. I was completely out of it, I'd just walked out on Lucas, I was switched off. I didn't say anything. Not a word."

"And him?"

She puts on a silly precious voice and speaks with her

mouth wide open: "Blah blah blah, I'm *sooo* glad to see you, why don't we get together *tonight,* blah blah, oh really you know a nice bar? Blah blah blah, a glass of bubbly perhaps? Can my driver drop you off?"

Then she drops the voice and concludes: "Poor guy, what a dope he's turned into."

"You could tell that in two minutes?" asks Véronique doubtfully.

"Course I could, it was written all over his face, he was putting it on like crazy."

She doesn't get angry while blaming him. Michel's looking at her attentively out of the corner of his eye. He rubs his lips.

"So, that, 'Oh really, you know a nice bar,' means you've made a date for tonight?"

"He said he'd drop in here this evening. But I know guys like him: he won't. Anyway, see if I care, I'm not going to hang around all night."

Unwisely, Véronique asks: "Oh, you're doing something tonight?"

"Well, I was just going to ask you, I was hoping I might crash at your place."

VÉRONIQUE HAS AGREED at once to take her in: "But just for three or four days, okay?" Admiring the friendly, straightforward way she states her conditions, Gloria replies, "Of course, thanks, that's so cool," while telling herself that once she has her feet under the table, she'll manage to extend the stay.

Véro's living room: pale yellow walls, postcards pinned up with little clothes pegs, teapot in the shape of a blue elephant, cups with big Japanese fish on them, piles of videos and DVDs, books lined up neatly by size. The graphic albums are stacked on the floor, probably because they won't fit on the bookshelves. A Batman is sitting down in a corner, arms outstretched and no head. Must belong to some little nephew. Véronique has throngs of sisters, there were eight daughters in the family. All the others have reproduced in multiple copies. She often looks after a kid or two for a day. That's one of the secrets of her hospitality: she doesn't mind getting stains on the carpet.

They've hardly arrived before Véronique offers Gloria a spliff. "I wouldn't say no," anything to dull the anguish will be welcome tonight. While listening to her voice mail, Véronique has switched on the television and guess what, Eric's face fills the screen. Clean-shaven, dark blue suit, full of health and well-being. He's presenting a totally stupid game show, one that Gloria has never been able to understand. He teases the contestants, who all blush pink with pleasure before they make fools of themselves in front of the whole of France, giving ridiculous answers to dopey questions.

When she's at home, Gloria zaps it off as soon as it comes on. It's an acquired reflex. It doesn't make her feel in any way happy to have known in flesh and blood someone who's on TV. She thinks it just shouldn't happen. There are the little people on screen in one world, and then there's the big, real people in the other. If everyone stays in their place, it's fine—if not, it creates confusion. She doesn't dare ask Véro to switch channels, seeing that she seems to like the show.

Gloria comments, making her voice sound impressed:

"Well, get him, great, isn't it, the older he gets, the younger he looks. Nice to have lots of dough."

"Apparently they have loads of makeup on for the cameras. What did he look like for real?"

"Good-looking. Ghastly."

"You don't like him?"

"Couldn't care less. But I like to trash the people on TV. Good way to let off steam, eh?"

"And you *slept* with him?" asks Véro, right away. Gloria takes advantage of the moment to show off.

"Yeah, course. Mind you, in those days I slept with anyone at the drop of a hat, they had to run to get away from me."

Eric carries on hosting the show on the small screen, Véronique is staring at him, absolutely glued to it, as if the fact that someone she knows actually *went out* with him makes the program fantastic. Gloria drinks some tea, burns her tongue, makes a face and adds, "He wasn't as bad as all that. At least he was interested. Not like some guys who make a song and dance to get you into bed, and say, 'Okay for you?' after three pathetic little pokes."

Gloria follows Véro into the kitchen, spliff in hand. That familiar lump in her throat. She's trying to resist calling Lucas. She wants to tell him how sorry she is, how ashamed. She's lonely, she'd like him to say he loves her and wants her back. Only that's not what he would say. He'd say, "I've had it up to here," he'd say, "I can't take anymore of this." He'd say he was sorry, and would sound sincerely exhausted. And in less than two seconds, she'd have started snarling hysterically that she'd find him and kill him. She knows herself of old. So she's not going to call him, the same way you're not going to pick up a cigarette when you've just decided to give it up.

Be patient with the pain, suffer in silence, grit your teeth, wait.

Gloria unfolds an IKEA chair, such a weird color green, whoever designed it ought to be caught and questioned: Why did you make it that color? The tablecloth has a pattern of fruit. Everything in this house is pretty, it looks grown-up and at the same time definitely feminine. It actually says "respectable housewife," the kitchen is so well kept, everything in its place. Colored magnets on the fridge, pinned to photos of holidays, Christmas parties, friends laughing with their noses pressed up against the camera, red-eyed like rabbits.

The frozen vegetables are hissing in the frying pan, and the microwave is humming to warm up some mini pizzas. Between comfort and despair, Gloria is gently getting drowsy.

Lucas had taken fright. Too many tantrums, too many mornings when she would get up quietly to go and cry, lying in the empty bath, and end up on the bathroom floor, hitting herself and covering her stomach or her face with scratches. She liked to bang her head against the wall as well, scaring herself with the violence of the blows. It gave her a weird feeling inside her skull. An unusual echo. Your skull is a solid piece of work, in her experience. It can be fractured, yes, but it's fucking solid. She'd realized gradually that he was going to freak out. First it was the mornings, when he found her in that state, then the evenings when he got home. Then he started getting scared to put his arms around her, because he never knew what her reaction would be. He'd panic when she phoned him. He'd see her number come up on his phone and he wouldn't know what shape she'd be in.

And the worst of it was, she couldn't reproach him with anything. No cracks in his wall where she could hang on and attack him. Of course he didn't want to have a child with her. Who'd want to, with a madwoman?

She attacks her belly with her fingernails, as she's now in the habit of doing. So much so that it's covered with blue semicircular bruises and nail marks digging into the flesh. Or long red welts that take months to disappear where she's drawn blood. Stupid belly—prominent and empty.

She's at the age when women who haven't had children realize that they won't ever now. To be born a woman, the worst fate in practically every society. Just one trump card: the ability to give birth. And in her case, she's missed the boat. As with everything else. She's really missed out on everything, from start to finish.

Gloria sighs, then realizes that she's suddenly been seized with a burst of enthusiasm. Part of her is rubbing her hands with glee and rolling up her sleeves: *Right, who's next?* Through suffering, by a mysterious kind of emotional alchemy, the heart generates its own bursts of sunshine. Alas, they don't last long.

"Would you like some herbal tea?"

If Gloria wasn't sleeping here, she'd have snapped back: "That stuff? Stupid, money-saving, middle-class fad."

Instead, she asked, "No beer left?"

Terrible feeling as night falls, a cold monster is prowling around her, wanting to grab hold of her and suck out what remains of her reason. Or self-control.

Véronique has pulled a pile of children's exercise books out of her big black satchel. She puts them on her desk and starts marking them. Gloria is interested in what she's doing.

"You give them grades? Even in nursery classes?"

"Yes, I draw a little red man with his mouth down when something's wrong, and a green one with a smile when it's right. If it's just peculiar, I draw an orange man with a funny nose."

"Poor little kids," Gloria says with sympathy, "even when they're five years old, they get to feel they're failures."

"We have to assess them, it's compulsory. I don't know what to say really . . . it's not the worst thing we have to deal with just now."

"Yeah right, that's why you're on strike all the time."

"I'll let you take my place for a year, and you'd soon see whether we're on strike all the time. Three weeks and you'd be on your knees, then you'd know what I'm talking about."

The telephone rings. Véronique freezes, glances at the time, and picks up, looking anxious. It's the sort of time when you get bad news. Gloria watches the expression on her face, praying that it's not some serious crisis. She wants to be able to cry herself to sleep on her pillow, not to have to comfort the friend who's putting her up. But Véro stands stock-still, opens her eyes so wide she looks like she's had a face-lift, gasps, replies, "Yes yes yes," and holds out the phone, pointing to it and whispering excitedly, "It's *him*!" Gloria's heart is jumping under her ribs, she imagines it's Lucas.

"So, we meet for the first time in twenty years, and the first thing you do is stand me up!"

In other circumstances, indeed, she would be amused, or flattered, or mad with rage that he might imagine she'd forgotten the past . . . but this evening she's simply desperately disappointed that it's him.

She replies dully, "Sorry. I couldn't wait. But honestly, I didn't think you'd turn up."

He's super excited, in a good mood, cheerful.

"You're not far away, is that right? Jérémy told me. Come over here and join us! I'd so like to see you again."

He shouts the last bit, she pulls the phone away from her ear. If she had set out to impress Véro, she'd do exactly this. She wouldn't have minded basking in a little reflected glory, but all she feels is sad, like someone who's going to be sleeping alone because she's been thrown out again. She has tears brimming in her eyes and is in no mood to joke, she sighs and replies, "Listen, I'm going to be straight with you. What the fuck makes you think I want to see you?" She articulates every syllable. "You and your fucking stupid TV face, do you get it, go back to your studio and don't imagine for a *second* that I've forgotten anything, GET IT? ANYTHING AT ALL. Right, bye."

She hangs up. Now, as well as feeling sad, she feels ridiculous. Véronique stares at her in astonishment. Gloria feels tears running down her cheeks, her confused feelings are upsetting. She shrugs.

"Okay, it's silly to insult him. But it all started with him."

"What? Insulting people?"

"Having *anything* to do with men. Him, that prick, he was the first Hiroshima in my life. You have to understand, I don't care if for him it's all buried in the past, but for me . . ."

She's weeping softly now. Sweet tears running down to

her lips, she can feel the floodgates about to open, she'll be bawling soon. Véronique holds out a whole box of Kleenex and asks again, "Sure you don't want some herbal stuff?"

"You haven't got any pot left, have you?"

Véro goes to look in a drawer, finds a little joint and hands it over. Then she hesitates, but ends up asking all the same, "You really know each other *that* well?"

Funny how everyone's so interested in that.

She avoids talking about it, because it fascinates them so much, and that really drives them nuts.

"Big fucking deal. He's on TV, what's so special about that?"

"Well, to be honest, I really like his show."

"Well, to be honest back, are you out of your mind?"

She feels as though she's stuck in the last century, the olden days, when if you did something at home, you didn't go telling everyone about it next day. One of Gloria's big problems is that recently she hasn't stirred outside her bar. She's not up to speed with the huge changes that have happened to her contemporaries. For instance, their recent passion for watching trashy TV shows. As if it were fun, as if it were innocent, as if it were anything but pure surrender, and as such, totally unacceptable. She could give them a hard time about it, but she senses that other people are tired and discouraged. Not everyone is like her: still ready to go mad with rage and smash the place up. Most people need rest and something to amuse them, otherwise they wouldn't get up in the morning.

Véronique is avoiding her eyes, looking unhappy and embarrassed to have brought it up. She brings a prebaked pie out of the oven and cuts them two large slices. Gloria's irritation vanishes as she watches her, with a slight feeling of shame. It's not because her friend likes watching stupid TV shows that she's in this state. Gloria pushes out her lips to look like a duck, as if it is going to help her think, then decides to try and tell the story. But it won't come out easily, it was all a long time ago, and she hasn't thought it through properly since.

"You know quite well where I met him. Everyone knows it, in this stinking town full of hicks with nothing better to do than gossip about everyone."

At that moment, she understands what the "id" means that psychoanalysts go on about. Because right now, the id is talking through her. She can hear herself spitting out the words, spluttering as she speaks, aggressive and unhinged. But the moment when she "makes a decision" to express her anger, that exact moment, she can't quite reach it.

Once more, Véronique stiffens in her chair, embarrassed to have provoked this reaction. She apologizes: "I'm sorry, it's none of my business. I was acting like a groupie, it was indiscreet."

The nicest people are always the only ones who ever apologize for being annoying. Pity, that.

But Gloria's memory is stuck in a groove, she has a flashback to the same image, almost twenty years since it happened, the same image that stays with her: her father is standing in a corridor and watching her disappear. She's being dragged backward, held up under the arms by two men. Alongside her father are the doctor and her mother. They too are looking wretched. The pain spreads around her. As usual, she's the one causing the pain . . . To get back into her memory, she has to get past the barrier of that image: she'd dropped to the floor screaming, the two men had picked her up and forced her into that place, the institution where they were going to deal with her. For her own good. She's looking at her father: "No, no, please!" Her screams are hardly noticed. In this place they're used to them, she finds out later. And he watches her vanishing, his eyes are sad—never has she caused him so much pain. But she's the one who's being locked up, and who won't be able to bear it.

She must try and keep that image at bay, stop it from turning into a loop, or else . . . But that's exactly what happens. She holds her head in her hands, the first hot tears burn her eyelids as they well up, then they roll, comfortingly, down her cheeks and fall on the table.

"It was just after dying that I met Eric."

IT WAS IN 1985, days after Christmas. It had been snowing nonstop, the countryside was white everywhere, as it can be in eastern France.

An acquaintance, a fan of the Cure, always dressed in black, had taken advantage of his mother's absence to have parties at his place every night. He lived in Jarville, near the railway bridge. Gloria didn't know him well, but they'd bumped into each other that morning on the twenty-one bus. Impressed no doubt by her look, he'd invited her. Preferring to avoid long negotiations with her parents, she simply didn't tell them. As usual, and like many other teenagers at the time, she'd climbed out of the window and gone there on foot, it was only five minutes away.

They were listening to Lydia Lunch. Gloria was wearing a dog collar with a leash, far-out. She'd spent much of the evening walking around a bedroom, listening to the same song on loop. Other kids were out of it on the couch.

Two of them were necking, covered with studs and chains, the pair of them, very thin, like two little birds who'd fallen into the water. The bedroom floor was covered with a dark blue fitted carpet, scratchy to the touch, when you put your hands on it. Next door, the TV was on, playing Madonna's "Like a Virgin."

A nice evening, quite calm, until this boy called Léo arrived. He wasn't from Nancy, she'd never seen him before. In fact she'd never seen anything like him. A pun-kette's dreamboat: blond hair, androgynous beauty, but very masculine attitude, like a mischievous pixie. He was wearing a super-tight black biker jacket and short jeans over electric-blue creepers. She could hardly believe her eyes seeing him arrive. She'd stopped circling the room at once and joined his group of hangers-on. Even in her dreams, she hadn't imagined anyone looking like that. So perfectly perfect. A promise of total fulfilling happiness: a welcoming tropical jungle. Without even trying to speak directly to him, she'd found plenty of ways to be near the corner where he was. The little prince laughed a lot. Gloria wasn't the only one to be knocked out by his looks. The whole gang had spontaneously grouped itself around him. Whatever he said, there was always someone who found it hilarious and burst out laughing. He played it up, simpered, struck poses, came on a bit camp, but never lost anything of his masculine aura. Yet he was also acting the beautiful angel.

Luckily he ended up asking her, yes *her*, if she knew where he could find any acid. Gloria had shrugged, playing the girl who isn't shocked, knows her way around town, and likes to help visitors. Inside her head, everything was fizzing, exploding, going off like fireworks. But she stayed calm and just said, "Might be some at La Paix, it's a bar near the station, yeah, I think they might have some there. Or else the Campus, it's a club." She wasn't bullshitting, but she wasn't as certain as she was pretending either. She passed him the bottle of whiskey she was holding by the neck. She congratulated herself on having worn her lacy white tights and vinyl miniskirt with holes, which was too tight so it made her behind look great. She'd almost turned up in bleached combats and dark red Doc Martens. She'd have scared him off then, for sure.

So he had followed her out. They couldn't find any driver willing to take them into town. Great, they'd have to walk, just the two of them, to the bus stop. In the cold, which made you want to link arms. They'd filled their pockets with Kronenbourg cans and left the party together. In the white expanse outside, the carpet of snow crunching under their steps, the expression "walking on air" had made her beam with happiness.

She'd waited till they got to the bus shelter before counting . . . *three, four* . . . "Wanna sleep together?" She'd taken a big deep breath first and clenched her fists in her pockets. Didn't take it the wrong way, visibly flattered, not dismissive. "Okay if you like, but let's do the acid first." She'd stretched out her legs, sitting up against the glass panel of the bus shelter, stunned by the promise: they were going to sleep together. They sang "Should I Stay or Should I Go." She was amazed that a guy like this could even exist, and her mind was blown by the thought that he was talking to her. So, okay, life was less crap than she had imagined.

On top of that, they did find some acid at the first bar they went to. She liked taking it, even if it made her freak out, ever since that memorable night when she'd found herself, who knew how, in the park by the garden center where some fairground folk were setting up their swings and roundabouts. Léo wasn't taking much initiative, but he let her caress and kiss him, amicably enough. Gloria looked sideways at him, hard to believe it was really true that she was having a laugh with this boy. He was going back to Paris on New Year's Day for a rock concert at Juvisy. She slapped her thighs: incredible, she'd been planning to go to Paris then too, they could take the train together. He was as sweet as he was easygoing. He'd said, "Yeah, that'd be cool," without trying to get any advantage from his being so good-looking and exciting. They were waiting for the acid to work, hiding from the wind in another bus shelter, this time in the town center. When a car slowed down as it passed, Gloria had just noticed that the LSD was taking effect, because sounds were becoming a taste in her mouth and the air was full of colors. The car door slammed and her father surged up, a giant, raging with fury, he'd been driving around town for an hour looking for her—turned out someone had asked for her on the phone and they'd realized she wasn't in her room.

He had snatched her away—literally and roughly—from the arms of Prince Charming. She just had time to say, "See you tomorrow." Then in the car, sitting by her father who was yelling and banging the wheel with his fists, she'd begun to realize the acid was really hot stuff.

Now she was inside a huge grinder, with long steel teeth capable of piercing her innermost emotions. Words plunged in, great shards of glass, meaningless but super-charged with hostile power. She was shut in and clinging to the seat. Her father was attacking her with a frightening passion, all his frustration directed at her, like a flame-thrower. Normally she had ways, tricks, and mannerisms to deal with it but just then, her head bursting with LSD, she was visualizing his words as blows to her mental state, with some parts of it irredeemably smashed in.

Two days later, instead of simply slinking off without bothering them, in the normal way, she had taken the rash step (no doubt prompted by too much acid) of telling her folks where she was going. She'd invented a party in Paris, where there'd be parents in attendance, acoustic guitars, and folksinging. A case of teenage folly, assuming everyone else was stupid.

In the dining room, they were sitting side by side, watching TV. She'd cleared her throat and launched into her speech. Her father had said, "No!" without a second thought. Her mother hadn't said anything, just put on her martyred expression, meaning she couldn't bear Gloria to start making a scene.

She'd insisted. It was impossible to describe to them the way he smelled, the way his skin felt, or to make them realize what a fantastic erotic opportunity was on offer. She was even prepared to take the train and come back the same night. But they dug their heels in and didn't see why there was any dispute about it. "But I can't *not* go, don't you see? And why shouldn't I anyway? If I'm going to a party, Nancy or Paris, what's the difference? Except in one of them I'll enjoy myself, and if I can't go my entire *life* will be ruined, and I'll feel like I'm just nothing."

Suddenly her father got to his feet in a rage. It's easy to see where she gets her habit of yelling like one possessed, trying to wipe out her adversary, knock him down, send him flying. He'd begun his usual rant, saying they'd had enough, with her mother going, "You just don't realize," and then the first blow, to punish her for insisting, followed by another to teach her to lie down when she was getting a hiding.

Only then, for the first time ever, facing him, she'd picked up a chair and raised it to defend herself. Bad move. It made her father go absolutely crazy. She'd had some serious beatings in the past, but this one went beyond bounds, and in fact it was the last ever. That he was a violent man was one thing, that he wanted to discipline her was another, but at no time did he actually want to kill her. Her father loved Gloria. She had always believed him when he said he loved her more than anything in the world. But, logically enough, it was like her own love affairs later in life: they adored each other but couldn't live under the same roof. Let alone talk normally to each other.

That evening, she had tried to defend herself seriously, refusing to curl up in a corner protecting her arms as she normally did. This time, she wanted to get past him, run away, and somehow manage to join Léo in Paris.

A doctor had arrived, helped the two adults to pin her down, given her an injection. Cotton wool, at once her head was full of cotton wool. Then the house was full of firemen, and she was in a coma on the ground, surrounded by boots.

Waking up in a hospital: the psychiatric ward.

In the yard, behind the window with its thick iron bars, everything was white, covered in white. She came to, finding herself in a hospital gown she didn't recognize. No other clothes in the room. Or any furniture either, except a bedside table, screwed to the floor. Headache. White walls. A square room with a very high ceiling. She got up to open the door and ask what was going on, but the door was locked. Accustomed to trouble, at first she didn't panic. That would take a few more days. She pressed the button above the bed. A man came in, a black nurse, in a white uniform, very tough looking and sexy, but not at all punk. He asked, "Feeling better now? How are you?"

She smiled, because when she wasn't screaming her head off and hurting herself, she was usually sweet and smiling. In short, she tried to retain her humor, her dignity, and to stay calm. She tried playing the girl who can't remember anything. A girl this kind of thing never happens to, a girl who says, "What's going on? When can I go home? Are my parents here?" He said he didn't know, someone else would come. She insisted politely, "Could you tell them I've woken up? I need to leave now." She had only one thought in her head, catch the train that Léo would be on. She was well used to cops, teachers, counselors, social workers, janitors, etc., etc., the wretched fauna that surrounds problem teenagers. She was used to finding the right thing to say to them and disarming them. But this time it didn't seem to work, the nurse spread his hands in a gesture of powerlessness: "You'll have to see a psychiatrist before being discharged. You'll have to wait." He wasn't even unpleasant. He was paid to be there, and free to get out of the place, when she wasn't. Sitting on her bed, she looked at the walls again for a long time. Tall white walls, how totally boring was that? Before ringing the bell again. This time, the nurse was a woman, and visibly harassed. Gloria again asked politely when she could see the specialist, and the woman shook her head: "Not till tomorrow, it's New Year's, we've got twice the patients and half the staff." She was annoyed at being called out, and left at once.

Gloria shook her head. Tomorrow would be too late, impossible to get to the station by late morning. She'd been awake for two hours now, sitting twiddling her thumbs in this cold and hostile room. She knew it was probably not the best tactic in the world, but she couldn't stand this atmosphere anymore, so she threw her head back, took a deep breath and howled, for the first time. Then as nothing happened, she decided to carry on, howling nonstop and throwing herself against the walls. "Let me out, fuck it, I need to get the fuck out." She could see that she must look like a crazed bird, skidding around bashing its head against the wall. People came running pretty quickly, but she was too busy playing her part to calculate what they might do, and kept protesting, "But I haven't done anything," crying like a neglected child. You could tell at once that they were used to this, they very quickly overcame her and strapped her down on the bed, efficiently, with practiced hands. She felt herself dropping off to sleep before she had even stopped shouting. Like an animal in the slaughterhouse, slipping sideways, collapsing, giving one final shudder, and then it was over, she was out for the count.

She woke up, still strapped to the bed, feeling sick and groggy as if she'd swallowed stones. For a few seconds, she thought she must have been in an accident, until it all came back . . . Then she saw her father sitting, waiting, his hands clasped between his knees, his eyes looking empty with dark circles around them. His expression was so sad, she had never seen him like that before. Even if she had been free of the straps, she still would not have attacked him—she would rather have strangled herself. It was as if this was the only thing she had ever succeeded in doing— giving pain to everyone around her, pain to her father. *I didn't want to make my father cry, I didn't want to see him looking so sad, so devastated and powerless. I was desolate that he didn't understand. I didn't want things to be like this. I'd have preferred to comfort him, give him a hug, say anything he wanted me to say, be the person he wanted me to be, and be it willingly. I didn't want to make my father cry, but I didn't want a living death, crushed in the life he wanted for me.*

Seeing him sitting by her bed, as she lay there tied up, she could see his love, his anxiety, his unbearable pain. Her father was from Longwy, the son of a coal miner, and from a large and poor family. He was a perfect example of social mobility under the postwar French republic, the 1970s, education, meritocracy, and all the rest. For him it was impossible to understand that she didn't want a nine-to-five job, that she didn't believe in his world. His generation had believed in collective progress, corresponding to the amount of effort you put in. They'd had thirty years of economic improvement, the so-called *Trente Glorieuses*. She was only fifteen, but she already knew, like many kids her age, that it wasn't going to be the same again, it wouldn't work out like that for them. Punk rock was the first warning that the postwar world was in trouble, a condemnation of its hypocrisy, its inability to confront its old demons.

She began to groan, for lack of the right words, and even

in that moment, she wouldn't have been able to reproach him with anything. She closed her eyes again. He stood up by her bed, he was crying quietly, like a man not used to it. He wept and she groaned. But she didn't yet know that he was weeping for the death of his daughter, the one who'd gone into Brabois Central Hospital on December 29, 1985, and would never come out. Another Gloria would take her place, pretending to be the same one, with pieces missing from her heart and a brain split in two.

When she asked, without being able to look at him, when she'd be getting out, he'd said gently, "You've got to see some specialists. It'll take a few days."

Then, unable to stop herself, she'd opened her mouth and started howling once more. An unexpected hoarse cry coming from some low point in her body. At once, another nurse appeared: rolled her over onto her side, thrust a needle into her buttock, under the sheets—stop, it's all over, back to sleep.

On New Year's Eve, the dessert was lemon sorbet. They had to wake her up to ask if she wanted some—surely she would? Because they'd given her another shot, since she'd made another scene that morning upon waking up. She was obsessing about the concert she was missing, and the idea that she wasn't going to be there made her go crazy every time she remembered. She didn't have any cigarettes either, which was bad, but naturally nobody in the place would have allowed her to smoke them, because if she didn't have nicotine at least that was one less thing that was bad for her. Sugared lemon sorbet. She found that a sick joke. Her mouth felt sour, full of the horrible taste of enforced sleep. She'd eaten a spoonful all the same. She wasn't strapped down now. But nor was she in a state to get worked up. She'd fallen back heavily, letting a mouthful of lemon dribble onto her pillow. In her dream, an alligator lying on her stomach was keeping her warm, protecting her.

Next step, interview with the specialists: give the right answers, show she was squeaky clean, mentally clean. So everything was all right, yes, no health problems, no, she was eating okay, friends, yes, girls, boys, school, fine, nothing to explain a breakdown, no need to be in a mental ward . . . add a bit of humor. As a result, on January 2, they'd announced to her parents there was nothing wrong with her, her mental health was normal, so they'd have to take her back home.

She was in her room, they'd brought her the newspapers, but still no proper clothes. She could hear her father yelling at them in the corridor—no, she *wasn't* normal, she *wasn't* in perfect health. In the 1980s, psychiatry wasn't really fashionable yet, people thought of the brain like the engine of a car. He wanted them to say, "We've opened up her skull, fixed a few neurons, put a spot of oil in there, it should run sweet as a nut now."

In the end, instead of discharging her, they'd taken her by ambulance to Toul. After her previous sessions with the specialists, she wasn't too worried. They'd said, "Just one more interview," and she'd gone in there convinced she'd be out by nightfall. And be able to put on something different from badly fitting hospital gowns that didn't do up the back properly.

At Jeanne d'Arc Hospital, she'd been taken into the office of this handsome elderly man, graying at the temples, aged about sixty. She imagined the Nazis exactly like him: calm, free of doubts, perfectly satisfied with themselves, sitting in elegant surroundings where everything was tasteful, clean, and impressive.

He didn't like her dyed red hair. Straight away, in the tone of someone competent, who has spent time thinking about it, he'd announced that she *wished* to appear ugly and asked her why. Why did she do that, didn't she know she could look quite pretty if she tried? Not a very promising beginning, in Gloria's opinion. She didn't think she looked as bad as all that. Not repulsive anyway. On the other hand, she wasn't setting out to appeal to ancient psychiatrists with white hair. You can't please everyone, but this man was convinced that if she didn't look attractive to him, that was her fault. For once, hearing this, she resolved to keep her mouth shut.

He started asking questions about sex, staring hard at her, probably to gauge her reactions. She'd have liked to jump up on the desk and start kicking his head in, to teach him to live and let her live. But of course it wasn't the moment.

There was no way she was going to talk about sex to this weird old guy, completely uncool, in this room with the light coming through the blinds, in the heavy silence. She avoided his eyes and stammered out a few laconic replies. At least she felt entirely confident that she was bright in school terms, bright enough anyway to satisfy the questions of a man like him. Or else it would really have panicked her.

"Why do you think you're here?"

"That's just it, I don't know."

Wrong answer. One of those damned times when honesty is not the best policy. And she dug herself even deeper in.

"I'm here because my father started yelling at me and instead of keeping quiet, I answered back."

Wrong again, you could tell right away from the old guy's expression.

"And in your opinion, why are you refusing to be a woman?"

Gloria decided to keep her answers to herself. Because agreeing to be a woman means suffering in silence, not fighting back. *Yes, you asshole, that's the real answer.*

But for the moment she didn't know what to say instead. After all, she had breasts big enough to be in a Russ Meyer movie, she knew she had a sexy behind, and when she was allowed to get dressed she was quite happy to wear skirts (with holes in her tights, agreed). She'd threaded pink laces into her trainers, she never went out without makeup, red eyes, black lips, green nail polish, and she was the only girl she knew who could climb out at night wearing high heels.

The old guy had written pages of observations before he got back to what he considered crucial: "Why make yourself ugly? Why did you cut your hair like that? And dye it that color?"

If she'd been the lead singer in a group, it would have made good lyrics: *Help, I'm in the madhouse, way away from you, the shrinks just want me to have a new hairdo*—but of course here it wouldn't help at all.

So, keep your mouth shut again, hey ho, granddaddy, it's called punk! Nothing to do with whether I've got a pussy, a prick, or a pair of wings, come to that. But since this old man had probably never left his own backyard . . .

She was surprised that someone with all these qualifications, in charge of a hospital section, should be so completely stupid as not to realize—in 1986!—that she was just going through normal teenage years and that there were far more distressing forms of rebellion than dyeing your hair a bright color.

Still, she thought she'd convinced him. When he'd made her wait in the corridor while he talked with her parents, she hadn't worried one bit. Tongue in cheek, she'd convinced him that she was a nice reasonable girl, capable of answering questions, and not flying off the handle every couple of seconds.

He called her back in, sat her down between her mother and her father. She was expecting a sermon, advice, the kind of guff you got from counselors at school. When the words "And I think it would be best if you were to stay here with us for a while" were pronounced, Gloria closed her eyes, her mouth, her nose, her skin, closed down everything, to retreat deep, deep inside herself, inside her heart and her stomach. She'd gone away. Between her and the world, that was it, over, she bent her head and held her breath.

There are moments, like this, that change everything. What had seemed solid and unchanging crumbles in an instant and nothing will ever grow there again as it had before. She once more closed her mouth, her eyes, her nose, and swore she'd get out, get out without betraying herself, and above all without being cured.

She felt, rather than saw, her parents accepting the decision. How could these two adults, who were themselves exceptionally violent, who flew into tempers every day, how could these two adults, full of pain and depression, how could they not see that she was simply their daughter? How could they leave her here, in the hands of strangers? Interned. Locked up. Battened down.

Until they were in the corridor, she said not a word. In fact, she was waiting for something to happen. For the old order to reassert itself. For one of her parents to come down to earth and say, "She's coming home with us, we don't even know you, monsieur."

Finally, in the corridor, she had burst out, begging her father not to do it, "Don't leave me here, don't do it," she had begun to cry. "Not here, not again, I can't bear it, I'm begging you."

She'd never begged him for anything, certainly not in that tone of voice. His face had assumed an expression that she would often inspire by other means in other men, the expression of someone who's terribly sorry, but he's about to ruin your life.

When she'd taken it in that she was really going to have to stay there, she was stunned, knocked out, a foul taste in her mouth and revulsion in every bone. Her parents had brought her an overnight bag, but she wasn't allowed her own clothes or makeup—and of course they hadn't thought of cigarettes. They looked as if they were at a funeral, as if they hadn't slept. And *she* was the one reproaching herself, the one who felt guilty. Just like when she ended up on the floor, arms wound around her head to protect herself from her father's blows, and her mother would invariably help her to get up, whispering, in mournful tones, "Why did you get in such a state?" Except that *he* was the one with the aggression inside him. He must have suffered the same things as a child, humiliated and beaten every day. Some of your dad's sickness, some of your mother's, and then good luck to you, but oh my God, however did she get this way? How was she ever going to *not* drive other people mad, except by being someone else?

Afraid of her. They were afraid of her when they got in at night, turning the key in the front-door lock, what would she have been up to now? Afraid when the phone rang, what were they about to hear? She was their own inner demon. And yet, they'd done all they could to suppress it, deny it, but here it was, coming out again through their daughter's lips. They were afraid, they'd asked for help. And all anyone had been able to suggest was to lock her up among lunatics and stuff her full of mind-numbing drugs. The same pills she'd have paid for in a club or at a concert she now had to scheme ways of spitting out. Result: she hardly slept. At night, they regularly opened her door, glanced in, watching her. What for? No idea. Just out of habit? Or to make it clear there was no privacy. No way of protecting herself from their inquisition.

Waking up at Jeanne d'Arc, even before she opened her eyes, she would remember where she was, and then in a second the poison came flooding in. And it was even worse than a toothache, first because there was no chance of buying cigarettes, second because there was no knowing when she'd get out—some people had been there three years—and third because it wouldn't look at all good on a job application.

No books, no newspapers, no cigarettes. Just all these mad people together and one TV set for the whole floor. At first, she'd refused to leave her room, and since they were still a bit afraid of her, they'd put her in a single: great. Some wards had eight beds. Ever been in a room with eight deranged people on the night of a full moon? Not much fun. The shakers, the anorexics, old women looking lost, men plotting in the corridors, whispering that they're being followed, then trying to run away shrieking. There was one guy, about thirty years old, who had a real problem with her. Whenever he saw her, he'd run up and grab her arms just enough to hurt, and then he'd snarl: "You filthy whore, I know you're putting stuff on the toilet seats, so I'll get crabs, but it won't work, I tell you." He was utterly serious, totally into his fantasy. She would push him away, he would insist, she pushed him away harder, and started screaming to get rid of him, a nurse would appear and tell everyone off. She'd become blasé, very fast. There was a woman for instance, blond, about forty, impeccable hairdo and makeup, skimpy gown, skeletal body, who really freaked you out. She adored Gloria and would lie in wait for her and grab her, pulling her into her room to show her photos of her house, her daughters. Then she'd start crying and asking her if she thought she was thin, and Gloria would say, "Yes, you are a bit, but you're going to go home, don't upset yourself," and the other woman would carry on crying and spreading out on the bed the photos of the life she'd had before, that she was destroying. The worst thing was that most of the people in here were old. Between thirty and fifty, but to Gloria they were positively geriatric.

All that romantic talk about mental hospitals, how the real lunatics were outside and the ones locked up are the only good people, poetic souls, well, that took quite a knock. Here, they dribbled, they raved, they pissed themselves, they cried a lot, they groaned in the night when they weren't howling. Nothing funny about it, nothing poetic.

In her room, lying on her back, she stared at the ceiling and channeled her rage, her fear, her shame, and her frustration into a circle around her navel, a knot of dark energy. She waited. She observed everything, thinking, and refused to do any activities.

She left her square bedroom with its dark red walls for half an hour every other day for an interview with her therapist: a clueless, listless, and unmotivated woman. Gloria could sincerely understand why you wouldn't have much enthusiasm for your job if you worked at a supermarket checkout, say, or if you were a caretaker or shop assistant. But not to care about your job when you had the power to say *stay* or *go* to someone in a psychiatric prison, that was nihilism taken too far for her. And you were *obliged* to go and see this obtuse dark-haired woman who was looking after your case. She had protruding teeth and wore glasses with big black butterfly frames. Expensive designer ones. Refusing to go and see her was a big no-no. This woman was obsessed with drugs, that was the only thing that interested her.

At every session, Gloria had to answer questions, how much she took, how it affected her. And every time, she refused to say that this was the cause of all her problems, "No, you've got it wrong, I'm young, it's just for fun, to get high. I'm not hooked on anything, and I get over it really fast." The woman seemed to have cloth ears. There weren't a hundred ways you could answer her questions. She had her files. They were about the real world, and in them were written a certain number of received truths. She was a psychiatrist because she couldn't be a priest, she was as rigid as a conservative Catholic faced with someone who was into wife-swapping. This therapist wasn't unlike the education counselors back home, whom the children regarded with suspicion: "If doing what I'm told means ending up like you, I'm going to be a juvenile delinquent."

Every other day, this therapist was back asking the same questions: "What kind of drugs, when, who with, did you vomit, cry, were you a victim . . . ?" "No, madame, all I did was have a good laugh and enjoy myself. Before I was brought in here, I promise you, I had no complaints."

Very soon, she stopped playing too proud to answer, because she wanted to get out. She was too frustrated, locked in her room, and she knew quite well that they wanted her to say something. But she couldn't work out what. She tried, "If I say that I've been lying all the time, and actually, yes, I do drugs, I'm hooked. It's really hell, it's like in that book *Christiane F.* I've had to sell all my records to feed my habit, so can you please help me to stop? Then I can get out, okay?" But that didn't seem to work. "What if I told you I'd been raped when I was little? Can I go home now?"

So as to meet people, she'd started taking part in the group activities: ergotherapy, group sessions, role-playing, relaxation, music therapy, anything and everything. Uncomprehending art therapists tried to have a go at her head. They would say, with knowing looks: "Aha! I see you've drawn an eye." *Well spotted, dork.* Then she'd drawn the head of a girl, and it had *two* eyes. Many meaningful glances would be exchanged. She'd drawn two eyes now! And that was as far as it went. Experts? These people were *paid* to do this? She'd quite enjoyed the relaxation class, on the other hand, breathing in to inflate her stomach and thoracic cavity, her shoulder blades, so that her body felt heavy on the floor. At least nobody could pretend to understand anything she said here, since nobody asked her anything. The group therapy sessions weren't so good. Listening to these adults expressing themselves like wounded and humiliated children was the stuff of nightmares. She didn't need to know all that about these older people. They were revealing their innocence and their inability to grow up. Nothing to do with her. But she kept going back there with unhealthy curiosity. And anyway, otherwise it was so boring.

She'd made friends, soon after her arrival, with Isabelle, a little brunette who was a real laugh. She seemed just like a kid. For a few days, life seemed to have returned, they visited each other's rooms, exchanged T-shirts, and shared cigarettes. The first question anyone asked in this place was, "Why are you here?" Gloria always answered, "I haven't the faintest idea," and Isabelle had burst out in giggles, "Same here!" Her hair was dead straight, shiny, reaching halfway down her back. She laughed at everything.

Before Isabelle was transferred to another psychiatric unit, some well-intentioned people took Gloria aside—people who hadn't even given her the time of day the week before—and made it their business to fill her in: Isabelle was here because she had tortured her little girl, with cigarette burns and putting her hand on an electric hot plate. Gloria had looked each of these Good Samaritans in the eye and said, "Yes, I know," to show them she didn't care. But she did care. It freaked her out, in fact, that someone who was so cute, sweet, funny, etc., etc., could at the same time be capable of taking her little girl's hand and pressing it down on a hot plate to punish her.

She'd set about loving Isabelle even more, a sort of emotional contortion, but eventually the other girl had had to leave.

Life reverted to normal, and since she had to get used to *this*, she'd get used to it. At least from her room she could look out of the window, through the bars. She could see a parking lot, people getting in and out of cars.

If she went too far from the end of her corridor, a nurse would come running after her. It was impossible, for instance, to go down to the lower floor to buy a newspaper. Her father had to be with her for that. He came in from Nancy every two days. She saw her mother less often, since she found it too upsetting to come.

The spinal column of every day was the telephone. When it rang in the supervisor's office, everyone with a room on the corridor froze, all the doors opened, waiting for a name to be called. Someone from outside, from the real world, the world of people free to live without trying, people who didn't roll on the ground, didn't hear voices, and weren't possessed by evil spirits. In a comic and pathetic ballet, every time the phone rang in that little office, the doors opened in a sinister kind of synchronized movement, heads popped out, the lucky inmate walked along beaming and delighted, while all the others returned disappointed to their rooms or to the TV lounge.

There was a smell everywhere of old people and piss. One little old lady came trotting along whenever she saw Gloria, right up to her, and slapped her face. She had wicked eyes. She only reached up to Gloria's chest, which made her easy to deal with. Sordid, like everything else.

When Eric arrived there, he was sufficiently different for her to spot him at once. A funny guy, because there he was, blond and bourgeois, squeaky clean, and convinced his name was Karim. Well, it could have been, perhaps, but the address he gave seemed to rule it out. And he had this very odd way of talking in the slang of the housing estates. The *beurs*, second-generation young Arabs living in France, weren't fashionable yet, but they already existed. Still, *they* didn't talk in the really weird way Eric did. When he began to explain to the doctors, in a tone of confidentiality, that people on the radio spoke to him directly to warn him about an earthquake, he lost all credibility. The victim of some chemical imbalance, evidently, he was living in a parallel universe, and wearing expensive clothes. When Gloria had glimpsed him between two corridors, he had on a striking black-and-white sweater. Of course, to make him feel better and return to his senses, they quickly confiscated his clothes for the old hospital-gown look.

He spent his first day there chatting, affable and relaxed, with the young anorexics and the ancient crackpots, he could have talked to the walls and it wouldn't have surprised anyone. The only cool thing, in fact, about this kind of place was that no one would think of passing a disobliging remark. For instance, if someone took it into their head to scold a chair, get down on all fours, or sit on the floor, huddled up and singing old nursery rhymes, no one would turn a hair. They were left in more peace here than in the Paris metro. Eric obviously took himself for some kind of prophet, you could tell from his eyes and the way he put his hand on people's shoulders. If that was his speciality . . .

It took a week for his parents to catch up with him. In

fact, he had entirely recovered his memory, spontaneously, by the second morning in Jeanne d'Arc. The short circuit was over. But he didn't tell anyone. Because he wanted to get to know Gloria, who at first wasn't too keen.

She'd realized that she appealed to him in a lot of ways, which was not exactly flattering, since she had no wish to get involved with some weirdo who believed in aliens.

The day after Eric arrived, a woman in a white coat had come into Gloria's room. Whether she was a psychiatrist or someone who cleaned the toilets or just a troublemaker, she didn't say, all she wanted was for Gloria to stop playing her music so loudly—on her Walkman! In that place, one of the basic principles, no doubt for everyone's good, was that anyone could just walk into your room at any time to tell you anything. At night for instance, they'd open the door wide, several times, letting the light in, to look at you. Perhaps to check if you were lying on your back when, this week, you were meant to lie on your side. Another thing they checked was that no one was having it off with anyone else. Not at all advisable, mad people getting together. Apparently they'd only harm each other. It's a well-known fact, cuddles are very bad for them and don't help anyone recover. (You had to wonder who were the ones with the most damaged heads, the staff or the patients.) So in this woman had stormed, in a great rage. Gloria removed her headphones, politely, without showing how much she would have liked to go on listening to her Motörhead album uninterrupted by some killjoy.

And the woman had screamed, "We can hear it in the corridor!" grabbed the headphones, put them to her ear, and pulled a face. Not a rock fan, obviously. Intimidated, Gloria experimented with a goofy smile, meant to express,

"It takes all sorts, eh?" But the old witch didn't see it that way, and grabbed the Walkman with a toss of her shoulders. "You think you'll get better, listening to stuff like that?"

Gloria sat still for a couple of seconds, telling herself she didn't want to get in trouble, it was probably just a test. Even here, even these people, couldn't be so stupid, could they? As if there were any limits to the nastiness of the powerful. A voice in Gloria's head was telling her to stay calm and wait for her father to visit, so that he could ask for her Walkman to be returned. The same voice advised her to keep quiet and never mind that she'd spend a few days without her music. Rightly or wrongly, this cowardly voice lost the battle super fast, and Gloria hurled herself at the woman. Literally propelled herself at her, as if she were rediscovering reflexes from playing rugby (in some previous life perhaps?). She'd flung her into the corridor, where the woman fell over backward, the confiscated Walkman in her pocket. Gloria, on her knees astride her, had grabbed her by the hair. And before the other slimeballs could muster the gumption to come running and pull her off, she had time to draw a little blood from the back of her head. She was screaming in the woman's ear: "You whore, you bitch, you can't stop me listening to Motörhead, hear me, you can't do this to me!" Yelling at the top of her voice, hoping the woman would be deaf for the rest of her life. That would make it worth creating havoc. Ruin her life, filthy cow, so she'd never hear properly again. At the time this had seemed important.

As a result, Gloria was deprived of music, exactly and precisely the only thing that kept her company until the end of her stay. Yet another thing that would help her get better, "rebuild herself," as *they* called it. Fuckers, with their crap methods.

That was the other thing you absolutely had to understand before they'd let you out of there: they could do *anything* they liked, and all you could do was keep your mouth shut. As time went on, Gloria learned that this was a very basic lesson. Which a lot of people know about, in fact.

Eric had been in the corridor that day, the woman had literally landed at his feet and he had stood quite still while Gloria was shaking her, yelling mad insults at her. He had observed the scene with the utmost attention. And a slight, knowing smile had crossed his lips.

Next day, breakfast time (if you could bear to eat it), 6:00 a.m. The future belongs to those who get up early, all right, but could someone please tell her the point of getting mental patients up so soon, given that everyone was totally fed up with being here? Oh well. Refectory tables, you were supposed to find a place for yourself. Gloria could never find a seat. Balancing her tray in one hand, it was tricky. What with the residents she wanted to avoid, the ones she made nervous, and the tables that were already full, she often had to go around the room several times before sitting down. Every morning, the anorexics, who had been forced to eat a bit of defrosted bread, were already vomiting. One mouthful and they puked up three whole meals. The nurses were instructed not to let them go to the toilets on their own, but they escaped. One old woman was chewing on her hand, which, like her arms, was covered with scabs and scars. She must have become unhinged long ago, before they invented modern ways of self-harming, so she ate her own flesh. This was pretty upsetting to see, especially on an empty stomach. One man, graying temples, metal-rimmed glasses, tracksuit top—typical gym teacher—used to sob hard, with tears running down his cheeks, then calm down before starting to howl in distress. It just took him like that, and he added to the local color. In this cacophony of wrecked souls, what depressed Gloria most every morning was that the coffee was lukewarm and bitter and served with powdered milk, whereas she liked her coffee boiling hot and laced with cold milk—real milk. She was propped up over her bowl, almost dozing off. Eric had appeared out of nowhere and sat down beside her. She'd noticed that he was looking at her with a dazed air, as if rooted to the spot. But she hadn't grasped straight away that this was serious affection.

As polite and poised as if they were meeting in a normal café—easy to see he hadn't been there long—he asked her, "Do you listen to a lot of music?"

She didn't know what to reply.

"Same as everyone."

He laughed. "No, I don't think so, I saw you fighting for the right to listen to Motörhead. That's not like everyone, no way."

At the time, this had gone to her head, thinking that it attracted him to have seen her freak out the day before, and then to remember it next morning, as if it were funny. Every tantrum of this kind made them all the more determined to keep her there, and the longer she stayed, the more frequent and extravagant the scenes became. You had to admit that if she were looking for a trigger for tantrums, she'd come to exactly the right place.

She clenched her fists without answering, she found this boy a bit of a jerk anyway. He was tearing his bread into little pieces, which he then ate like a sparrow, in tiny bites, chewing them very slowly. He was almost as tall as she was, but very fragile looking, with curly hair, sharp features. His gray eyes darted around the canteen, with real cruelty perceptible in them. He stooped slightly, giving an impression of intelligence and vivacity, but it made you feel uneasy. He stayed looking thoughtful for a while, visibly not distressed to be in this place, then he remarked, "I never get in a rage like that. I'd really like it to happen to me."

His voice was high-pitched, but pleasant.

"Oh come on, man, you don't even know your own name. But you know that you never get in a rage?"

"Yes, yes! I know, weird isn't it, the brain, I haven't stopped thinking about that since yesterday. It surprises me too, it really surprises me, I've forgotten my name, my address, my work, my friends, but *what* I am, myself, that seems to have stayed clear. Well, at least I can ask myself the question, that's something."

He was very calm, making out like some character in a dream, expressing himself slowly, as if it were painful to be waking up completely. She thought it must be the meds they were giving him, making him high, getting special treatment. But as she discovered later, he was always like that: in his own world, with occasional blazing outbursts. He looked at her over the coffee bowl he was holding in both hands.

"Apart from Motörhead, what do you listen to?"

"Motörhead."

"Oh, she has a sense of humor, I see."

"Don't you like Motörhead?"

"Frankly, if I didn't like them, I *certainly* wouldn't tell you. I don't want to get beaten up . . ."

This started him off laughing, she was already getting used to him. He had a slight coughing fit afterward and put his hand in front of his mouth, his hands were precise and delicate. White with long, thin fingers. He was refined without being feminine. Extraordinary to discover among all these crazy people in gowns, a rich kid who had remained a rich kid. She was about to get up and ask him to leave her alone, once and for all. Then he added, "I prefer the Stooges, New York Dolls, Generation X, that kind of music. Not as powerful as Lemmy but more twisted, I think, I prefer it."

She stayed sitting down. She would have been unable to identify any of the bands he mentioned if she had heard them. But she recognized all the names, the list operated as a good password, nothing but quality stuff, old guys.

"So you remember the *music* you used to listen to as well?"

"Are you working for them, or what?"

His smile showed his front teeth, his canines slightly too long and pointed, gave him something of a vampire look, which Gloria found suited him.

She was watching out for one of the servers who was in charge of refilling coffee cups. When she turned her head back, he was devouring her with his eyes. Remaining a little reticent, she was nevertheless becoming intrigued. You could sense at once that he wasn't really calm and peaceful, contrary to his apparent attitude. First of all, he wasn't at all upset or angry at finding himself among the insane. He was taking it too well for it to be genuine.

Gloria started talking again. "But you don't just listen to punk music, do you?"

"I listen to everything really. It's my thing. I like it all, jazz, rock, hard rock . . ."

This was the 1980s, people who listened to a bit of everything didn't really listen to anything much. She insisted: "Okay, okay, it's fine to be open-minded and educated, but what bands?"

"Polnareff."

"Oh, so you're a poof?"

He was content simply to give her a doubtful look, almost pityingly. She appreciated the effectiveness and economy of expression: in two seconds, he'd made her feel really stupid.

"Sorry, I must be mixing him up with someone?"

"With Frankie Goes to Hollywood?"

"No, with that guy who sings 'Où sont les femmes.'"

He immediately began a brief but very accurate imitation of the singer she meant, singing and wriggling on his chair, shaking his arms and his torso. A thin, high-pitched voice.

"Go on, you *are* a bit gay, aren't you?"

"No, not really."

"Peculiar to like Polnareff though."

"It's not my fault if you only go for one kind of music."

"At our age though, it's weird, isn't it?"

"It's nothing to do with age, stop it. You're being thick, thick, give up!"

"And you remember *that* all right, do you, that you like Polnareff, isn't that weird too?"

"Yeah, a bit more. But stop frowning. It really, really doesn't suit you."

When something made him laugh, he looked like a child, his eyes changed and betrayed their animal power. A funny guy altogether, with the rodent-like teeth he showed when he smiled. She felt herself beginning to be won over—to feel less alone.

As he relaxed and declared that he could be nasty as well, and since Gloria, whatever her doctors said, was all woman, she started wanting to sleep with him. She certainly liked his hands.

He hesitated, and looked at her, trying to make something out. Feeling she was being assessed, she immediately wanted to be attractive to him. He leaned a little toward her, their shoulders touched.

"Can you keep a secret?"

She couldn't prevent a little nervous giggle.

"Who do you think I'd tell, here?"

"When I woke up this morning, I could remember everything perfectly well. My name, my local disco, and even that I don't really like coffee first thing in the morning."

"Oh really? But you still don't get it, do you? Your secret's neither here nor there, if you really want to be in here, you can tell them your real name. They'll keep you just the same. It's not as if people are fighting to get in here, it's not selective . . ."

"Yes, but I want us to get to know each other better."

"Well, that's flattering . . ."

She didn't believe this for a second, and it must have been in her voice because he frowned, embarrassed.

"You're not very encouraging. Don't you want to get to know me?"

"I'd sit and chat with a German-speaking goat, I'm so lonely here."

"Good, because I'm much more fun than a goat."

"So how come you lost your memory?"

"I must have had too much Rohypnol."

"I hate that kind of stuff. Last time I had some, I ended up head down, asleep on the floor, through a whole concert of the Cure."

"In Vandoeuvre?"

"Were you there?"

"No, but I've got this friend, he talks about it all the time."

"So you really *do* know about punk."

"I keep up with stuff. But what I really like is Polnareff."

"And you're not queer? Never mind, I get it."

She made him laugh and he gave her some funny looks. Gloria was starting to feel disturbed, wondering on one hand whether she wanted to go to bed with him, and on the other whether he too was thinking of this, or whether he wasn't interested at all. She tried not to ask herself that question for the moment.

Eric must have read her thoughts, since he said, "Look, I'm not trying to chat you up or anything, I just wanted . . . I'd just like it if we could maybe have a smoke together, just talk a bit . . ."

"You've got some cigarettes?"

Her eagerness could not have been more obvious if she had rubbed her hands together. She suggested, "I've got a little stuff and some papers—spliff?"

He agreed and raised his hands in the air, arms up straight. Gloria said, "You look a bit like a cat."

"I was doing a boxer who's won the fight, but okay, too bad."

"Oh really? Sorry, but you did look like a cat."

"You wouldn't be a castrating kind of girl would you?"

"Me? You must be joking? Well-known for it."

She'd hidden in a pot of Nivea a little ball of dope that

a friend had brought her, a boy she hardly knew but who had decided to take an interest in her case. He came to see her by car, brought her some rag dolls with funny faces, the Cabbage Patch Kids, and he hid little pieces of shit in their pockets. "That's really kind of you," she had said with enthusiasm, wondering whether this guy was really cool, had nothing better to do, felt concerned, or just wanted to sleep with her. In which case it wasn't worth going to all the trouble. She liked the dolls anyway, they made her room look more cozy.

Her stay in a psychiatric hospital had become something weird, cool, all-or-nothing, as viewed by her friends, girls or boys. The ones who came to see her were not at all the ones she would have expected. Her best mates, the boys (and the one girl) for whom she would have gone to hell and back before she had been locked up, had never called or written. It was her school friends who had really been faithful. They would often phone, tell her funny stories, some sent newspapers or cassettes.

She pretended to be a girl who was neither surprised nor wounded, nothing that could make her mother say, "See I told you so." She was determined to be Miss Josephine Cool, but actually it was weird that her wildest friends had dropped her so brutally. When one of them had gone to prison, she had written to him, even sent him some money. She'd learned as well that there were plenty of jerks out there who thought it quite normal that she was in here. "Yeah, Gloria, well she dropped too much acid, she's fucked-up." As if anything at all could justify her being locked up here with horrible and incompetent slimeballs who didn't even have the slightest idea how to put someone back on her feet. After all, you had to be soft in the head to expect a person without even a garden to walk and sit in to make a complete recovery of mental balance, if all you provided was a lousy canteen meal, an hour in the TV lounge, and a few sedatives.

When she'd found out that several people she knew had found the decision *understandable,* she'd had to stifle tears of rage, burying her head in the pillow. *Please God, don't let anyone come into my room just now.* Die, rather than admit how she felt. Hard to believe that these kids, who listen to punk music morning to night, could just accept it if one of their gang gets locked up. You had to suppose that it gave them street cred or something, she'd find out when she got out. Some of them, tucked in at night by their mamas, never having taken a risk in their lives, were now *pleased* about what was happening to her, because that made it all more serious: hey, we're punks, it's dangerous.

Eric had already discovered a secluded place where you could smoke in peace and quiet, cigarettes or even a joint. Gloria was amazed that he had found it so quickly.

It was an empty courtyard, entirely surrounded by buildings, and reached by corridors she didn't know about. There was a small bench in the middle, deep in the snow that was still covering everything. It must be a special place for people who wanted to smoke in summer. It was bitterly cold. Gloria stamped her feet against the bench. She rolled up, gritting her teeth, stuffing the joint as much as possible with frozen fingers. She asked him, "How come you've still got cigarettes? Did you buy some before you got here or what?"

"I had plenty of cash with me when I arrived. I bought some off Pierrot, don't know if you know him, he's the one who . . ."

"I don't talk to anyone here."

"Have you been here long?"

"Two months, maybe not as much. Yeah, coming up to two months. Not hard to work out, I came in on January the third."

"Must get pissed off if you don't talk to anyone."

"At first I didn't plan to do that, but . . . what's he look like, your Pierrot?"

"He's a really nice guy."

"Not weird, then?"

"Well, he is a bit, you know, away with the fairies. At first sight, he looks okay, just this guy that used to work in a bank. Mind you, after about five minutes he'll start telling you that he's being followed, for instance, he gets on the train, someone's following him—it's the government that's after him. If he goes to the swimming pool, they follow him, if he phones, they listen in. And now that they've got him up here, they're still following him. He told me for instance in his sessions with the shrink, they're taping him . . ."

"That's just what I mean. I'm fed up with these people, their nutty ideas . . . it's all so trivial. I don't want to chat with someone who works in a bank, that would so totally depress me."

"Working in a bank, that'd depress you?"

"Why, do you think it's *romantic* or something? It'd really turn me on, eh? Chatting to him about how he gets up every morning to go and be yelled at in a stinking office with colleagues who hate him and then at the end of the month get just enough money to pay the bills? I'm too young, can't you see, too young for compromises. Why should I bore my ass off talking to old squares? They don't even know who the Stooges are."

"So why are you here?"

"My parents."

"And?"

"I don't know what got into them, but it was nothing to do with me."

"Did they want to go away on holiday or something?"

"Dunno. They're pretty uptight anyway. I'd rather they'd've dumped me at the side of the road."

She was acting the girl who's quite confident that she's here because her parents have somehow gone crazy. She sincerely thought she believed this. But deep inside, the intimate enemy was watching and collaborating with the shrinks and therapists, deep inside, she was convincing herself that there really was something wrong with her. You don't get locked up by chance. Not in places like this.

She'd pulled hard on the joint, enjoying the burning thrill in her throat and a lungful of nicotine.

"But how did you manage to find this place? I haven't had such a good time since, well, since I got here . . . "

"It's my Boy Scout training, be prepared . . . "

It was a long time since she'd been able to smoke and she found his remark funny enough almost to make her roll on the ground laughing. Once she'd calmed down, she breathed deeply with pleasure. She passed the joint to Eric and surprised herself smiling at him in a dopey way. Next moment, he had a coughing fit, and it set them both off in gales of laughter. They returned to the refectory for lunch, freezing cold, but ecstatic. Gloria was relieved he hadn't tried to put his arm around her to keep her warm. She didn't need someone who clung to her. He looked at her with wide eyes, finding she looked disturbingly like Greta Garbo. Every time she made some feeble joke, he'd fall about in delight, in fits of laughter. He was beyond in love with her. It was passion.

In other circumstances, she'd have avoided him. He was just too precious, physically and intellectually. He lacked seriousness, toughness, virility. She couldn't care less about guys who camped it up, except when they wanted to make love to her. Which, paradoxically, happened to her quite often. But she'd learned to be wary since one boy *like that* had really shaken her by jumping out of a second floor window, just to piss her off. At the time, she'd refused to feel guilty about this. It had even taken several other people to hold her back from running over to lay into him when he was lying on the ground. But since then, she'd avoided vulnerable-looking homosexuals because she was sure they'd get her into some inextricable trouble.

But for now she was only too glad to be able to talk to someone who'd heard of Stray Cats, Joy Division, and the Cramps, too relieved to be able to talk about what interested her. To have confidence in someone else's judgment. Eric was reattaching her to the world she loved. He knew about music. And that was fine by her.

They would stay in her room, with the door wide open, otherwise the staff would go ape worrying they were sleeping together. His own room was occupied by four people, one of them an old man who wandered and never spoke, but occasionally broke out and became violent without a word, which was much more impressive than if he'd been yelling. Without a word, he'd head straight for a glass door and demolish it by crashing his head against it. She'd seen him do it once. In later years, she often modeled her style on his. For instance, if she really wanted to disrupt an evening, she'd adopt the old man's tactics and break a window—using some object so as not to hurt her head, but not saying a word.

Hervé, one of her mates from her "gang," was one of the few who came to see her, but they wouldn't let him in—he was too drunk. Never mind, just to hear him chanting in the courtyard, "Let Gloria out, let Gloria out!" from two floors up, had cheered her spirits. Then he had taken up a position under her window, a stroke of luck, and played *Macadam Massacre* at top volume. She'd clung to her window bars, singing along at the top of her voice, hoping he could hear her. And since indeed that was the case, it had taken the police to get him away. He must have said to himself, since I've come all this way, might as well really mix it.

Lying across her bed, Eric listened to her stories. She wasn't usually talkative but she had some leeway to make up, weeks of silence, and above all she wanted to tell him more about her life outside, before, the kind of girl she was before this happened to her.

From the moment she and Eric got together, she forgot to spend all day raving about when they'd let her go and started playing jokes instead. For instance, following one of the attendants with her questions, especially if he blushed easily: "Tell me, would sodomy damage the brain?" Eric adored this, he had a talent for pushing her to do silly things. He made her talk, be funny. He was like the answer to a prayer, this boy arriving in the chamber of horrors.

But one afternoon, his parents finally found out where he was. Eric and Gloria were both in her room. They were listening to Wunderbach, she was humming, lying on her front, as she watched him draw on the cover of a note-book, squares inside triangles. He was telling her he'd seen Stray Cats live in concert. She replied she had this school friend—she wore a green-and-white Teddy jacket, this girl from her old school—she'd taped two whole cassettes for her of Stray Cats and drawn pretty covers for her, not bad at all. A doctor had come to fetch Eric. He didn't even warn them they should say goodbye. It must have been one of their therapeutic principles: never confuse an interned being with a human being.

Recognizing his parents at the end of the corridor, he'd simply said hello to them. Without pretending to be happy, or surprised, or furious, or not to remember. No fuss, but plenty of style. He was surrendering. He waved from the end of the corridor to Gloria, then quickly put his hand on his heart.

She looked at his parents, bourgeois, serious, looking out of place in this setting and appalled to find themselves there. The mother with her ponytail and casual clothes, the kind of woman who does her own gardening, and the husband who could have come straight off a golf course. Pathetic and very upright. Relieved to see him there and safe and sound—his mother had wanted to pat his fore-head and he had just shied away and stared at her, quickly.

Gloria didn't understand exactly whether it was see-ing him standing there looking so cold and dignified, or whether it was because he was leaving, but for the first time, she regretted having always managed to avoid sleep-ing with him. She liked him, that was the truth.

She didn't want to be there without him. She preferred not to hang around watching him walk away and realizing what was happening. Alone again in the institution, for a time always unspecified. A day, a lifetime . . . it depended on other people.

He'd left her his Walkman when he went. She put the headphones on and began to cry.

SHE FINALLY GOT out of the hospital about five weeks after him. The whole time she remained there, he'd written to her every day. He sent her little pellets of dope, hidden inside cassettes, cigarettes, or detective novels, which she read at once, it made the days go by quicker. Once he had left, she fell head over heels in love.

Every morning, a letter would arrive from him. At first she'd played casual, just looking for the gift. But soon she really wanted to read the letter and admitted it readily. She replied every day, he'd sent her envelopes and stamps, everything she needed. He was funny on paper, much more so than in the flesh. His writing was small and regular, sloping, very clear, a bit feminine, not too much, just enough to be seductive. He'd started talking dirty in his letters and that wowed her, it made her chuckle, all alone. She masturbated several times a day, thinking what they would do when she got out.

Overall, Eric provided her with a shield against the place, a shield against her pain. She thought about him when she woke up, the worst moment of the day: when she remembered where she was. He accompanied her virtually, helping to drive away the horror and anguish of the possibility that she might never get out.

Life went on. Every therapist she saw was just like the

others: all self-satisfied and simpleminded. "And what do *you* think about it?" they would say, looking penetratingly at her. They liked to screw up their eyes as if they were deep in thought. But it was obvious they understood nothing. She felt like taking them by the shoulders and booting them outside. "Get a life! Meet people, travel, listen to music, read something, get your own mind sorted out, you might be ready after that to come back and meddle with other people's."

The anger grew thicker inside her, took root in her heart, went in deep.

And then one day, the head doctor simply announced she was leaving. She bit back the comment: "Oh yeah, so you think I'm *cured* now, do you?"

Her father had brought two big sports bags to carry the stuff she'd acquired in four months. She felt blank as she packed up. Not anxious, not happy, not excited. Blank, as if broken.

In the car on the way back, the twenty kilometers to Nancy. Trees along the road, it wasn't yet a double highway. A few big stores, furniture, DIY warehouses. The snow had melted. It was spring already, with the first colors appearing. She and her father didn't exchange a word. She was no longer furious, or sad, or guilty. She was blank, as if in suspended animation, drained. She'd gone to earth, retreated inside herself somewhere. As if she'd been at the edge of icy water, or a polluted stream from which one has to retreat carefully. Her father seemed the same, as if scalded. She'd always known him with a beard, ever since she had been born he'd had a beard. Now he'd shaved it off, it made him look younger, naked, almost indecent. Vulnerable too. But if in her there was a glimmer of desperate tenderness for him, and if in him there was a twinge of regret or anxiety, neither one of them showed the slightest emotion. Two strangers, sitting very calmly in a spotless white Renault, going home a few days before Easter.

She didn't know it yet, but it takes time for critical events to register, developing like a plant in the soul, bearing their fruit and declaring themselves part of reality. To allow the symptoms to manifest themselves, as they would say in the hospital. Gloria would say, "The time it takes for it to hit."

Nothing would ever be the same again. And at the back of her mind always the question, *Who would I have been if this hadn't happened to me?*

Her mother, waiting for them at home, had cooked fries, Gloria's favorite, especially when she was little. She liked peeling the potatoes onto a newspaper spread across her lap, taking care not to peel too much off, but also trying to make a single peeling from one potato. Then wiping the potatoes with a clean tea towel—you had to take one from the drawer, next to the cutlery drawer under the tabletop. Then you put them in the wire basket to make the fries. The rest her mother did, handling the pan.

But this time she hadn't been there to help prepare everything. And she wasn't a little girl anymore. She hadn't thought properly, not at all. She had imagined this day, coming out of the hospital, thousands of times. Everything she was going to do the minute her nose was outside, the people she'd call, all the stuff she'd find in her bedroom. She would play a 45 on the record player, find her old clothes, put on makeup, telephone her friend Florence. Even taking a bus had seemed like something special when she was locked up.

Only now she was back home, it felt like nothing at all. Tomato ketchup on the little kitchen table, just big enough for the three of them to eat at. Nothing, ever, the same again. Her mother had prepared this celebration meal, but her features were drawn, she was avoiding Gloria's eyes. She was ill at ease. Nothing ever the same again. No appetite, just enough to nibble a few fries.

She felt confused, as if drained, neither aggressive nor amused, observing things almost automatically. Her parents looked tired. She would have preferred them to be full of energy and hostile to her, so that she could start hating them. But it wasn't so simple. In families, things are rarely cut and dried.

There was a new fridge. The old one had been on its last legs for a while. Life had gone on.

She found the courage to say, "No thanks, I'm not hungry," when she was offered the chocolate cake, a little overbaked, which her mother had made. This false birthday meal reminded her of the tea parties in the hospital, oddly enough. Full circle. When she saw her father's face on hearing she had no appetite, she'd immediately said, "Oh well, perhaps just a little piece." As if she couldn't "do that to them," refuse them the pleasure of seeing her eat what they had prepared.

She had been away four months, and on her return it was spooky, she found everyone both exactly the same and changed, all the people she'd been dreaming of seeing. Everything seemed kind of disjointed, she was out of sync. At first, coming out of the hospital, her feeling was fury at everything she'd been missing. But while she had been making herself sick thinking this way, of all the good times she'd lost out on, nothing had really changed. People she'd adored just "before," now seemed boring and stupid. Superficial. This word, which would never have occurred to her six months earlier, now kept occurring apropos of everything. Superficial. She'd lost her flexibility and tolerance for her immediate group of friends. She was damaged. Nothing was as she had hoped and imagined for four months.

In town, she'd bumped into Frédérique, a young bisexual well known in the district, bold, brilliant, often funny, and usually surprising. He came from Haut du Lièvre, a low-income neighborhood, and was intriguingly beautiful. He could make music with a washing machine and sing without opening his mouth. Naïveté, thinking it was decadent, the insouciance of the 1980s . . . His voice was always husky, and he cultivated an air of vagueness. Everyone knew he spent hours cruising around Place Carnot, looking for men. He'd thrown his arms around Gloria and given her a big hug. He was a sufficiently odd person for her not to resent him for never writing to her, and anyway they didn't know each other that well. But at last, someone seemed to understand where she was coming from. A sad place. So he hugged her, this guy who was always sarcastic, a crook really, with absolutely no moral sense. But he was the only *fucking* person who offered her some tenderness, right there in the street, who saw she needed something to hang on to. *Hold me, never let me go.*

To celebrate, he'd pulled out a little matchbox, two tabs

of acid and slipped them into her hand: "To help you get your bearings, good to see you back, big girl."

Just a little acid and bingo—all the joys of a really bad trip. Before it had even started working, she'd walked away from her friend Laura without warning. Bursting with overvivid ideas, she felt on the point of exploding, bombarded with crazy absurdities, images, and concepts, all visually unbearable. She was wearing her high-laced Doc Martens and they began to make her freak out, she was walking along the street and the sun was beating down and the Docs seemed to have a will of their own, as if some Nazi punk spell had been cast on them and they were going to force her to cut children's throats. Where they led she would have to follow.

Luckily they were content simply to take her back home, but the comedown was terrible. With the sun as well, brilliant, blinding, full in her face, scouring out the back of her eyes. On the way, she'd hallucinated she kept meeting the same guy, disguised as a painter, an office worker, a little boy, but always the same individual who stared at her and tried to make her understand—nonverbally of course—that some very bad stuff was about to happen. He was carrying a ladder, then two streets farther on she saw him with a briefcase, next, at the bus stop, the same man was standing with a baby clasped to his chest, and later there he was again, carrying a traveling bag. Told like that, it sounds like nothing, but at the time it was a nightmare. Luckily when she got home no one was in, she'd curled up in a ball in a corner of her room, and then, a false good idea or a real flash of intuition, she'd put on a 45 of the Béruriers, "Nada Nada," on her record player, an old one, you just had to put the needle arm in the high position for the record to keep replaying as long as you wanted. Until night fell and her parents came home from work, "Nada Nada" on loop, a needle penetrating her brain, her guts, all her white corpuscles, loading them with fear, stifled anger, hate. Since then, every time she'd tried to drop acid, it hadn't been good. Yet it was something she'd really liked doing, acid trips. Simply a sign that all her neurons were poisoned with anguish.

Generally, once she was out of the hospital, she found the whole world disappointing, without daring to admit it or complain.

Almost as soon as she was back home, she'd written to Eric, but as it was the Easter holidays, he was away. This was in the days before mobile phones, so if someone wasn't there, you just had to wait for them to get back, nothing else for it.

She'd been enrolled now as a boarder in a school twenty minutes from Nancy by train. She'd have to go there without seeing him again. In the end, that suited her. She felt somehow embarrassed by their idyll. Like memories of exotic countries, fantastic in real sunshine, pathetic when you see them on TV. Out of its setting, their story lost much of its charm, and she felt apprehensive at the thought of seeing him in the streets of her hometown.

She'd thought obsessively about him for days. She'd written pages and pages to him, laying bare everything about herself, without being afraid of his opinion. She'd read his letters, she knew him better than any of her childhood friends. And he was crazy about her. That felt nice. He often spoke about the way she threw spectacular tantrums. *Good*, she thought, *just as well, because I won't disappoint him on that score.* But it was astonishing—both tempting and terrifying—to be loved precisely for what she was most afraid of in herself. He spoke about what he was listening to while he wrote. Since they'd met, he'd started following more youth music, punk and psycho. There were a lot of things she liked about him, his laid-back quality, his ability to pick up on codes and issues, to come up with a view about different bands. But she didn't want to introduce him to her friends or go to concerts with him, or anything really. It had been a little hospital love affair, not something for the broad light of day.

The fifth day after she came home, she became a boarder in Lunéville, out in the sticks. She'd arrived at her new school with an orange crew cut, a safety pin in one ear, four piercings in the other, a heavy chain around her neck, wearing an army surplus coat with NUCLEAR YES PLEASE on the back in bleach and her old trainers—she'd given away the maroon Docs the day after the bad trip.

So after the Easter break, Gloria found herself sitting in the Lunéville train, on her way to school. The carriages hadn't changed since the 1950s: a musty smell, torn seats, black-and-white photos of landscapes above your head. There was no heating, so early every Monday morning she had to huddle in her seat. The windows were covered with icy condensation. She preferred to get up at dawn rather than take her time on Sunday night, because then the train was full of soldiers and she hated being in a compartment with a group of boys.

This state boarding school was a lot less horrendous than she'd expected. Not full of punk rockers, naturally, because it was out in the middle of nowhere. But the local teenagers were mostly good-natured, neither easily impressed nor wanting to show off. They could hold their alcohol well, had a sense of humor and patience. Nobody over-reacted about her appearance, or her record, or anything. Nothing like the nightmare she'd expected. She quickly made two friends among the girls, strong Lorraine accents but good company. They listened to Exploited, which, with cows and tractors all around, gave you an extra kick.

Eric was delighted she was out of the hospital. She wrote in reply that she wasn't allowed outside school grounds. In fact, she regularly escaped to go for a beer and have a night out. She could perfectly well have arranged to meet him.

She preferred not to tell him straight out that she didn't want to see him now. She hoped he'd get over it without too much trouble, but it looked as if that was going to be difficult. Ideally, she'd have liked it best simply to go on writing each other letters. It would have suited her to have, on one hand, a grand epistolary passion, and on the other, real life with real boys. Without a threatening bridge link-ing them together.

The boarders picked up their post in the evenings, after classes, from pigeonholes in the lobby of the residence. Almost every day, there would be a white envelope with his address on the back. The paper changed sometimes, or the color of the ink. A brief note or a thick bundle. This was her regular rendezvous. She liked the prestige it gave her among the other girls. But she wasn't going to open up to them. It was her own business. Her link. Often, she didn't read the letter right through. But she would have been in despair if nothing had arrived, or if the few sentences she did read hadn't been loving and passionate. She knew the words he liked best, his expressions, the jokes he'd tell. It was sweet and reassuring, a landmark. So she wasn't quite alone. In her letters back, she kept clumsily putting off the moment of seeing him again. But he wouldn't listen: he wanted sex. He'd loved getting her letters, writing, all that stuff, but now it was time to fuck. He talked about her body in almost every line. It was hard to ignore. Gloria was not keen at all. She was the kind of girl—there were quite a few of them around in those days—who couldn't reconcile sexual attraction with intellectual companionship. There was too much tenderness between the two of them, too many discussions on paper, too many confidences. That took her outside her erotic safety zone. A long way outside, in fact.

She wrote him things like, "Wouldn't you prefer for us to run through the countryside hand in hand?" pretending this was a joke. She was afraid that sex wouldn't work, that it would be embarrassing, awkward. She knew enough about it to be aware that intercourse can seem very long when you're not in the mood. Very long and very prosaic.

But for the first time in her short life, she couldn't manage to be brutal, to tell him she'd changed her mind. It would have been easy just to stop writing, even simpler to send him a short note along the lines of, "Do me a favor, get lost." But although she didn't want them even to meet, let alone touch each other, she didn't want to lose him either. Obscurely, she felt she couldn't allow herself to do without him. Or not entirely. He gave her moral support, bombarded her with his love, his esteem, his respect, his taste for her.

She managed to stall for a few weeks, keeping him hanging on without giving him a date. She pretended she didn't go home on weekends, whereas every Friday night she was back at the Campus, her local nightclub.

In May she was expelled from the school. She'd been stealing cash from girls in her class, taking it from their bags in the cloakroom during gym lessons. It wasn't the cleverest thing she'd ever done. At the time, she was in the habit of stealing. The moment circumstances made it possible to pinch something, she told herself it was provocation. Everywhere. All the time. She felt she was in a kind of cosmic test. Having the feeling that some mad education specialist had put cameras everywhere, and that it was her duty to show this person that she didn't care and was going to steal anyway. These were years when she was playing games, but in a confused state of mind. Anyway, everything cost such a lot of money, beer and cigarettes for a start, and after all you had to live. So some stupid local girl had complained that she'd lost five fifty-franc notes (it was still francs in those days). Hard to deny it when the exact sum was found in her pocket. She'd denied it anyway, on principle. Summoned to see the headmistress: fiftyish, small and plump with huge breasts, lots of makeup, big tortoiseshell-rimmed glasses and a smile. She was *sincerely* sorry it hadn't worked out, and wished Gloria better luck elsewhere, as she told her firmly she would have to leave. Gloria was not unduly distressed at her expulsion: she didn't mind school, but she preferred it in town.

Her parents hadn't made a fuss, not the way they would have before the hospital interlude. In the family, these days, everyone avoided making scenes. They had enrolled her next in the Lycée Chopin, not far from the city center. You had to take two buses to get there, it meant getting up rather early. But this was a lycée with no lodge at the gate, so the pupils could come and go without reporting to anyone. Gloria loved this. And the lycée was a little way off center, so the local bars were mostly full of high school students. Better and better, as she told herself.

She hadn't written to Eric to tell him about her latest escapades. She had stopped opening his letters, which were forwarded from the boarding school. She just piled them up, unopened, one on top of the other. Category: the past.

One Saturday afternoon, not long afterward, the whole gang was at the Foy. A chic bar, with windows looking onto Place Stanislas. Leather banquette seats, marble tabletops, glittering chandeliers.

As usual, the proprietress was sulking, wondering, as she did every day, what she had done to turn her establishment—normally catering to tourists and the well-off—into the rendezvous of choice for all the local punks.

Gloria was drinking shandies, because at the time, although she liked getting drunk, she didn't like the taste of alcohol, preferring sweet things.

There were a whole lot of them in the bar that day: Victor, shaved head, gray jacket, fan of German bands. Mathilde, a divine anorexic, eyes entirely redesigned with eyeliner, thirty centimeters of black hair impeccably gelled up on top of her head. Léonore, a punkette with a shaved head, blue eye shadow, long nails, very short skirts. Little Lorelei, scarlet hair, crucifixes everywhere, a walking religious festival, wearing her crosses right way up, upside down, in her ears, around her neck, on her wrists, green miniskirt, red tights with black stripes, two front teeth missing. Poulbot, a tall girl with curly fair hair, a friendly face, a big mouth, and a long skirt, thirties style. Plus a big guy called Herbert and his mate Roger, not what you would call intellectuals, in their green bomber jackets and rolled-up jeans. At the time, there weren't so many punk rockers in Nancy that it was worth picking fights with skinheads. They left that kind of thing to the Parisians, not enough talent locally.

Night was falling when Ratus arrived, looking the worse for wear. Ratus, an authentic punk rocker, way ahead of everyone else. Seniority among punks was a sign of street cred, it gave you prestige and various advantages. One of the rare points in common between punk and the civil service.

The story was that Ratus had run into a gang of neo-fascists, a mixture of mods plus two skinheads with southern accents. When they saw him, they'd started insulting him, calling him a filthy stinking punk. He had advised them politely to go fuck themselves, and they had all fallen on him.

He'd hardly finished telling his tale than everyone was on their feet—apart from a few girls with overcomplicated outfits, and the odd boy who wasn't keen on a fight. Once they'd paid—this took a good twenty minutes, what with finding enough coins between them—the gang was on its way, determined to persevere all night if they had to, to find the motherfuckers and give them hell.

They cheered each other on with howls of laughter. Their bad luck, eh, Ratus, they didn't know who they'd picked on, or they'd have stayed home with their mamas, doing their nails. Herbert was carrying a small police baton inside his jacket—just in case, he said, and now the moment had come. One of nature's vigilantes. He ended up, poor dope, spending ten years in prison, what a waste. Roger had gone to fetch a pickax handle from his car—again, you never knew, might come in useful. And Victor was fingering his teargas canister. Gloria, like Ratus, had simply smashed a Kronenbourg bottle against the pavement. She held the bottleneck in one hand, while a full beer bottle was doing the rounds. When they finished one, they stopped to buy some more.

Gloria adored this kind of escapade. She loved being in a gang, looking for trouble, the intoxicating rush of adrenaline, just before. Fear, mingled with determination. She loved the fellow feeling, the camaraderie it created at once. And she loved being a lone girl in a crowd of boys, without it being a big deal. She took this as a proof of her worth, "Good as a boy, you are," whereas it was just proof that the world is badly organized. Herbert was yelling at the top of his voice, "Here we go, last pogo in Nancy!" a local adaptation of the "Hymne de La Souris Verte."

On their way, they asked passersby for directions, sometimes politely, sometimes threateningly. A young kid—an apprentice amphetamine dealer—guessed at once who they were after.

"I saw them just now, they're at the Excelsior. They're waiting for me, 'cause I'm supposed to take them some stuff. I didn't find none, so they can wait. So what did they do?"

They'd reached Place Saint-Evre now. Moving along, almost at military pace, in a group, this time it was Roger who was howling "Ethylique" in a sepulchral voice. As they approached the bar, Victor signaled for them to stop and be quiet. "I'll take a look on my own, but not go in. See where they are, so we can rush them." The Excel was a café near the station, lots of glass frontage.

Then in they went. Roger, the biggest of them, signaled to Gloria to keep beside him in the frontline, "Come with me, a girl psychopath always impresses 'em." She knew how to behave, alongside the leader, his trusty sidekick. Baring her teeth in a sinister grin, like in an ultraviolent film. She wasn't planning on using her broken glass on anyone, it was just to look good and scary. Unless the situation deteriorated badly, she was thinking of dropping the bottle, pushing over some tables and throwing chairs. Noisy and visual, but not really dangerous. As for the others, she couldn't have sworn they were thinking the same way. But it was up to the assholes facing them to understand and get out of there fast.

They had walked the length of the bar, a dozen of them, with everyone staring. Silence had quickly fallen in the room. A tableful of young boys, shaven heads and crew cuts, wearing lodens and khakis, was waiting for them as indicated.

Gloria put on her broadest smile, like in a Western, life was good.

She didn't recognize him at first. The group of boys stood up, with mocking grins, ready for a fight. Not having found their amphetamines, they'd had plenty to drink instead, they were up for it too. A few waiters intervened, pushing everyone toward the exit.

"If you're going to make trouble, do it outside."

Wasted effort. The first fisticuffs were the signal for the start. Gloria had barely had time to aim a kick at the balls of a teddy boy—quite cute-looking actually, she noted—

before someone had grabbed her sleeve and was dragging her outside, yelling, "Run, the pigs, the pigs!" She was propelled forward, the first to make it through the revolving door, losing her breath she went so fast. Two seconds later and she'd have been picked up—a vanload of police was in the area and had spotted them immediately. Still running, she could hear their whistles and male voices ordering her to stand still at once, which she took good care not to do. Gasping for air, she made it to Place Carnot and slowed down. The guy who had warned her did the same, and only then did Gloria recognize him. He'd shaved his skull, it made him look quite different. He'd put on weight. His face had lost its androgynous, almost unreal beauty. But his body, his overall appearance, was a lot more attractive. He now gave off a more powerful, more animal air, something that wasn't there two months earlier. He was wearing a Harrington jacket and cutoff jeans.

They both stopped to catch their breath, side by side, Gloria managed to get out a few words: "Fabulous! So romantic!"

Eric smiled as he looked at her. They were under a streetlamp. He signaled that he agreed, his hand on his heart, trying to recover. Pointing at her he said, "I'd never seen you in punk gear before, suits you, bitch! Why did you throw me over?"

"Dunno what you mean!" Overcome by a convenient coughing fit, she had to lean against the wall, sliding down to squatting. She smiled up at him. "Scared you, eh? What were you doing with that bunch of morons anyway?"

"Mates from the South, not morons, quite the opposite. What possessed you, coming in and picking a fight?"

"They beat up one of our pals!"

"What, that tramp? Pal of yours?"

He had crouched down beside her. With a sniff, she leaned over to look at his badges. He put his arm around her waist. She read "Skrewdriver" and "Komintern" and pulled away, shocked.

"Know who they are, those pukey bands?"

She stood up, making a face of total outrage, so as to be able to leave him.

"You go around with fascists, you listen to shitty groups! What do you think you're doing, little boy? Growing some balls? I wouldn't do it that way."

She sneaked a glance at their reflection in the bus-shelter window and thought they made a nice couple. A Destroy punkette and a psychopathic skinhead, impressive, no? Plus "we met in the mental ward," very modern, in her view. Still, not a reason to let herself soften toward him. Not that at the time she was too fussy about what people thought. On the contrary, the more outrageous it was the more she was up for it.

It was just a strategy so that she could leave him there without having to explain. Yes, she was glad to meet him again, and amused by the circumstances. But she had to find her way back to the others and get away from him. She didn't want to explain why she'd stopped writing to him. Too confusing. Best just to split.

She was about to get angry and walk away when she saw Herbert running across the square. She just had time to wave to him and hear him yell without slowing down: "Get away FAST. Cops everywhere, they're after us."

Eric grabbed her hand firmly. "I live around the corner, come on." And since she was hesitating: "Want to get clobbered and blamed for everything in the bar? Hurry!"

She consented, struck by his common sense.

He did indeed live about two streets away from Place Carnot. In the entrance hall, she started to wonder what the hell she was doing there. Wide wooden stairs smelling of furniture polish, silence. Gloria was spitting like a cat, it was too quiet and peaceful, arrogance and opulence, too much for her to bear. Everything that as a teenager she feared: order and prosperity.

She stopped on the stairs, exactly like a mule that refuses to budge.

"Look, never mind, I don't want to come in. Your parents will be there."

"We won't see them. Don't worry, I'm not going to introduce you to them right now, mademoiselle vanishing act."

Gloria shook her head, obstinately.

"Don't make me laugh. Just leave me here for five minutes. I'll go home, I'll get away with it."

Eric sighed, and sat down beside her on the stairs.

"You're pushing it. You're lucky, you know, every time I see you, you're trying to beat someone up, and that really turns me on."

"It turns you on?"

"Yeah. Makes me really want to fuck you. Already before, it was quite strong, but now, seeing you . . ."

"Oh really?" Gloria asked, impressed by such certainty. She felt her reluctance melting. All the reluctance of the last few weeks. He put his hand over hers.

"See, frankly, you look a bit crappy in that punkette gear. But since it's you, I like it. Any other girl, looking like that, I'd feel like vomiting. But you, well, you turn me on. I don't know why. You just turn me on. Coming?"

She rolled her eyes up to heaven, like a saint ready for sacrifice. Then she stood up. Dusted off her behind and asked, "Is it a long way up, to your place?"

"Yes, but we don't have to take the stairs."

They went up in the elevator, and when they were in front of a huge door, a door so imposing that it could have been a dentist's office, he rang the bell. The door was opened by someone Gloria thought might be his sister. Very beautiful, youngish, but sad-looking. He greeted her and she signaled to them silently, in complicity, indicating they should tiptoe along to the right. The apartment seemed as big as a hypermarket. They went up a flight of stairs, then along a narrow corridor with gray carpeting and high ceilings. His bedroom, on the top floor right, was spacious, with several windows. Gloria understood better now why he so much wanted her to go back home with him. He explained that since he'd spent that week in the hospital, his status had completely changed—he was regarded as seriously ill now. And that wasn't bad at all, because everyone tried to be really nice to him, concerned. It was cool.

Hi-fi speakers, record collection, tape recorder, TV, video games, consoles, model airplanes. Gloria was both touched and appalled that he wasn't ashamed to let her in to see all this.

He had some good weed, she'd slumped onto his bed and dropped off to sleep. He'd woken her not long after, carrying a load of chocolate cakes. He rolled another spliff. They watched *Mad Max*. She had almost nodded off against his shoulder, it felt nice. They were getting used to each other. He kissed her on the lips, his tongue was delicate and nervous. She regretted coming here.

Then things moved fast and in a couple of seconds her clothes were off and he was on top of her and fucking her. With great enthusiasm. They were both aroused by what had happened earlier. Having managed to escape so successfully, Gloria consented to return his passion, feeling for his skin with her mouth, scratching his back as if to mark out the territory. She didn't take her eyes off him, his eyes were half-shut, concentrating, he was plowing into her as if his life depended on it. She would have preferred to go gently, more slowly, but she'd noticed that it wasn't worth even trying to say that to a boy his age, not the first time anyway. They both fell asleep immediately.

In the morning, he fetched them two bowls of black coffee, a demi-baguette, and a pot of Nutella. She almost fainted with gratitude. A whole pot of Nutella, hardly started! "No one else is home." They listened to the Meteors, then the Cramps, then "Surfin' Bird," at top volume in this bedroom belonging to a well-behaved little boy. They howled as they jumped on the bed. He kept putting his arms around her and hugging her too tightly. "I'm so glad I found you again, Gloria, I missed you." She liked him to say that. And she felt it was resurfacing fast, the pleasure she felt at being with him. This time with nobody watching them.

They made love all day, sometimes on the carpeted floor like youngsters. She was finally getting used to him, wriggling, rubbing up against him, laughing with content. Since saying, "I didn't know how much I wanted it," they had had time to warm up. She came, almost inadvertently, which didn't happen often. In fact, never with a guy. On her own, yes, anytime she wanted. But not with someone else. It hadn't bothered her before. She was a girl, she wasn't going to fuss, she wanted to please the boy, and was quite content if that made him happy. So it had taken her by surprise, and even disconcerted her a little now, to find that with him she could come. Just like the first time she'd masturbated, she knew what it would feel like, she wasn't born yesterday. But she was puzzled that it was happening. At fifteen, she had imagined she would be frigid all her life. Which hadn't surprised her then, there were so few things she got right. But Eric was feline, he undulated over her, worked on her to possess her, whatever the cost, to the far end of the end of something she didn't yet know she could be. When they began again, she understood. It was almost frightening, another thing about him that would count for a lot with her. His tongue was diabolically competent. As often with her lovers, she'd learned in a day to appreciate what only the day before seemed a fault. As for him, he was like a kid at Christmas with a new toy, he wanted to play all day long.

His parents were back home, but they didn't come to his room. She'd had enough now, cloistered in his pad, it felt like being held in a luxurious aquarium. "Come on, we'll go out." He disappeared to nick some cash from somewhere in the house and in ten minutes was back with five hundred francs.

"Where did you get that?"

"It was lying about."

Later his mother would give him hell, discovering he'd pinched money from the household budget.

Outside in the street it was getting dark. Eric had taken Gloria by the hand, and she felt uncomfortable. Afraid of meeting anyone she knew. She wasn't quite ready to acknowledge him. Too precious, too new, too teddy-boyish, too blond, too delicate, too *everything*. Now she was ill at ease. She was beginning to plan how to get rid of him and go join her usual friends. Then they'd bumped into Victor, and the two boys had got on fine. They'd gone over the bust-up of the day before and began to reenact it live, going mad with excitement, miming the actions, inventing extra twists. Gloria, feeling left out, chewed her lips, thinking about the flagrant injustice of male solidarity. Always ready to be best pals, just like that, whereas if she wanted to get three little sentences out of them and a bit of consideration, she was obliged to move mountains of motivation. Seeing how easily Eric fit in, she began to relax a little though, and was more willing to let him hold her hand. That evening, the three of them went to some practice rooms—the basement of a warehouse for fitted kitchens, fixed up for them by the father of one of the gang—to watch a band rehearsing. They'd bought several six-packs of beer. They sat in a corner, the band was doing a Joy Division cover. For Gloria, this kind of place, the atmosphere—deafening drum kit, electric guitar, amplifiers on full blast—felt like being a trout returning to its river. Wraparound sound, for once she was exactly where she wanted to be.

During a break, everyone shook hands all around and, standing with Roger, she told the drummer about what had happened the night before. She could hear Eric somewhere behind her asking if he could have a go on the guitar, and she stiffened with shame for him. She thought it was being a total twat to ask to play instruments when you didn't know how. She could have done with a spade to dig a hole right there and jump inside and never come out.

When she heard him start to play, she remembered just in time to look cool with it. He played better than anyone she'd ever heard, holding the guitar the right way, low down. She listened, arms folded, unimpressed girl, just lending an ear. Inside she was thinking, *Wow, I hadn't got you down as this good.*

He wanted her to sleep at his place again, but when she called home to tell them she was staying with a girlfriend, her mother had answered icily that that very friend had been ringing the house all evening. "You should have warned her, my girl."

Eric bought her a last glass at the bar by the bus stop. She tried not to be too enthusiastic, she thought she'd noticed that it put boys off if girls seemed too keen right away. But really she wanted to climb all over him, touch him, slip her hands under his sweater, make little loving sounds, kiss the back of his neck, stroke his back, and for want of being able to give way to her feelings, she started acting like the girlfriend from hell, finishing off her shandy while giving him the benefit of her theories.

"See, if you play guitar, it's not *quite* so bad you being an upper-class snob, because being a guitarist trumps being a snob. See what I mean?"

"Are you that kind of girl? Groupie? Chases around after bands?"

"You bet! Drives me crazy when a guy can really play. Like you, if you saw a girl with super-sexy fishnet stockings, that'd turn you on, wouldn't it?"

"Yeah, all right, I get that."

"So okay, explain to me how it's less stupid to get horny when you see a girl's stockings than to get wet when you hear a guitar solo."

"Getting you wet isn't the point of the guitar solo . . ."

"Oh really, that's what you think, is it?"

She caught the last bus, the twenty-one, eight o'clock, one that would take her straight home. Night had fallen during the journey, and she watched the streets she knew by heart as they went past. It was the first time a boy had been mad about her and at the same time impressed her this much. As a rule she attracted stupid assholes.

IN JUNE 1986 she read in *Best* that Bérurier Noir would be playing at Saint-Etienne with OTH. Eric had suggested they go see them. They were meeting every day now, one way or another. That they were meant for each other was beyond discussion for both of them. They weren't old enough yet to realize that the future lasts a long time, and sooner or later things get complicated.

That evening, he'd gone home to fetch a rucksack and "some stuff" while she waited for him down in the street, a bottle of Kronenbourg in her hand. She'd wanted to show him how easy it would be to steal a Renault 5, but she got confused trying to hot-wire it, and in the end they'd taken the train, since Eric had enough on him to pay for both their tickets. Less exciting, but more reliable. It was a night train, hours and hours in an empty carriage. They fell on each other and to their great regret, nobody caught them at it.

She was used to coming every time with him now. She was convinced, like a good little Catholic at heart, that this was because she was in love. The future would tell her otherwise about orgasms, it was more complicated than yes or no.

In Lyon they trailed around the station and met a guy from Longwy, easily spotted by his red Mohawk, who was going to the same concert and could take them by car. Eric had a knack for getting on with people, he wasn't afraid of linking up with them, cracking jokes. Gloria was happy enough to go by road, but this guy drove in his own special way, and it was a miracle they didn't have a head-on crash. He stopped at every gas station. She had a feeling of freedom, possibilities, intoxication. It was fun to look at the other people in their cars and be glad she wasn't living their lives. She wasn't that little girl being driven around without any choice, or that wife sitting alongside the hubby in the driver's seat, or that secretary on her way to a course. She didn't have to be someone normal. In the 1980s dyeing your hair green still caused a sensation. For lots of people it meant the unknown, danger, being part of something special, like knowing a secret.

In the car, they prepared for the evening by listening to *Macadam Massacre* at full volume, yelling along with it: "*Adonowonabébé adonowanabébémalo.*" Speed, the motorway, a new friend, the bass beat banging out. This music, which she'd been listening to all the time for the last few years, had two contradictory effects: a fantastic sense of relief, a loss of repression, and yet, at the same time, it also conjured up deep anguish. Without resolving it, it spoke to her about *that*: being locked up, terrorized, being in the dark.

They completely lost their way and by the time they got to the concert, OTH had already started their gig. They were singing "Euthanasie pour les rockers": "*Tu finiras clodo, finiras clodo / Je finirai riche, et mon vieux chien aura sa niche / Heureusement y aura l'euthanasie pour les vieux rockers*

/ *Euthanasie pour les vieux rockers*" ("You'll end up on the streets, you'll end up on the streets / I'll make a pile of dough, my old dog will lie low / Old rockers, put 'em to sleep / Old rockers, put 'em to sleep!"). The concert was in a great hangar out in the middle of nowhere. Losers, pariahs, junkies, good-for-nothings, all quite happy to meet up in the same place. There was some sort of confrontation with a gang of skins, but Gloria was so out of it she couldn't really remember afterward what had happened.

Beer, plenty of beer, Coca-Cola, whiskey, more beer, and as soon as the bass started up, a powerful primal basic sound, a thousand people jumping up and down. As if at a signal. A chaotic psychic crowd movement, a fabulous collective jam. All through the concert that energy had to come out, bodies against bodies, crashing into complete strangers, sweating and yelling. Letting go.

At the end of the concert, Eric, who always had an idea where he was heading, took her by the hand, there were fields all around. They had sex in the grass, like randy rabbits, it was scratchy on Gloria's back, she could feel prickles on her thighs.

Hitchhiking back to Lyon took all night. They'd been picked up by a scary-looking soldier—is there any other kind?—who looked like he would rape young couples and then chop them up. Gloria didn't close her eyes the whole trip. Eric, more relaxed, was snoring peacefully, head on her shoulder. The driver didn't open his mouth the entire time, his hands gripping the wheel, jaw jutting out and determined. He dropped them off on a motorway exit just outside Lyon. They were stuck, because it was impossible to cross the road, and dangerous for motorists to slow down. Since they had no choice, they accepted it philosophically.

The main thing was not to give up, they repeated to reassure themselves, stuck on the edge of a motorway with cars rushing past at top speed all around them. In the end an old banger took the crazy risk of stopping, four kids inside it, on their way back from the same concert, wearing polka-dot shirts and sailor's caps, and still as drunk as skunks from the night before. They all piled in together as far as Lyon city center.

Eric and Gloria had tried to sneak onto the Nancy train without tickets, but were spotted very quickly by a zealous inspector who took the opportunity, when the train stopped in the middle of nowhere, to make them get off. Night was falling. They set off on foot, trudging a long way, not anxious, but without any other option than to press on through the countryside. Finally, they reached an engine shed, where there was no one to find them.

She came straddling him, to sex it up. Dawn was breaking. It was like being on a journey, except that the train was stuck in a shed, with grass growing between the rails. Surreal. Both violent and very gentle. She tried to be as wicked as she could. She liked to feel that he was losing his head. She felt for caresses, movements so as to feel him trembling and clinging to her. The sensation of climbing, then opening like a lotus blossom inside. It took her by surprise every time, a great powerful wave surging up between her legs. Every color of the rainbow. Then the gallop. Just had to hang on, not to miss the climax, that was important. There was a huge space inside her that she'd never realized existed before. Sometimes, in spite of everything, she got distracted, started thinking of something else and missed the moment. It wasn't automatic, it was even rather tricky to manage, taking off.

So she sometimes faked it, struck attitudes, and although she'd never seen a porn film in her life—in those days only addicts and people with subscriptions to a certain TV channel did that, and they weren't numerous—she spontaneously mimicked all the poses of the genre. Even when the earth didn't shake, he was magnetic, embraced her, and transported her. He said it was because of her, she was a sexy witch. She pretended to believe him. But she knew it was the two of them, their coming together that took them to this fantastic place. They had fallen asleep huddled together.

GLORIA WAS FASCINATED. Every time he took her to his place, his parents were appalled. And didn't conceal it. Brilliant, exactly the effect she wanted to have on the old killjoys. Eric's mother, a handsome dark-haired woman, elegant and authoritarian, gave her the kind of agonized stare that Gloria took as a compliment—it meant she'd made the right impact.

The summer holidays arrived. To Gloria and Eric, it was an ideal opportunity to go to London, to buy hair dye and records, striped tights and studded belts.

For the first few days of the holidays, the sun blazed down. Gloria had bought an orange wig and wore a fluorescent green miniskirt. She peered at herself in every shop window, thought she looked sensational. Eric, more restrained, had found a gray cloth cap and splurged on brand-new Doc Martens. They were on their way back from Parenthèses, a record shop, when Gloria started planning decisively.

"We'll have to work through July. Got anything lined up? I can get a job at the Mammouth supermarket, my dad knows the guy who hires temps. That's to pay for the ferry. Once we get over there we'll work something out."

Eric shook his head, obedient little boy.

"No, in July I'll have to stay with my parents, we always go to our house in the country."

"What about August, will they let you go then?"

"No, they won't, but they'll leave me alone. They want me to stay in Nancy with a tutor."

"A what!"

"A tutor to help me study. It's to get me up to the level of this place they've enrolled me in next term."

"They're going to *pay* someone to make you do your vacation assignments?"

"Well, yeah, that's their plan. But I'll talk to my father in July, try and get him to have a word with my mother."

"And if she says no?"

"I'll pretend to give in, but one morning I'll get the train and by the time they tell the cops, we'll be in London, cool. I've got a bit of money hidden away, I want to get a synthesizer."

"A tutor! God, what a performance, just to pass your baccalauréat!"

GLORIA PUT IN a month's work at Mammouth, shelving packets of biscuits from six in the morning. By the time the customers arrived pushing their trolleys and ready to complain, the packets had to be lined up properly. The first days were fine, she'd enjoyed taking risks on the sly, sampling all the biscuits. It was strictly forbidden to open any product, let alone eat it. Anything found open was taken out back and thrown in a bin—scrupulously mixed with inedible trash, in case it attracted groups of "scroungers" to the garbage. After ten days, she had tasted all the varieties they had on offer and was tired of them. She'd made friends with the gangling teenager—another temp—who was in charge of the candy department. She popped over to see him and pinched packets of Carambars or little chocolate bears. It gave her a thrill, like living dangerously.

It was her first paid job, she was just sixteen. It made her decide that once she was grown-up, she'd certainly rather tramp the streets than spend her life on her knees from dawn to dusk in a supermarket smelling of detergent, with artificial light beaming down on you, having to suffer in silence the nasty remarks of frustrated supervisors. (This was a youthful vow she was never able to keep. Her whole life thereafter consisted of dead-end jobs of the same kind.)

They were writing to each other every day again. The trip to London was taking on the dimensions of a honeymoon. Gloria didn't even go out on weekends, so as not to spend a centime of the precious sum she was saving up for their departure. Eric was seething in the country house: "Last summer we didn't know each other, but I was already fed up with it . . . This year it's not just that it's boring, I'm realizing how stupid they are, how arrogant, how cowardly . . . This is the last time I give in to them."

Gloria said nothing to this, but found it peculiar anyway to be going on holiday with your parents when you were seventeen—more like a mama's boy than a tough skinhead. He wrote: "My dad is so totally a stupid bastard.

He said no to London right away. They really hate you. If you could hear them, you'd be proud of yourself. Anyone would think you were more of a threat than the entire Red Army, and let me tell you, around here the Red Army isn't flavor of the month!"

She laughed when she read his letters. She sent him mixtapes.

On August 1 Gloria had completed her month, collected her pay. She was ready for a long lazy morning. But at dawn, Eric tapped on her window.

She lived in a housing estate where many people had converted their basements into bedrooms or offices or utility rooms. Her windows were barred because when she had moved into this room, she'd invited too many friends to come and sleep over.

She had gone upstairs to open the door, and met her mother—an insomniac—trailing around in a blue dressing gown, looking weary. Gloria had apologized. "It's just Eric, I don't know what he wants, but he's here."

Her mother had simply rolled her eyes, without a word.

The time in the hospital had made the whole family calm down. Gloria asked for fewer outrageous permissions and no longer shouted at them. Her parents forbade fewer things. An uneasy status quo. Nobody wanted to go through the mental-ward stage again. As a result, her father, so as to keep himself out of the way, worked twice as many hours as before, which was some achievement. If he was never there, there was less risk of an explosion.

In Gloria's room she had an old barstool. Eric perched on it. He seemed disoriented.

"I've run away. I can't stand them anymore."

He was looking tanned from his holiday. Still half-asleep, Gloria didn't know what to say.

"You want us to leave for London right now?"

"London's out, I'm sorry, I don't want to get caught at the border on the way back. I don't want to go back home. EVER. Know what I mean?"

"What happened?"

"Everyone was so weird in the country. They were all being super nice to me, the uncles and aunts, but my mother and father too. Treating me like a prince, but putting on pressure as well. I think it must have been to make me go off you, you see? A new strategy, nastier but not stupid. Half emotional blackmail, half manipulation, half—"

"You can't have three halves, but go on."

He smiled for the first time. But at once, he had to clench his teeth and his eyes filled with the tears he had been holding back.

"They didn't lecture me. I even tried to talk to them two or three times, get them to see my point of view. I was so goddamn stupid, I thought they were listening, and I told myself they'd come round in time . . ."

"So, what's the problem?"

"Let me finish. You don't know my sister, Amandine, well, generally she's a pain in the neck. Her tactics are always to say yes, yes, and then she does exactly what she wants behind their backs. She steals from them, she likes poking around, finding money, pills . . . That's the way she's always been, Amandine, since she was little, she pokes her nose into everything. She's sure there are family secrets, that's her romantic streak. And she's good at finding things out, plenty of practice. Soon as anyone's back's turned, she'll be into their bag, soon as the house is empty, she's rooting around in drawers. There's less than four years between us, and yeah, we scrap a lot, but well, we *are* brother and sister, you understand?"

"No, I don't understand, I'm an only child."

"Two kids in the same house, we may not always get along, but well, fact is we're fond of each other. So at the end of the holidays, I could *tell* something was wrong. She was being way too aggressive toward my parents. Never seen her like that before, usually she's more devious, Amandine, she very rarely tackles them head-on. So I didn't know what was going on, and with me, instead of teasing me and provoking me as usual, she was kind of embarrassed, looking at me sideways, watching me."

"Hey, the suspense is killing me, get on with it."

"So one night she comes to see me—big deal. She acts like the elder sister, asks me a lot of questions about myself, us, drugs, life, how I see things . . . just amazing from someone whose main aim in life since I've been around is to make me stay out of her way."

"I know what it is, she's pregnant! And they're saying she's got to have an abortion?"

"No, no, nobody has abortions in our family. Or if they do, they keep it quiet. Let me finish, nearly there. So I'm suspicious, and I get ratty, I ask her questions too. She doesn't say anything, not even to tell me to get lost, or that I'm an idiot, etc., she just looks at me with tears in her eyes and trembling lips . . . and finally she lets me into the secret—that the rest of the family all knows about, except for her, and *she* only found out when she chanced on the enrollment forms—at the end of August, they're planning to send me to a military academy in Switzerland! With walls as high as a prison, no question of getting out, even for Christmas. The idea is to discipline me, put me back on the straight and narrow."

"Are you sure your sister isn't making all this up?"

"Amandine found the fucking *forms* in my mother's desk. She usually keeps it locked, but that day one of the grooms had been injured, she'd had to go out in a hurry."

"A groom? You're really weird, your family, you have grooms?"

"We keep horses, we're not going to hire lifeguards."

"But is it just so we can't see each other, you and me? That's why they want you locked up?"

"Partly. My mother's terrified you'll get pregnant."

"Well, you can set her mind at rest, we do abortions super quick in my family. Anyway I'm on the pill, what would I do with a kid, at my age?"

"She thinks you'd pressure me into marrying you and then . . ."

"Love you to bits, baby, but I don't want to marry anyone. She's nuts, your mother."

" . . . for the child support, alimony."

"Oh really, how does she know I haven't got a nice little job with good pay and everything?"

Gloria starts packing her bag, in other words collecting her cassettes and some makeup essentials.

"Right, well, the good news about all that is we can go off on our big adventure."

"But I don't want to make you miss out on your final year exams, just because—"

"Are you kidding? I couldn't care less about my exams, anyway I'd never get a job. That's at least one thing your mother got right."

SHE'D THROWN HER travel bag out the window, asking Eric to pick it up. He would leave the house first and wait for her at the bar on the corner, the Petit Palais, so as not to alert her parents.

Gloria had stayed alone in her bedroom. She was saying goodbye to her childhood possessions, and wanted to write a letter to her father and mother. She was very young, and thought sincerely at that moment that she wouldn't be seeing them again. This definitive departure reconciled her to them, and filled her with an affection for them she had not felt for a long time. It was like an ordeal by fire, as invisible tender hands pulled her and begged her. But she had to go. *Life means moving on, you'll have to get used to leaving people behind*, she told herself, to bolster her courage. She tore up several versions, getting lost every time in sentimental effusions that made tears come to her eyes as she sat alone. In the end, she simply wrote: "Don't worry. Thanks for everything, love you lots."

She went out wearing a T-shirt, no jacket, telling her mother, who was reading the paper in a corner of the kitchen, that she was going to buy cigarettes. As the gate squeaked, she still had tears in her eyes—she was running away like a man, like a coward. The little street on her block was suddenly charged with sweet memories. Happy days leave less trace than traumas—until they're in the past. *Family, I'll miss you a bit*, was the way Gloria thought of it, with melancholy.

Two hundred meters down the road, she had put it all out of her mind.

THEY SPENT THE whole of the month of August in

Paris, so happy and trouble free that they were surprised such a life could exist. Coming out of the Gare de l'Est, they had gone straight to New Rose, off the Boulevard Saint-Michel. In front of the record shop, a few skinheads were hanging around. Eric went right up to them as if they were a friendly group of wolf cubs. Like it did every time, his natural manner won them over, and one tough skinhead with a lot of teeth missing took them under his wing. He put them up at Juvisy for the whole month, in an apartment belonging to his mother, who'd gone off on holiday with Club Med. They went back every night by the last train, brazenly scaring all the other passengers in their carriage. It was weird to see this great brute in his little-boy bedroom. The mother had locked the sitting room and her own bedroom, to keep him from making a mess of them. Eric and Gloria slept on the kitchen floor. Every morning, all three took turns perfecting their look in the bathroom: one shaving his head, the second gelling his Mohawk, the third curling her blond hair—before they went off to spend the day in central Paris, hanging around the Fontaine des Innocents and the Forum des Halles, opposite the Père Tranquille restaurant. They spent the time chatting, telling each other stories or real-life adventures, and panhandling. In those days, Paris wasn't full of beggars, so people quite readily gave cash to these runaway teenagers, with their wayward looks and strange outfits.

One of them would describe how he'd been beaten up the day before, another was angry because someone in the group had given a Nazi salute in front of some old ladies, the discussion would degenerate. One guy would turn up with a newly traded Walkman and want everyone to listen to Crass. Another would arrive and try to grab his headset, and another lively discussion followed. Their days were punctuated by getting stopped and searched, the cops were the only "normal" adults they really met, briefly, now and then. The rest of the time, there was no one around to bawl them out over little things, they were inside their punk bubble, very pleased with themselves. On the margins of society.

Then the skinhead's mother got back from her holiday. Gloria and Eric had just met a punk from Marseille who was following Bérurier Noir around from concert to concert. They jumped a train as far as Troyes with him.

When they got there, the station had been invaded by a whole crowd of punks: all it needed was some black flags. Blue hair, red Mohawks, bottles of Valstar, bovver boots, coming from all directions, everyone was at home there. A lot of youth with big grins, still in possession of all their teeth, beginner street kids, delighted to be there, wrapped up in their old sleeping bags. They greeted one another more or less cordially, going with the flow. Eric and Gloria were immediately adopted by some punks from southwest France who had glue to share around, unbelievable accents, and many tales to tell.

The concert was like Brazilian carnival for French kids: lots of fun and partying, but with an undercurrent of rage, of grating madness.

After that, Eric and Gloria followed their new gang to Besançon, a town reputed for its well-organized soup kitchen. The local cops tried to persuade them to move on somewhere else. The police spent their time arresting youths at random, taking first one then another into custody. They all learned the drill, how to spell their names according to police regulations, how to sleep on the floor, leave their shoelaces and belts at the desk, regularly have their money confiscated, receive punches in the police station in front of the others, get handcuffed to radiators. It gave them stories to tell later. It became routine, among these young people, made them feel they were genuine down-and-outs, true punks.

One evening, all high on Coca-Cola and red wine, the gang decided to get back to Toulouse in stolen cars. There were fifteen of them. The first car they tried, a Fiat, wouldn't start. They all tried pushing it, trying to get the engine to kick in by rolling it downhill. Upon which it crashed into another car . . . belonging to the police. The cops were aggressive at first, not realizing it hadn't been on purpose. After that, they kept asking, "But what would fifteen of you be doing in a Fiat?" Good question—why had they gone along in such a big group to steal a car?

Eric was enjoying their freedom more than Gloria. He had to get his own revenge for discipline and ambition. To get drunk on beer, singing silly songs, was exactly what he wanted, it made him feel much better. As a couple they were popular, always welcome. It was fun being the two of them.

Another time, Gloria and Eric, having spent several hours sniffing glue, had decided to rob a tobacconist's shop, after a Parabellum concert in Grenoble. Unwisely, Eric thought it would be a good idea to start by jumping on the roof. Gloria thought that sounded like a great plan and followed him up. They bounced up and down like mad creatures, sincerely hoping the roof would give way, so that they could help themselves to what was inside. Since the owner hadn't foreseen that anyone might try to rob the shop via the roof, no alarms went off. Not that they needed to. The pair of them were making a racket fit to wake the whole town. The sight had so flabbergasted the shopkeeper, who turned up quickly, that they had time to get away.

Another time though, Eric's obsession with roofs paid off. They managed to get into a little supermarket several nights in a row, pinching alcohol and savory biscuits, avoiding the night watchmen, crouching down between the shelves, keeping still, thrilled to bits. Very exciting. Then some of their mates caught on and overdid things. The roof was soon security-proofed.

All this time, other people their age were learning about real life in school or university, or already in jobs. People of their generation were learning to be competitive, disciplined, learning not to set their sights too high, not to ask questions, and that money is what matters most in this world. Eric and Gloria were learning nothing at all, they were having a good time and taking their revenge for all the past pain . . . In different ways, both of them would eventually realize what a very poor preparation punk rock had been for later life. Too much fun, too much utopianism. Getting back into reality wouldn't be a pleasant experience.

But for now, they didn't leave each other's side for a second. They fucked when they felt like, they lost all inhibitions, they panhandled together, they went to charity shops together when it got cold, looking for warm sweaters, they went together to the public baths . . . Besançon, Montpellier, Toulouse, Paris. Then it was autumn and really cold outside, so they bedded down together in the same sleeping bag. It was a time of student demonstrations, about which they couldn't care less, but throwing stones at the police then running away, breaking shop windows, and fighting skinheads was still just as exciting. They stayed in Paris for a few weeks.

At Nation metro station, they spent hours doing nothing but lounging around and chatting about passersby. There were regular scuffles. Eric liked picking fights with soldiers. He'd found some mates who shared his taste. Gloria loved hiding behind him when he started to mix it with them, he would give her the sign and she'd come forward to give them a head butt. They were never expecting that a girl would be the first to strike a blow. Let alone that she'd hit so hard. They'd run away after that, often pursued by the companions of the guy on the ground. They'd be laughing about it for days afterward. Being stupid had become an article of faith. They were beaten up themselves too. They patched each other up as best they could, with handkerchiefs and spit, or else they would go into a pharmacy and ask for help. Sometimes they'd be given top-notch dressings for their injuries, other times they'd be chased out with threats to call the police. Occasionally they managed to grab a prescription for amphetamines, and then they would walk around in a group for nights on end, high as kites, talking nonstop.

They had all declared losses, using false names and dates of birth so as to avoid their parents being alerted, since they were minors.

In October they were in Évry, a town outside Paris, a big gang of them. Sleeping in the staircases of a tower block, since nobody used the stairs, especially on the thirteenth floor where they were squatting. That morning, someone had brought up a whole tray of croissants "found" in front of a canteen.

Since it was cold, they spent the day hanging around in the entrance to a shopping mall, where they were all copped by the police, because some madwoman had accused them of nicking her purse while she was window-shopping. They were bundled into the same cell, girls and boys together, for once. Gloria clung to Eric, she had the beginnings of a cold with a high temperature, and she dozed off while the others quarreled or joked. One tall guy, prematurely aged with drugs, had hidden a dirty syringe in his pillow, which he had been allowed to keep. He was being scolded by the others, who told him that was filthy and dangerous. Then in the middle of the quarrel they had fallen about laughing. "Are you nuts or what, did you think you were going to able to find some H in the cop shop?" and they all found it hilarious. Gloria had dozed off again. One of the cops came for Eric. It didn't worry her, that was the usual tactic, pick the kids off one by one, take their photo, threaten them, etc. She was used to it, so she didn't protest. At about five in the morning, they were all told to scram—in fact, the woman had been making it up, and the cops had no intention of making out a lot of paperwork for all these time-wasting kids. She had asked where Eric was, and the duty sergeant told her to get lost. She decided to wait at the mall all that day. Since she was feeling ill, she dosed herself on cough syrup with codeine, so she was feeling a bit high, and still didn't worry until the evening. He hadn't reappeared. That was more weird. The first three days, two friends with the self-chosen nicknames of Sid and Waty had kept her company, trying to find any information from the police station, but they just kept being sent away. Had he been charged with some offense? They went to the law courts, all five of them, but there was no trace of him there either. Or anywhere else. Gloria made light of it—"It'll be okay, no worries"—until the friends shook her awake. "Stop taking that syrup, Gloria, wake up. You can see he's not here anymore. They can't keep someone for five days, even if Pasqua's minister of the interior. They must have taken him back home. He's still a minor, isn't he? You should go back to Nancy, see if he's there." She benefited from the others' general benevolence and kindness because of their status as the mascot couple.

The gang went to Paris for a festival where the Wampas, Los Carayos, and two or three other groups were playing. She found herself all on her own. It was a long time since that had been the case, and it changed everything. Sleeping in a group of twelve in corridors, drinking beer, and exchanging stories was fine. But loitering in the cold all day, she simply became a vulnerable girl, the target of really annoying men, who hung around her and had to be yelled at to make them go away, because they all wanted to talk to her, buy her a meal, help her—and then fuck her over, one way or another.

In the end, she gave up thinking Eric would reappear. She returned from Évry to Paris. Once there, she went around asking everyone if they'd seen Eric. She tried to call his home, she tried to call friends in Nancy, she begged in the street all day to get enough money to telephone. Nothing, nobody had seen him, nobody knew anything. She was afraid they'd killed him. Did they do that sometimes? At the police station? Kill a kid, sodomize the corpse, and throw it in the river? She was afraid. For the first time in her life, she was fed up with being a layabout, hanging around with young deadbeats like herself. She'd had enough of their stories about being beaten up, always the same old stuff all the time. And she realized she didn't have a plan B, was fed up with being cold and dirty.

One day instead of begging, she'd sat down in the metro station and started to cry. An old lady had come to sit by her and console her. Gloria had smiled nicely at her through her tears. The old woman reminded her of something, a whole world it seemed she'd left a few months before, a world she had thought she would never return to. The sweet atmosphere of childhood.

Something had given way inside her, making her less toxic. She had really enjoyed those two minutes of compassion, she had liked the gloved hand patting her back. Before she left, the old lady had slipped her a fifty-franc note. Like a kind, complicit grandmother. That had made Gloria cry even harder.

Eric must be back in Nancy. She waited for a through train, so as not to be chucked off at some isolated station on the way. When she arrived, she realized why she had been putting this moment off for so long: the terrible sensation of being back at square one, waking up—in a flea-bitten state what was more—from a beautiful dream of being together. The end of the idyll. She tried to convince herself that she was worrying about nothing.

She dragged herself all around town asking people she knew whether they had seen Eric, but no, nobody knew anything here either. She was wearing a big red anorak from the Salvation Army store, and had picked up some kind of eczema, which disfigured her face. She felt a certain incomprehension in the eyes of her former friends. No one wanted to put her up. She slept in the railway station until it closed. And again, even in the state she was in, she had to keep walking the streets till the station reopened, because all the wolves on the prowl kept trying to pick her up, and unless she really insulted them, they kept on insisting. Once she started yelling at them, they called her a filthy whore or a stupid tramp and tried to attack her. As if it were totally scandalous that she dared refuse the help and company of the first dumb scumbag to come along. She was just a girl, with no right to be on the street at night, or any right to choose who she wanted to go along with. Nothing but a girl, who belonged to the first comer, no choice. So she had to walk as if she were heading somewhere, not talking to people because she had a date. The only way to avoid violence was to tell lies: "I'm waiting for someone." "I'm already spoken for."

She was so lonely that she felt stunned.

Next day, she sat down at a corner where she knew her father came past on his way to work every morning. When he arrived, she didn't dare look him in the eye. She had lost a lot of her arrogance. She was expecting a torrent of anger, like when she played truant from school as a little girl. But he just hugged her without a word, appalled to see the state she was in, and said nothing at all. Once more, she felt ashamed to be bringing all this on him. He had taken her home, called her mother to tell her Gloria was back, and had made her eggs and coffee. He was glad to see her, glad and sad at once. She had told herself it was really stupid the way they loved each other, without ever understanding or doing the right thing at the right time. Her parents asked nothing from her. Neither of them. They took her to the doctor for her skin disorder. She had to have some ultraviolet sessions at a dermatologist. She let herself be manipulated, like a little girl.

When she tried ringing Eric's house, his parents hung up. They soon changed their number. They must've known where he was, otherwise they would have cracked and asked her for news of him. But they didn't ask anything, just hung up. They knew where he was, all right.

Gloria worried away at the problem from every angle, and inevitably started to lose her head. They *must* be able to talk to each other, or at least write, know when they might meet. They must be able to communicate. She called hospitals, boarding schools, as soon as her parents were out she took down the directory and called anywhere she could think of, but with no result.

She found it strange that Eric hadn't even thought to write to her home address. She wondered if he was cloistered somewhere where he couldn't send letters, but even if you're in prison, you get to write. Not for a second, during the three weeks that this had lasted, not for a second did she imagine that perhaps he didn't want to write to her. The idea never occurred to her.

WAKING UP WAS unbearable, after the first moment of oblivion. Then it became a ritual, she would think to herself, *I'm fine this morning*, before it would all come flooding back, why she wasn't fine at all. The corpse of a beast weighing many tons seemed to be pressing down on her body. She was suffocating, and at the same time harboring a panic attack, a creature with long talons, lodged in her throat trying to break out and scratching at her internal walls. Fury such as she had never before known that made her groan out loud, a wounded animal, blinded by her own blood, choking, fighting, spitting out her sense of loss and anguish, her back broken and pinning her to the bed. Later, every time she read some junkie's account of what it was like to come off hard drugs, she'd be reminded of those days. Except that in those descriptions of overcoming addiction, there wasn't that phenomenal hate, turned against herself as much as against anyone else she met.

She waited anxiously for the postman, for a phone call. She haunted bars, simply in hopes of finding someone who might know something. Abandoning all dignity, any attempt at attitude, not caring what other people might think, she'd rush up to new arrivals: "You haven't seen Eric, have you? Heard anything about him?" But no, nobody, nothing.

It was during that fortnight that Michel had approached her. One night she had ended up in the Téméraire, a night-club in the old town, having met up that evening with Roger, who said it was important for her to have some fun, and had dragged her there. She had sat sulking while sinking several beers. Tears in her eyes, she couldn't stand anything those days, she found people noisy, self-centered, phony. She had no desire anymore to joke or take any interest in the thousands of tedious things everyone else found fascinating. In the end, a boorish local had pushed up too close against her, and she had spat in his face before leaving the bar like the poor distracted wretch she was becoming. Michel, who had been standing at the counter alone, had followed her out and taken her arm. They had never spoken, but she knew perfectly well who he was.

Michel was a fixture, everyone knew him. To start with his legend, he'd been there when the Sex Pistols played the Chalet du Lac in 1976. People said he'd met Patrick Eudeline, Johnny Thunders, Siouxsie, and Lux Interior. His look was always irreproachable, and he had a wicked attitude: sexy, cold, and cultivated. If Michel decided some record was cool, the rest of Nancy nodded in agreement. Same way, if Michel said a film sucked, they all sneered at it. He was the cat who knew where it was at. He was capable of making everyone listen to the "fridge" track of a record made by Ganz Neit, a local group that had recorded the sound of a fridge for twenty minutes. If Michel found that worthwhile, then the sound of a fridge became really exciting. Even in the improbable swamp where she found herself, Gloria was well aware of her luck, to be picked up by Michel in the street. That he was interested in her, when she wouldn't have dared even ask him the time. In the small number of things she respected, Michel's opinion would have come top of the list. His concern for her had taken her absolutely by surprise. For two whole minutes she'd stopped wanting to die.

Later, when she knew him better, he'd tell her many times that he'd been struck by the expression on her face when she'd come into the bar. Her fury and pain, obvious all over the room, had seemed familiar and admirable to him. At any rate, he'd caught up with her and asked, "Are you okay? Do you want to be alone?" She couldn't stop crying, and he deployed all his charm to console her. Flattered and intrigued, she'd repeated between sniffs that she should be going home, while wishing he'd hold her back, which he had done. He wasn't trying to pick her up, there was no ambiguity about it, he was acting more like her big brother. She told him her story and he was touched. The urban romantic myth of despair. He was truly kind, she could hardly believe it. The feeling between them then wasn't exactly peace and love, a bit more hard-edged than that, sharper, each watching their words.

He'd walked her along, talking about this and that, going to some lengths to distract her, and had taken her to a bar near where he lived at the time, behind La Pépinière, the big park in the city center. The owner was a jovial, old-fashioned guy in shirtsleeves and suspenders who served them sandwiches with a little glass of Côtes du Rhône. Michel had the reputation of being on heroin, which was quite true and even that day when he was clean, he barely sipped a little wine. It was extraordinary that a guy as furiously punk as this could be on good terms with the old-world café proprietor, just as it was amazing that his brain didn't miss a trick. When she mentioned that Eric had a nineteen-year-old sister who was in the advanced *hypokhâgne* class in the Lycée Poincaré, his face lit up.

"Well, you should go and see her!"

"I tried, they wouldn't let me set foot in the fucking lycée!"

"Do you know her, have you ever seen her?"

"Just for a moment, in a corridor once. How could I know that one day I'd need to ask her something, a girl like that?"

She made him smile. She could sense that she attracted him, like an adopted little sister. She hadn't tried to be clever or to act the punkette, yet it was obvious that she and her story appealed to him. He'd decided to help her, and at midday next day he called her: "Listen, it's great, my ex-fiancée is in the same class, she knows who your boyfriend's sister is. She's going to have a word with her today, I'll know more tonight. Do you want to come around for supper?"

Well, of course she did, with a feeling that her blood was starting to flow again through her veins and waking up her brain. Of course she did.

Michel's apartment was candlelit, it had a spooky atmosphere, like going to eat with a vampire. There were posters from a Cramps concert, another of the film *Out of the Blue*, piles of books taller than Gloria, discs by Gainsbourg on the floor with some by Trisomie 21. The curtains were heavy, thick, wine colored. They listened to an experimental Hungarian group.

Gloria had drunk nothing, she was paralyzed with shyness. The ex-fiancée was friendly enough, but intimidatingly beautiful. Two older people with that confidence and the way of exchanging clever witty remarks that more grown-up people seem to have when you're only sixteen. A tall creature, red-haired with pale skin, blood-red nails, wearing mittens and a long vintage skirt. She had pale eyes, you couldn't see exactly whether they were blue or green. She spoke very slowly and expressed herself impeccably.

Gloria had perched on the edge of a chair and was afraid of falling off, of doing something ludicrous, clumsy. Michel was heating up water for pasta. It was so improbable to watch this local punk hero do something as ordinary and domestic as cook pasta. And at the same time it was sublime. It meant he had nothing to prove, or else that you could be a punk and still do boring everyday stuff.

She had asked the older girl with her eyes, and the Goth

had almost smiled. "Yes, I had a talk with Amandine." She felt better already, at last something was happening, she felt more at home, she felt she was coming back to life.

Just as well, because what followed wasn't going to be much to her liking.

"He's in Switzerland, in a high-discipline school."

"His shitty family! I knew it, I was sure. Did she say where?"

"No, I tried, but she was very cagey. I don't know what her brother's like, but Amandine is pretty smart."

"Yeah, he's clever too. And he has an ordinary name. What kind of a name is Amandine, for God's sake? In that family they don't seem to realize . . . They think they're living in a fairy tale. But do you know her well?"

The beautiful creature smiled again. Gloria wondered what it was about her that made everyone laugh. The older girl went on.

"No, but we're in the same class, I went to see her about some homework. And I brought up the subject of my little brother, Eloy. I said he knew her brother from Saint-Cyr and was wondering what he was doing now."

"Oh really, your brother?" said Gloria, opening a fresh packet of Camels, surprised by all these coincidences.

"No, it's completely false," Michel commented with a sly grin, "but Sylvie lies like a trooper." This struck a false note, too deliberate if it was meant as a compliment, and they exchanged a short but not entirely friendly look, before she carried on.

"I don't even have a little brother. But I do know a younger boy called Eloy who went to Saint-Cyr. Well, anyway," Sylvie went on, "Amandine dodged the question:

'Oh, he's in another school now, don't want to talk about it.' Well, it excited me, I love it when people clam up."

Michel remarked, "Yeah, when people stand up to you, you love it. It's when they give in that it's harder."

And Gloria started to tell herself that it suited him to have an excuse to ask this former girlfriend for a favor. It wasn't hard to see that she still had an effect on him.

"So I started to look concerned, and I tried acting very sad: 'Oh, boys that age, they can be so difficult can't they?' I was almost in tears over this, and she kept on being distant for a bit, but in the end we found ourselves having a nice cup of tea in the Excel, and she told me everything. How he took drugs, how he'd picked up all these STDs."

The Goth put her hand on Gloria's arm.

"I'm just saying what *she* said, I'm not saying we need to believe her."

Gloria, who didn't see any harm in it, said, "So what, I'm a punk, I'm not scared of getting crabs."

It had been a spontaneous remark, but she saw that she'd scored another point with Michel. It pleased her greatly, though she was far from suspecting that twenty years later he'd still be her best friend. He liked her attitude, her abruptness, and he appreciated her pale eyes and blond hair. He liked the way she looked at record covers, turning them over and over and asking off-the-wall questions. He liked it that she was in love, and desperately unhappy in love, that she had burned her wings and was suffering, and that she made a loud noise falling to earth. She reminded him of himself: she was a version, in the shape of a 1980s girl, of the way he had been as a teenager. He was feeling lonely at the time. A lot of his friends had died, others had left Nancy for Paris or to go abroad. His sweetheart had abandoned him for someone else the year before, and he wasn't over it yet, but too proud to let that show. He liked this Gloria kid, a blond punkette with a child's round cheeks, who sulked in bars and was looking everywhere for her boyfriend. The Goth went on.

"Apparently the mother just adores her little boy, it's a bit over the top, in fact. Her husband and daughter, she couldn't care less about them—but her son, he's her whole life. So she made herself ill, and he went missing for three months. And in that time, the mother finds she's got breast cancer, get the picture, bring out the violins. So to cut a long story short, the police found the kid, in a terrible state, and then there was a family council, the whole bit, and if you're a minor in cases like that, you know you have to go before the youth magistrates . . . Well, they gave him the works."

"I know . . ."

"So his mother, she was devastated, just having to go to the tribunal she was weeping buckets. In the end, it turns out they've got an uncle in Switzerland who knows the head of this school. It's not a military academy, it's worse, a kind of boot camp. A gilded cage, specializing in psychopaths and I don't know what."

By now Gloria was like a motorway interchange, pierced through with violent currents whirling, clashing, fertilizing each other. She was relieved to find out where he was and to get the beginning of an explanation. It was a pity not to know the exact town, but her brain was processing information at top speed. Even if she had to hunt down all the private reformatory schools in Switzerland, well that was humanly possible, it wasn't as if they'd sent him to Oklahoma. The cancer story didn't mean much to her, no need to think long to imagine all the direct implications there. Sylvie had made it clear that "for the exact town, I had to give up, because she did describe the school a bit, and it's worse than if you tried to get someone out of Charles III," the Nancy jail. Gloria affected a neutral expression, indicating, "You don't know what I'm capable of." Sylvie went on.

"It's officially an establishment for difficult youngsters. In fact, they're mostly junkies, you know? Have you seen someone who's on hard drugs and they're in some program to get off them, but they really don't want to? They don't get any craftier or tougher or quicker. You wouldn't believe the lengths they go to, to get their hands on what they want, whatever the cost. So an establishment where they really, really can't get any drugs for months on end, it's got to be worse than a prison, believe me when I tell you."

Michel confirmed this with a knowing look. "Even in the middle of nowhere, even in a plane, even in a hospital, if you want to, you can find the stuff, the craving makes you like superman. She's telling you the truth. If the kids in that place can't get ahold of anything, they must be locked down with triple locks."

Gloria scratched her throat, not wanting to give in yet to the obvious. And it was taking her some time. "Oh, surely they must be able to get out?"

The Goth concluded: "Sorry, nope. His family can go and see him in the spring, not before. But he won't get out of there till he's finished the baccalauréat exams, so—minimum two years, if I understand right."

"So, they did it, he *knew* they would, they've clapped him in jail . . ."

"You know, what I picked up about Amandine's family,

you should be careful not to tangle with them, they're one of the richest families in the region. You don't get as well off as that by letting your kids do what they want. They'd rather one of their kids die than fritter away their fortune. Otherwise it'd be a free-for-all, and you have no *idea* how much there is at stake."

Michel nodded again in agreement

"Yeah, great big inheritance, too much status to lose, they bring their kids up to obey. Otherwise they wouldn't be able to pass on their power from father to son for centuries and centuries, and just think what a disaster that would be . . ."

Gloria wanted to go on believing there was some way of reaching him, once she had the address. Evidence had never intimidated her. She was unwilling to understand.

THE NEXT FEW days she spent riding buses. She looked out of the windows at the city, at the people who got on, she went to sleep or jumped out to have a drink, steal a bottle of beer, or look at sweaters in some shop window. She would walk along for a few meters, catch the first bus that came along, and stay on it to the terminus, staring down the man opposite, then get off, change buses, and so on. She was in suspended animation. Those first days, she rejected the idea that he wouldn't find a way out. Eric would be knocking at her window one night or one morning. His parents would have given up, or he'd have been able to escape. She was waiting, full of calm energy. Completely stunned, in reality.

One day, at about five in the afternoon, Gloria was struck by the obvious. She had to write to him, if only to tell him how well she was doing, that she wasn't suffering. That she'd wait for him.

So she took a bus, this time with a destination: Eric's parents' house.

She pushed open the street door, and the feel of the stairwell brought a lump to her throat. A kaleidoscope of impressions, voices, whispers, memories jostling in her head as she walked up the stairs to their landing, surprised by the clarity as well as the anarchic confusion of the moments they had spent together. "Both together," these words were waltzing in her heart, filling her with fervor. Nothing would separate them. Certainly not a few years.

His mother answered the door: severely dressed, gray suit, looking a bit like the former justice minister Simone Veil, but less distinguished. There were strands of gray in her hair, as if in accusation. Illness had aged her, she'd lost weight. Gloria had prepared her little speech. Calmly, she wanted to persuade Eric's mother to pass on a letter, just a note if necessary. If she wouldn't give her the address, could she at least let her communicate briefly with her exiled son? But the mother slammed the door in her face as soon as she recognized her. Calmer still, Gloria leaned on the bell. She could feel the blood hammering in her temples, with a heavy regular pulse. Pressure built up inside her. Then the father came out, furious. Gloria burst into tears, begged him to listen to her, but he didn't want to know, he was very sure of his position: she was not to come near them again or he'd call the police. Then, without premeditation, finding it inevitable "because I had to do something," she collapsed onto the big thick doormat on the landing, screaming and writhing like in a scene from *The Exorcist*. She heard the neighbors on the other floors opening their doors to see what was going on, asking each other. She heard the nearest ones, across the landing, move up to peer out through their peepholes. She found herself pathetic, yet at the same time doing exactly the right thing, this was really what she wanted to do, to cry out all the tears in her body, banging her head against a closed door. A perverse voice inside her was saying, *Let them call the police, the bastards, at least I'll have spoiled their evening.* Insidiously, the rage inside her had reached its boiling point. From tears she moved on to insults, at first quietly, then screaming out loud: "So you've locked your son away, but that wasn't enough, oh no! Not for you, you rich slobs! Just to send him a letter, I've got to make a scene, cry my eyes out. But he doesn't belong to *you*, do you *hear* me? *You're* the wasters round here! Shitty bourgeois assholes!" Getting back to her feet, she threw her head back, drawing in as much breath as she could so that everyone would hear her invective. She imagined that this kind of family would be petrified of scandal, so she did her best to provide one. Then it occurred to her that this would really make Eric laugh, it was exactly the kind of tantrum he adored, and Gloria choked, torn between pain and rage. She had no idea what to do next, but she didn't want to leave for home, not yet, she hadn't gone far enough. She wanted the police to be called, she wanted everything to go through to the bitter end. She had begun to aim a series of kicks at the front door, getting more and more violent, hurling herself against it as hard as she could, taking longer runs at it and howling like a banshee. Now all the neighbors were glued to their peepholes, but nobody dared venture out, and she was running up and down, out of breath on the confined landing, aiming for full impact against the door, her whole body landing with great thuds. She flung herself at it in a frenzy and—quite unexpectedly—the door gave way before the police got there. She lost her balance and sprawled, amazed, on the floor of their entrance hall. Delicious smells of cooking, comfort, the ruins of a nice evening. She stood up, her left shoulder was indescribably painful, but for the moment that was a side issue. "Where are you, you bastards! I'm glad I've got in here, now I'm going to bust your balls!" The father tried to grab hold of her, she had the reflex of pulling a coat stand over onto him, and then the presence of mind to kick in the sitting-room door, a table, and a window, with the help of a minibar. Amandine, pale in the face, tried to calm her down, but Gloria had only to look her in the eye to send her reeling back. "As for you, you bitch, you've been in league with them! When your brother gets out, and he'll never *ever* be the same after this, think about what I'm telling you now. You *bitch*, you let them do this to him. You hear me? You'll remember this, like it or not, you'll remember what I'm saying." She was so convinced of what she was shouting that she must have been convincing in turn, since his sister staggered backward, her eyes full of tears. It was as if she'd cast a spell on her, and it brought immediate relief to be able to return some of the pain these people had inflicted on her. But it didn't last. Because five minutes later she was just feeling pathetic. At which point, Gloria, at something of a loss, since no one was trying to stop her, attacked what was left of the sitting-room door.

When the cops finally got there, appearances were, naturally, completely against her, and there was plenty of good cause for the householders to lodge a complaint.

Gloria allowed herself to be handcuffed without a word, exhausted after all this wildness. But on the stairs, thinking that the bastards hadn't yet had all they deserved, she started yelling again at the top of her lungs, "All I wanted was to get to write him a *letter*, you filthy fascists, damn you to hell for what you've done to me, let me *write* to him, you have no right, hear me, no right at all to keep us apart!"

At the police station, she took out her shoelaces, emptied her pockets, and showed them she wasn't wearing a belt. She was quite calm. She had no voice left to make her statement, her hands were aching, she'd cut her forearm quite deeply, her neck ached and her shoulder was dislocated. She was calm and sad. She kept repeating, "All I wanted to do was write to him, just write him a note," vaguely, under her breath, partly because it was true, partly to make an impression on the police, so that they wouldn't be too hard on her. And indeed it seemed to work, they were more understanding with her than usual.

She had been arrested under her real name, and since she was under eighteen, they'd had to call her father and wait for him to come and get her. She collected her things and got into the car without a word. On the way, her father said resignedly, "If you think that's the way to get them to let you see him . . ." It pierced her to the heart again, you would think she'd never get tired of this. She opened the car door and flung herself out onto the road. This time, she sprained a shoulder and an ankle, and they had to take her to the hospital. She could sense her father had had enough, but that he was still determined to get her cared for and to say nothing. Later, she was to produce the same result with other men, with her crazy way of experiencing pain, always turning it into a big performance, something that would often have her ending up in the emergency ward.

One of the doctors thought to give her a powerful sedative and at last she went to sleep. She didn't want to be there at all, she didn't want to know anymore.

Within the next two weeks, Eric's parents moved away. She heard later that they'd gone to Paris. But no one was able to give her their address.

She was afraid of meeting Michel again in a bar, afraid that he would have found out what happened, and be angry with her, but instead, he smiled when they bumped into each other, stifled a broader grin and commented: "So, when you're not pleased, you certainly let the whole world know, eh?" as if it were a compliment, and he bought her a drink. She was still just as surprised that he treated her as a friend. She could listen to him talk for afternoons on end. He told her anecdotes, he commented on the news, he read the papers, he had enthusiasms, made jokes, got angry. He fascinated her, he was an education.

They'd meet every afternoon at the Petit Théâtre, a bar on the edge of the old town. He'd read his newspaper, she'd draw in a little sketchbook.

She felt torn to pieces, it hurt so much to be herself that she could feel no change in the pain. Michel told her, "You're like a nineteenth-century heroine, it's as if you're going to die of a broken heart," and indeed her face changed, showed marks of grief, the circles around her eyes deepened.

Eric's parents brought charges. Her own parents tried to get her to take an interest in the case that was coming up, because it was important, but it was wasted effort. She was so listless that she allowed her mother to advise her how to dress for the occasion. Then she listened to the lawyer appointed by the court, some arrogant young idiot. She waited, sitting between her parents in the big modern building, one with that horrible cold architecture, where they told you the verdict. They came to tell her she was sentenced to pay a fine along with an injunction against ever going near Eric's parents' home again. She couldn't care less, they didn't live there now anyway.

A fortnight after this outburst she went back to school. One morning when she was cutting class and sitting at home listening to Bérurier Noir's *Concerto Pour Détraqués* full blast, she saw the postman arrive and almost automatically went to see if there were anything for her. There was. A letter with a Swiss postmark. And immediately she realized that she shouldn't rush to open it, because it wasn't the letter she was hoping for. She put it on the kitchen table, in their tiny kitchen with its blue walls, and the tablecloth with its floral pattern.

She took a few deep breaths, hesitating to open it, then poured a shot into a mustard glass and drank half of it off, holding her breath. She hated the taste of whiskey. She was afraid to open the envelope.

IT WAS TIME, he said, to "pull himself together," to "come out of it," to "face reality." He'd thought hard, he didn't want to ruin his life, he wanted to study. He knew she would understand, and that since his mother was ill, "He couldn't do this to her." He insisted that it had been hard making this decision, but they couldn't go on seeing each other. It had been painful for him too, especially the first days—again, she'd understand, wouldn't she?

Tiny handwriting, compressed and suddenly cramped, too regular, observing the margins, too correct, too mean, too infuriating. And he hoped she'd understand!

She understood fucking nothing. Above all, how he could have written such a cold letter, so inappropriate, so unexpected? What was she supposed to understand? She felt ashamed, for him as much as for her, as she read the letter. She felt wicked and stupid, an idiot in hell. To have waited so trustingly. To have felt so good with him. To have believed even for a second, to have imagined it could be happening to her, true love—beautiful, luminous, and without complications. "You poor fool," she kept telling herself, "that'll teach you about life, you stupid fucking idiot." She hated herself, in waves of anger, then it turned against him, "Mama's boy, go lick your mama's ass, do whatever she says, stupid, weak fucking coward!" Her head whirled, she was betrayed, humiliated, abandoned, furious, mad with rage . . . and deeply unhappy.

When had he started lying? Had he always known he'd go back home when they were together that summer? Had he been bored secretly, had he regretted running away, had he wanted to go home? Had she been so naive she hadn't realized it at the time? Now she didn't miss him at all—or not the same way. In the time it took her to read that letter, she had armed herself head to foot with scorn. Something inside her had retracted, closed in on itself, and would never be exposed ever again.

These things weren't meant for her: happiness, complicity, a soul mate, love.

"His dear mama, his schoolbooks, being reasonable, not doing anything out of turn . . . stupid, mediocre, mean-spirited fucking little idiot." She'd have liked to have him in front of her for two minutes. With time to tell him a thing or two. She beat her brains to the bone, she dug deep inside herself for the wounding things she'd say when she saw him again. And for several days she rehearsed in silence the moment when they next bumped into each other.

Next day, at the counter of a café, she'd met Roger again and called to him from the other end of the bar: "You told me not to trust him! Well, know what? You were abso-fucking-lutely right." She'd had too much to drink. Roger listened patiently to her story and was kind and sympathetic, agreeing with her how appalling it was. He bought her a few beers. Gloria, being well brought up, bought him a few as well. She couldn't get over his being so thoughtful and concerned. That was the good aspect of that terrible time: people were warmer and more attentive than she had expected. He ran a few theories past her.

"It's this government's fault, the socialists, bunch of hypocrites, pretending we're all in it together, rich and poor, brown and white, Jews and Protestants, well forget it. In the end it's just everyone for himself and it never works, their big society. Socialist politicians just want to be able to fuck black girls with a good conscience, believe me . . ."

Then the evening got wilder and more confusing. Roger started a fight, but Gloria couldn't work out why he was grasping the head of this young fair-haired guy under his arm and bashing him. They'd had to run away because the bartender was furious. Perhaps the blond boy worked there, she wasn't sure. Anyway, a bit later she and Roger were standing on the roof of a car, arm in arm, concentrating hard on getting the words of a song by Renaud right: "*Et la blonde du sixième / Le hash elle aime*" ("The blond on the sixth floor / Hash is what she's for"). Soon afterward, as far as she could remember, they were in a bedroom, in a hostel for young workers and they were fucking. She found out that night that he talked nonstop during the act. She wasn't used to that, it made her lose concentration. It was quite funny.

In the morning, big hangover, dry mouth, bruised all over. She left before he woke up, not finding him such fun the next day.

Outside, the light was too bright, it hurt her eyes. She stopped to drink a black coffee. There was a lump in her throat. She'd never sleep with Eric again. Never again curl up alongside someone believing so hard that they loved each other to distraction. It wasn't even a decision. She just knew, and unlike most of the ideas you get when you're a teenager, it was true. It hurt so badly that she couldn't even cry.

THAT NIGHT, AFTER Véronique is in bed, Gloria spends a good fifteen minutes trying to unfold the sofa bed, without success. She gives up and decides not to bother. "For all the sleep I'd get anyway," she tells herself as she paces around the bookshelves, hands in her pockets, head to one side, trying to read the titles. Then she tries the medicine cabinet, finds nothing but a little cough syrup containing codeine, and finishes off the bottle. Sometimes it helps her sleep. Inside her head there is a confusion of things, she's too tired to put any order to the thoughts, memories, and pangs of anguish going on there. She feels as though she's riding an old-fashioned Mobylette the wrong way up a motorway, trying to avoid trucks and cars coming at her, thirty-five tonners speeding toward her, like in a Mario Kart game, rolling her over, knocking her out, then sending her flying into the wilderness. In this chaos, it's hard to distinguish what really hurts, the old episodes from her adolescence or thinking about her parents, both dead now, and vanished with them is all that time of her life. She's inexorably cut off from it. She knows that Eric is an orphan too, she read it somewhere. Does he get sad every Christmas like she does? She wants to call Lucas, she hasn't lost the reflex yet of counting on him when she's had too much to take. Just yesterday, he was still her partner, her other half. Gloria would like to extinguish all these thoughts, lie down, drowse off, and be able to leave herself behind.

Poking around among Véronique's things she finds a CD compilation of Janis Joplin. Joplin, astride a huge motorbike, is laughing as she looks straight at the camera.

Gloria puts on the CD very low and crouches between the speakers. She tries to concentrate on the music, wiping everything else out. Filling her head with sound.

How many times, in how many different situations, has she retreated into herself just like now? She has been listening to Janis Joplin since she was a kid. Accompanied by her, as if by a big sister.

In the early 1980s a girl who worked in the market, older than Gloria, orange hair, shabby leather jacket, class act, told her that Janis Joplin was the leader of all lost girls.

She'd advised Gloria to make her a personal patron saint, whenever she was unhappy in love, or when she was looking for dope and couldn't find it, or when she had nowhere to sleep and was sick of being in the street, or if she wanted a job. In fact, on any occasion, she should make a little altar to Janis, the urban goddess, light candles to her and make her offerings such as a nice big spliff, a can of Kronenbourg, a pretty garter belt, whatever you like, depending on your mood.

Gloria had met this girl at a party after a concert by the Stranglers and KaS Product at the Pulsation Jazz Festival. She'd taken two packets of Mercalm, antiseasickness pills that were supposed to give you a high, but had just sent her off to sleep, sitting down, with her head on the table. When she came out of it she chatted with the people still at the party. She had never known whether the older girl was nuts or just kidding. She never met her again to find out. But at any rate, she liked the idea, and often in her life she had built little altars so that good ole Janis, patron saint of wild girls who've gone over the top, would come to her aid. She had bought a secondhand Joplin vinyl LP, chosen because of the sleeve by Crumb, and had left it lying about in full view so that she looked like a rock buff. And by pretending, Gloria ended up being genuinely touched and then supported by those tracks.

Day breaks and Véronique's alarm goes off. Gloria curls up on the sofa pretending to be asleep, she aches all over as if she'd spent the night fighting. When the apartment's empty again, she gets up—black coffee, cold shower— then lies down in front of the TV, watching kids' shows.

She can't concentrate on anything. The emptiness is like a white flash, within reach, imminent.

For the first time in two decades she feels like talking to Eric. She has hated him with such intensity until now that it has never occurred to her. He'd written, apart from the famous letter about returning to the straight and narrow, perhaps three times in twenty years. Flattering her ego perhaps, vaguely, but disgusting in fact. *Stupid twat, I don't want anything to do with you. You think just because you're famous, I'm going to care about what's been happening to you?* She had told herself he was writing to her because he liked being the kind of a guy "who doesn't deny his past." Or out of guilt. Or because he simply got off on it. *Well nothing doing, buster.* Every time she got one of these letters it had surprised her, only slightly interested her, and she'd forgotten about it within ten minutes. *It's over, the past, nothing to do with me, finito.* He was a useless prick and she'd been taken for a ride, end of story. She wasn't going to spend all day thinking about it.

That afternoon, she trails along to the Royal. Jérémy greets her with a shout.

"Hey, you're a star! Everyone was expecting you last night."

Michel is already sitting there. With his pretty bitch of a girlfriend. Gloria reflects that it's odd to be so in love and already in the bar by two o'clock. Then she deduces from it that their pretense of being a happy couple is coming apart. She's willing to take a bet: in a couple of weeks that girl will be gone.

Vanessa has always looked at Gloria with that slightly amazed contempt of girls who divide the world into two categories: those who make an effort and the others. Boxing in the second category, Gloria has never actually been worried by this lack of sympathy. But today the deal's completely changed.

"Where the heck were *you* last night?"

She hasn't even had time to sit down, kiss people, take off her coat. The other girl, beside herself with excitement, is talking to her as if they are old friends.

"You missed it all! Eric was so disappointed. We had a fab evening, such a pity you weren't there!"

Sneaking a glance at Michel, taking a deep breath, and looking puzzled, Gloria rubs hard at her eyes with the flat of her hand, hoping that after this reality will seem plausible. But Vanessa slides along the seat toward her, coming on full strength and with a big smile.

"I didn't know you knew Eric Muyr! Wow, that's fantastic! Michel had never told me."

Her voice is embarrassingly eager. Gloria is paralyzed with shame for Michel, who's acting like he's not taking much notice, but his face is livid and fixed in an awkward smile. She forces herself to reply with a pretense of friendliness.

"Oh, you know, when I used to know him he was just a snotty teenager—it was in the olden days . . . like people say, that doesn't make us feel any younger."

She's secretly praying Vanessa will gather she doesn't want to talk to her. Certainly not in this girly, best-friends way.

She's shocked, actually. For one thing, that anyone can be so half-witted as to be impressed by someone on TV, and for another that Vanessa has completely changed her manner toward her so shamelessly. She could at least have had the hypocrisy to approach her more discreetly, make a little attempt at being friendly first . . . Well, Gloria certainly prefers people who are manipulative to those who make fools of themselves. She scrutinizes Michel's expression for anything that confirms her intuition: he's going to detach himself, this girl is too much, he's going to send her back to her mother.

Instead of that, however, Vanessa, now acting like her best friend, leans over and announces proudly, "Guess what! Michel and I are going to move away. I wanted to be the first to tell you. We're going to live in Lyon! You'll come and see us, won't you?"

Gloria freezes her face, so as to show nothing at all of what she feels, and turns toward Michel, who explains, more quietly, "She's got family there. She can get a job in journalism. Me too."

"You too? What? The Lyon press? They have papers there? They have restaurants, not newspapers, wake up!"

"Yeah, they *do* have newspapers, I'll be able to write stuff . . . It'll be interesting. A change of scene, a change of life, you'll see."

Gloria swallows, her smile is almost pained.

"Well, that's fantastic, congratulations! And good luck!"

Beside herself with excitement, Vanessa jumps up. "Let's celebrate! Champagne anyone?"

Michel raises his eyebrows in surprise. Gloria shakes her head. "I prefer beer, if it's all the same to you."

Taking advantage while the bimbo goes to bother Jérémy at the bar, Michel tries to sugar the pill.

"I'm in love. I've never done this, gone off with a girl

to settle somewhere. I want to try things I've never done."

"You couldn't just take up surfing? Like everyone else?"

"Do you want to take over my apartment?"

"Ah! First good news of the day."

"I don't want to move my stuff right away, maybe in three months. Just so's to not be bothered, not have to rush and so on. If you want to stay there while I'm away that could be fixed. Then if you wanted to take it over, you know, for good."

"That would really suit me. I've got no income, no references, I don't have any of the things you need to rent . . ."

"It's okay, you have all the qualifications!"

"Well, if I could sublet for a bit, it would help me out. I'm gonna end up homeless, if this goes on, so . . ."

But actually, it doesn't really suit her, being all alone again.

Vanessa comes back to the table with two beers. Her phone is making a ghastly noise, supposed to be this disco music but in fact it's something eardrum piercing. Vanessa answers and moves away because the signal inside the bar isn't too good, so she goes out onto the street, walking up and down in the cold, chatting.

Michel takes a piece of paper from his jacket pocket while she's outside.

"Eric asked me to give you his number. I'm giving it to you while Vanessa isn't here, otherwise she'd copy it and start bothering him . . . She's a bit . . ."

" . . . of a groupie."

"Well, yeah, a bit, she is . . ."

He scratches his neck thoughtfully.

"You were right not to come here last night, you'd have been really pissed off, watching everyone hanging around him. It was freaky, you know, really freaky."

"It was, like, 'We're in the backwoods here.'"

"Yeah, pretty shameless. Even people you and I like, they were hanging around him, trying to talk to him, get close, stare at him. Midnight here, you should have seen the place, CRAWLING! People phoned each other to tell them about it. I felt a bit bad for him."

"He must be used to it."

"Not sure you could get used to that. Kind of humiliating. I think he tries not to get caught in that kind of situation. We had a word or two. I didn't know him, in fact, apart from . . ."

"Ah well, what goes around comes around, that's how we met, you and me, after all."

"And since then, we've stuck together, haven't we?"

"Yeah, except now you're going seven hundred kilometers away, so of course that won't change our relations . . ."

He's ill at ease, as unhappy as she is. She unfolds the paper with the phone number he's given her.

"Hey, I could always call him and tell him I'm broke, he's absolutely loaded."

"He's in Nancy till tonight, I think. Call him if you like. He seemed genuinely keen to see you. I didn't imagine him the way he is."

"He doesn't look as good as on TV, don't you think?"

"Not physically, but I was thinking he'd be a total bastard, guess I was prejudiced."

"Prejudices, prejudices—usually justified."

She puts the number in her pocket, telling herself that she doesn't have a phone anymore anyway. Then she drinks off her beer, lifting her elbow high, without a word and without looking at him, and waits for Michel to do the same, picks up his glass, and goes to the counter. Jérémy is rinsing glasses, he looks tired from all his efforts the night before. He shakes his head.

"Oh, he was really disappointed you didn't turn up. You didn't say, honestly, he was really . . ."

"Look, I can't be bothered with him, okay? You're not going to be on at me for months just because when I was fifteen I used to know this asshole who's on TV."

That was telling him. She's fed up with bad news, fed up that everyone forgets she's just broken up with her man. In short, she is mega pissed off with everything.

Gloria spends the afternoon sitting at the same table. Vanessa keeps buying her drinks, her glass is empty one minute, refilled the next. She really wants to be best friends. And well, that's not a bad way to try. Then the loving couple leaves the bar. Gloria doesn't feel like going to Véronique's place, no desire to chat. She wonders what to do, feels terrible, sinister, thinks about hanging herself or jumping off a bridge, when Salim turns up, a tall black guy, always with a smile, stereotypical Caribbean. Good-looking, elegant, reliably willing to lend a hand. Suddenly she changes her mind and asks to borrow his phone.

"I've lost mine, do you mind, can I use yours?"

He slaps his thighs with laughter.

"Can't fool me! You didn't lose it, I saw Lucas last night, he told me all about it."

"Oh, he couldn't keep his big mouth shut, could he?"

"He was in despair. Know what, Gloria? You're a wild woman, you're impossible to tame. What you want is a real man, someone who can properly keep you in order."

And he taps his chest, boastingly.

Gloria smiles.

"Oh right, sure, if I was with someone like you, who screws anything that moves, I'd calm down."

"Why do you say that? What do you mean? Okay, you can borrow my phone. Just don't throw it at the wall, okay?"

She calls Eric. In fact, she'd prefer it if she got through to his voice mail and could say, "Too bad," but he must be one of those people who think they have to be available all the time for any call.

He sounds happy, natural, and surprised in a nice way, he acts as if they were seeing each other every day.

"What about tonight, shall we dine together?"

Gloria cooks, goes home to eat, sometimes has a meal in a restaurant, but she doesn't usually "dine." And the word makes her laugh, she feels suddenly as if she's in a French film.

"Okay, let's *dine.* So, where do people dine?"

"I'll meet you in Place Stanislas, in the Foy? Eight o'clock."

She agrees to everything and realizes as she's talking that she's more drunk than she thought. And more impressed, which is really annoying.

After finishing the call, she drinks several black coffees—which are on the house the minute she says, "I'm *dining* with Eric tonight, so I'd better be in good shape."

Jérémy bustles around her, "Try and come back here afterward, it's great business for the bar if a celeb comes in to have a drink. Do try to come over . . ."

She starts to wonder whether she really wants to do this or to chicken out. She goes back to Véro's place. As the alcohol loses its potency, the adolescent anguish of going on a date starts to kick in. Gloria isn't someone who normally has to overcome such anguish. She's been in infuriating situations, painful ones. Her life has few good points, except that she's used to it. She sees the same people all the time in more or less the same places. She knows them all by heart. She's rarely intimidated by a new situation. And not sure she likes it.

"WHAT ARE YOU thinking about?"

"That it's been twenty years. And I didn't imagine it this way."

"How did you imagine it?"

"That I'd be punching you in the face, of course. I dreamed too often of breaking every bone in your body by throwing rocks, oh, many times, many times. Then after a bit, I stopped thinking about it anymore."

He's drinking martinis, she thinks that's snobbish.

Everyone in the place is looking at him. He doesn't seem to notice. Gloria is shocked every time someone comes up to their table, interrupts them in midsentence, to say how much they admire him, ask for an autograph, or ask him why the time of the show's been changed. He replies, politely but distantly, he has a technique to get it over quickly.

She comments: "So now you belong to everybody."

"It's the magic world of TV. I'm not complaining. But still, if you don't mind, I've booked us to have dinner at the restaurant in my hotel. It's very fancy, I'm warning you. But we'd be in peace there for two seconds."

"Oh, me, you know, long as they have fries."

He hasn't changed that much physically. Tall, thin, he's kept that litheness of a young man, a supple, energetic animal. His hands are very white, well cared for, but enormous. They contradict the rest of his body, they seem as if inhabited by some surprising, worrying strength. He's acquired great authority, a calm authority that might be taken for charisma or virility, but it's pretty attractive whatever it is.

He seems sincerely moved. She's watching for the catch, the trick, the problem, what does this asshole want with her and how long is he going to go on looking at her with those silly big eyes? But she has a tendency to lower her guard, thinking he's just glad to see her, still finds her amusing, whatever she does. In that respect he hasn't changed perhaps. She only has to turn her head or open her mouth for him to burst out laughing, he's entertained and under her spell. That is still quite a pleasant feeling. But a bit surreal now.

He takes advantage of a couple of minutes when nobody has come to their table to talk about TV to lean toward her.

"And how *are* you? Well? How's your life, that sort of stuff?"

"Am I happy? No. I'm on benefits. Or when I have a job, it's minimum wage. It kind of makes life less pleasant, I can tell you. I've no regrets, if I could do it over again, I'd do the same, but no, I'm not happy. I'd *like* to have a car, I'd like to be able to go away on holiday, I'd like to buy a CD Walkman, and not have to line up at the post office on the first of the month, just to have enough to pay my phone bill."

"Okay, I see, in material terms, things aren't so good, but what about the rest?"

"You don't get it, my friend. I'm on *benefits*. That affects all the rest. I'm in debt up to here, there isn't any 'rest.' I'm dead broke, end of story."

She wants him to feel guilty, to feel bad, as if he were indirectly responsible. On the other hand, she has no intention of telling him about the fiasco of her love life.

She turns the question back to him.

"And you? You're happy, I guess?"

"No. And please don't give me a lot of grief because I'm depressed although I'm loaded. That's just the way it is. I'm not in a good place. For some years now. And it doesn't get any better."

"Oh I see, I was surprised you wanted to see me so much—but it's because you're depressed."

"I wouldn't have put it quite that way. You think you're an expert at cheering people up?"

In his eyes, there's that same amused, playful light that she had completely forgotten. And which still touches her. She feels her throat constrict. A mother—the embodiment of trailer trash, a big blond, with masses of makeup, perching on high-soled trainers that Loana was wearing four years ago—comes into the bar with her two kids who are already heading for obese. The kids have lovely faces, big clear eyes, delightful smiles. The mother wants an autograph. Gloria thinks about making this the moment to make her getaway. She's beginning to feel moved, touched. She doesn't want to feel this way. It would be inappropriate. And ridiculous.

"I often think about you, Blondie. I wonder how you're doing. I was so sad, you know, when you never replied to any of my letters, never called."

"Memory failing you again? You should think yourself

lucky I've even agreed to *dine* with someone who's on TV. I'd forgotten you called me Blondie."

"Does that bother you too?"

"No, I like it."

"*I'd* forgotten how aggressive you can be. It makes me laugh. I can relax when you get cross, I always used to, back in the day."

"Ah well, don't worry, I'm still aggressive all right."

"It's weird, you haven't changed a bit."

"Stop kidding. I've put on weight, my skin's shot to pieces, I've lost one or two teeth, my fingers are yellow with nicotine, my hair'll soon start falling out. You must have got a weird picture of me fixed in your brain if you think I haven't changed."

He looks hard at her, head to one side, agrees, and his big smile shows off his perfect teeth.

"You're right, Blondie, you're a realist. That must be why I want to fuck you so much."

"You poor pervert. What brings you to Nancy anyway?"

Gloria has answered him quickly and leans against the back of the seat, lighting up while he explains how it works, making TV shows in provincial France. She listens, amused, relaxed, not fearful. At least that's how it looks on the surface. Inside, there's total panic and alarm. She heard perfectly well what he said. She's playing for as much time as possible.

The restaurant where he takes her impresses her and prompts a nervous burst of laughter. Between two hiccups, she manages to say, "I didn't know people were allowed to SET FOOT in here . . ."

"If it bores you, we can get room service."

"No, it doesn't bore me at all. But it's strange. It feels like eating in a museum. Quite funny, really. Not ideal for your digestion, but funny as an experience . . ."

Then she collapses laughing again. Nothing in this place is normal, not the waiters, not the chandeliers, not the seats, the napkins, the glasses, the plates, the table-cloths . . . It's as if everything is labeled *refined*, *elegant*, so overpowering that it's stifling. She regains her composure, clears her throat, and has the distinct feeling that she's a woman from the backwoods lost in some remote palace.

Three waiters stand around their table. It's impossible to drain her glass without one of them hurrying to refill it. She leans toward Eric and whispers, "Are they going to stand behind us all night?"

He nods and remarks with a blasé expression, "They're not listening. Between ourselves, I don't think they could care less what we're talking about."

She sits like Tony Montana in *Scarface*, back braced against the chair, thighs apart. She smiles.

"I daren't even drink the water in my glass. Understand? You're too used to it. Do they serve beer here?"

He doesn't take his eyes off her. He's acting as if he's an attentive suitor. It has been years since any man treated her this way. As if she were an enchanted creature. Strange, not unpleasant, but somehow odd as an atmosphere. He's attracted to her, and it doesn't wear off. On the contrary, the more they relax, the more considerate, playful, drawn to her, and seductive he becomes.

He tells her his life story, with much name-dropping of celebrities, the way she might talk about the habitués of the Royal. She's on the lookout, but she can't detect any affectation, it's just what his everyday life is now, with people in his profession. He often repeats that he feels lonely, insisting on it: lonely at home, lonely when he goes on holiday, lonely in the morning, lonely with all his success, and lonely with his depression. He doesn't seem to be doing it on purpose, but this solitude comes up as a leitmotif.

In the end she says, "Come on, don't do a Kurt Cobain on me. You look pretty good, things can't be as bad as you say . . ."

Eric finds that hilarious, like everything she says. Gloria is taken aback by the way the evening is turning out. Big surprise that she suddenly wants him.

She is torn between waking him up: "Hey ho, this is twenty years on, I don't have this effect on anyone." And another wish, just as tempting, to take advantage of the situation, without making a fuss, without thinking too much. Since sooner or later she'll have to sleep with a man who isn't Lucas. So it might as well be a guy who's dying to do it. And it might as well be with a super good-looking guy with an impeccable suit, expensive shoes, and who's shaved recently. She can't make the connection between the man sitting opposite her and the boy who broke her heart almost twenty years ago. Some of his gestures, though, touch off something in her, like an electric shock, and make her incapable of reasoning more than a minute at a time, and her desire for him is so great that it surges up in waves and completely undoes her. It's his fault, she tells herself in an effort to calm down, he should have been less explicit.

How long has it been since she felt so light? Everything had become tragic, serious, gloomy. How long ago since she felt herself deeply moved? Boom, a magnetic boom deep inside, an enjoyable feeling of loss of control.

"You turn me on even more than I remember, and even

then, in my memories it was pretty good. I've been wanting to get you into bed since we met in town in the rain, haven't thought of anything else the whole time."

"Concentrate on something else, we're not going to start at the table. Or maybe yes? I don't know the local customs. I don't have any place of my own. Do you have a room in the hotel?"

She's talking too much and too fast, she empties her glass and holds back.

To anyone observing them from a distance, Gloria simply seems unfazed by his suggestion and is giving as good as she gets. They might also simply think she's had a bit too much to drink.

"BUT YOU DON'T have a girlfriend? Why not? Christ, you must be difficult."

The bedroom is in the same style as the restaurant: improbable. Gloria walks around the huge room and looks down from the window at Place Stanislas. Leaning her forehead on the glass, she thinks in the future she'll always think of this moment, this view from above, every time she crosses the square.

"You're lucky you left Nancy. Such a little town. I feel I'm so useless to have stayed here."

Eric takes a shower as soon as they reach the room. He's left her a silver tube full of coke: "While you wait."

"Okay, big boy, take your time then."

She lays out the longest line she's ever had all to herself, and it represents about as much as she's ever taken since childhood. When he comes out of the shower, she feels relieved that he's fully dressed. He returns her question.

"And you don't have a man in your life?"

"If I did, it wouldn't be reasonable to be here, would it?"

"But seriously, money apart, you're really unhappy?"

"Doesn't seem to be in the stars for me. When we were kids, we already thought I wouldn't be happy. But we didn't realize quite how disturbed I'd be."

"What happened to you?"

"Well, nothing. That's the point, nothing. Apart from watching some of my friends die, some getting to be complacent prigs, others getting into terrible messes, others trying as hard as they could and still getting nowhere. If it had just been me who was a failure, I'd have said it was up to me to get a grip. But it wasn't anything personal. Nothing goes right for me now. Like lots of people, you'll tell me. I don't like the euro, don't like CDs, computers, email, I don't like the way things are now, I don't like modern bands, I don't like my face, I can't stand the tarts prancing around on TV, I don't like working . . ."

"Hush, it's all over, I'm here now."

"Oh, big deal, that really comforts me."

Gloria points at the long line of coke she's fixed him on the walnut coffee table. He rubs his eyes, then dares to say, "Shall we fuck first?"

"Oh yeah, *that* was your idea, wasn't it?"

"You don't have to. You don't want to?"

"Why should I feel I have to? Are you thinking of paying me or something?"

"I didn't want to come on too strong."

"Well, you are, make no mistake, you are coming on strong. And if you want to pay me, well, if the price is right, I won't take it amiss, you know."

She's still playing for time with this kind of banter, but she knows she's going to have to do it. She practically wrenches the door off the minibar opening it, goes into ecstasy over the minibottles of Jack Daniel's, drinks two, and feels him come up behind her, take her around the waist and pull her toward him. She tells herself she's way past the age for her heart to be pounding like this, and lets herself fall back.

A really enormous bed, with a mattress half-soft, half-firm. Eric must have slept with millions of girls, or perhaps he just met one who explained things to him. Whatever it was, he has become a leisurely, expert, and considerate lover. He keeps his eyes open, she likes seeing that look, it holds both vice and trust. Gloria goes through all the motions, makes the right sounds and fakes it, without really committing herself. She doesn't let go for a second. Because the situation is so strange, because she's taken too much cocaine, because she is suspicious. There's a feeling of arousal but it's distant. She looks around the bedroom, which is several times bigger than any apartment she's ever lived in. She looks at his wristwatch, a heavy one in precious metal. She strokes his shoulders, and low down on his back. She agrees to try everything, turn every which way.

The geopolitical debate going on between the sheets gives her the weird impression that for the first time she's gone to bed with a grown-up. While still moaning and wriggling, she is trying to work out what makes it different, now that they are naked in bed and fucking, what makes him different from anyone else.

It's his attitude, his gestures, everything she knows about him. It both attracts her and paralyzes her at the same time: an adult, a man. This is a grown-up story. She's aroused, but it scares her stiff, she's afraid not to meet expectations. Bombarded with thoughts running through her head. After a while, she starts to move her pelvis more sensually and faster, dancing at the end of his prick and moaning in a convincing way. She's in a hurry for him to come, then they can stop fucking and snort some more coke.

He sends down for a bottle of champagne. She doesn't know whether she thinks this is a ridiculous or a marvelous idea. She's wrapped in a white bathrobe belonging to the hotel, never has she felt anything so soft and comfortable. She purrs with delight. He's as pleased as punch, absolutely ecstatic now that he's had his pleasure. He tells her it hasn't been as good as this in twenty years, no other girl comes up to her ankle, he fumbles in his case and finds a tiny knife with an ivory handle to cut some fine lines of coke. A practiced hand. He's radiant, compliments spill out of his mouth, he's so delighted at finding her again. Not that she really wants to bring up the subject, but sooner or later it'll be inevitable.

"If you have such a good memory of how we were as kids, why did you dump me like that?"

She's surprised to see that he is genuinely embarrassed, as if it had happened last month. She's also surprised to feel her own anger rising intact inside her, and she adds, bitingly: "How could you do it? How could you do a thing like that, Eric?"

And then he bursts into tears, this grown-up, this monsieur, he breaks down and offers any amount of excuses. Not explanations, but excuses and regrets. The only real reason he manages to give is still the same after twenty years. "I couldn't do that to my mother."

"I've missed you so much."

"That's funny. You must have met lots of people in your television world."

"People don't wipe each other out. Not necessarily. You and me, that's my secret history. And it matters . . ."

"You didn't answer, a while back, when I asked you if you had a girlfriend."

"They make me sick. I always seem to go for girls who are totally impossible."

Gloria bursts out laughing.

"Ah yes, that certainly fits, you always liked really difficult girls, I can vouch for that."

More champagne, more coke, a bit more sex, she's agreeing with everything he says, she's even started to make a little speech saying there isn't so much difference between someone on benefits and a TV presenter. She doesn't believe a word of it, but the drugs have pummeled her brain so hard that all her ideas are in tiny fragments. Next day, when she's sobered up, she'll be ashamed at talking such a lot of nonsense.

Very soon, the coke starts to affect her throat, she has to have some more, and it's still not enough to calm her anguish. For the first time in her life, there's more than she can absorb. Lying on her stomach on the bed, she says, "So much, it's kind of comforting."

He comes and sits astride her back and massages the nape of her neck. A sudden flash of lightning, a mental chasm, twenty years ago, the same position, the same gestures. How happy she'd been with him, the calm it had brought, the sweet certainty, the need for nothing else. A feeling of total bliss. For the last time in her life. Suddenly she sees clearly how bitter and lacking in magic the years in between have been. She knew this man at a turning point in time, the last months of maximum innocence. She was already sleeping around, taking acid and drinking whiskey from the bottle, stealing from old women's handbags, hitting herself with a baseball bat, and she'd thought she'd seen it all, she was an old experienced person. And then this boy, the first and the last, had made her truly happy. Before breaking her in two.

Gloria crosses her fingers and stretches with her arms behind her head, leaning back to declare: "You were always good at being Prince Charming, rock-and-roll style."

As the dawn breaks, he explains, while rolling some joints of pure grass, "I understand, I do, that you're still furious with me. I knew it then, when I wrote that letter from the Swiss school, I knew I shouldn't have. But until I wrote exactly what they wanted me to, they wouldn't leave me alone. I know it's hard for you to understand that, because giving in isn't the kind of thing *you'd* do. But try to imagine . . . "

"Oh, you know, I did try, at times."

"I was locked up for two years minimum there. And my mother, with her cancer, I thought I'd never see her again and I was sure it was all my fault . . . Please try and understand, Blondie, try not to be always just seeing it from where you are. I never forgot you, never denied you, it wasn't a case of 'wake up to real life.' I was trapped, they didn't give me the choice. But I couldn't get you out of my head, out of my heart. Sometimes, as time went by, I thought I had, but then some thing, some little detail always brought you right back for me. Do you believe me?"

"Oh, I don't think I care anymore, Eric, it's too late now.

What kind of grass is this? It must've grown on Neptune, it's *unbelievable*. Don't look at me like that, it's no big deal. We're so far apart now, I'm not angry at you anymore."

"When you're in my situation, nobody feels close. That's what's so strange."

"Asking for pity now?"

"When you're in my situation, that's just the point, nobody pities you, and that's so awful in the end. I want to be able to complain like everyone else . . . I have a right to, don't I? I have to pay a shrink, otherwise nobody in the world will hear my groans. It's not fair."

"Oh, cool it, Eric, you're getting tiring. If with all your cash you haven't found a shoulder to cry on, it's because you're not gifted for it, that's all. Is there anymore of that extraterrestrial grass?"

They spend the day in the bedroom with the TV on, too exhausted to keep up a conversation. They grind their teeth and see stars under their eyelids, then collapse into an uneasy sleep for a few hours. And that night, Sunday, Eric has to leave. He has to record a show on Monday.

It's raining, a sort of gray drizzle. Gloria is determined not to be affected. She's completely high, and feels in top form. Not knowing where to go, she heads for the Royal, where she has a big success. Still stoned, the sounds are echoing around in her skull and it takes her a little while just to reply when someone says, "Hi." She slips into a banquette alongside Michel, who is alone, she is glad to see. And he asks right away, "So you had sex?"

She lies, says no, with the would-be comic face of a girl who regrets it, so as not to have to talk about it. She claims: "No, we just took these fantastic drugs."

"I can see that, lucky beggar."

"No, no sex. Can you imagine the kind of girl he can pull?"

Michel nods—a little too fast for her taste. How quickly it resurfaces, the pleasure of receiving compliments.

From the loudspeakers, the first notes of "We Are Family" start to play and she improvises a little dance with her hands, looking dopey. Michel smiles and she asks him: "So, when are you leaving?"

"We've started packing . . . Oh, I hate moving, so much hassle."

"That's life, you've got to get on with it. That's how it is."

Then Gloria slumps into drowsiness as he opens a newspaper.

TUESDAY, IN THE post office, an old lady is practically lying across an official's desk. He is trying to make her understand that she can't withdraw any cash. He keeps repeating "TOMORROW" loudly and clearly. She's wearing a shabby dressing gown and has very little hair left. She doesn't understand. The official explains, at a loss for what to do, "They don't pay out on Mondays, you've only got forty centimes in your account, come back tomorrow, TOMORROW." She moves away, the next person takes her place.

In the queue, there's a little kid who's annoying everyone by talking too loudly, while his mother tells him to be quiet in the soft voice of a perpetual victim. Gloria glances at her and finally mutters: "If he doesn't hear his mother saying no when he's four, how's he ever going to listen to girls who say no when he's fifteen?" The woman, who hadn't asked her anything, turns around, at a loss. Taken aback. Visibly, she hasn't understood what Gloria's got against her. A black guy in a pink suit is standing stiffly upright, an idiot with a Walkman is listening to Slayer turned up loud, a fat man with a mustache is staring into nowhere. A woman complains that there's *always* a line at the post office. Gloria, never at a loss for something to say, looks her up and down and retorts: "Perhaps that's because you only come here at busy times, you silly bitch."

The people all look embarrassed. She's used to it. All day, she has to keep opening her big mouth for the slightest thing. She's beating her own records for aggression. The old woman has come back, still in her tatty dressing gown, and stands behind Gloria in the queue. She stinks of pee to high heaven. It's obvious she's forgotten she came in here five minutes ago. This makes Gloria terribly sad, she is unreasonably touched by everything at the moment. That's even worse to bear, tears of rage and impotence, bitter tears sting her eyes. She stays in the line, breathing too deeply.

Véronique appears, out of breath.

"Oh, I'm so glad you're still here! Eric just called!"

She touches Gloria's arm, she's so excited that she makes little animal noises.

"I spoke to him! Wow, I was like, how fantastic is that! He's very nice, isn't he? I wanted to be sure you had the message. I'm on the way to my dance class."

Still panting, she gives Gloria a pink Post-it in the shape of a heart, with scraps of tobacco clinging to the sticky bit. Eric's number has been carefully written on it in purple felt pen. Gloria shrugs.

"I've already got his number. But it was so sweet of you, thank you."

Véronique puts her hand on her arm to calm her, as she would with someone stupid, and explains clearly: "You've got his number and you haven't called him. That's just it, he *wants* you to call him. Well, not that it's an emergency or anything, but . . ."

"Yes, it was kind of him to leave me the choice whether to call him or not."

Véronique rolls her eyes, she's flushed with pleasure to have spoken to a TV personality. Gloria still can't get over the effect it has on them all. In her case, it isn't because he's famous that she's been thinking about him nonstop for the three days since he arrived. It's just because she's a fool, and already falling in love. Because she consulted the cards at Véronique's house, read her horoscope in the paper at the Royal. Because she's incorrigible. To her great shame, she's hardly had a thought for Lucas at all. As if a year had passed since their last quarrel. This has never happened to her before, to obliterate someone from her mind so fast. She thanks Véro again and apologizes.

"Look, I'm really sorry, I need to stay with you again tonight. I swear Michel told me they were moving out Monday. But for sure tomorrow. I've got the keys, I've found someone who's going to get my things from Lucas's. Tomorrow, I'll be out of your hair. And next week you must come visit me!"

"Doesn't matter, really, it's my pleasure, truly!"

Véronique goes out, her straw basket with her dance things under her arm. Gloria reassesses: three days to call her, well, he isn't just fooling around. She concentrates on looking sulky and above all resists the urge to dance the polka right there in the post office.

SHE PACKS ALL she can into her bag and hurries not to miss the train. At the station, she looks up at the clock, gets her ticket punched, picks up a newspaper, and as she's waiting to pay for it, recognizes Lucas going past, only a few feet away. She has just enough time to see that he looks drawn, in his brown eyes there's that miserable expression that she has never really noticed but which she knows by heart. In a shamefaced reflex, she turns her back without being sure whether he saw her or not. He goes on his way. She watches him disappear, his habit of stooping a little catches her in the throat suddenly. How can she be failing to regret him, even a little? Or putting it another way, how did she ever imagine she was really in love with him? She picks up her change for the paper and hurries toward her platform. This near miss makes her feel slightly ill at ease. She goes past some soldiers, arms at the ready, part of the government's antiterrorist dispositions. On the train, the places to put your luggage have been closed off for the same reason, with police tape across them. Consequently, people's bags are everywhere, piled up in the corridors.

Gloria finds a seat in a fairly empty carriage, opens her paper, but doesn't read it, gazing out at the landscape and thinking of other things. Her impatience, an undertow of fear, a delicious anticipation, a sensation long forgotten and yet familiar. It's like it was ten years ago, when going somewhere meant freedom, the promise of adventure. She's on the move, after years of immobility, which today seem like death to her. She's traveling toward something, it gives her a strange feeling in the pit of her stomach, sharp and intoxicating.

He's waiting for her at the station, at the end of the

platform. She recognizes him first and walks head down, thrown off-balance by her bulging bag. Having had to move out quickly, her worldly goods have been reduced drastically in size. She took advantage of that to come with all that's left: three sweaters, four pairs of trainers, not much else.

Eric rushes forward to meet her with a brilliant smile and reaches for her luggage, "Leave it to me," and then hugs her, slipping his hand underneath her sweater and up her back. Just like teenagers at the school gate. Gloria would like to savor the moment, but the lightheartedness that had filled her for the last few days has suddenly vanished, to be replaced by the beginnings of panic. She's no longer so sure she wants to go home with him, to see him, to have this physical contact. Perhaps she'd have done better to stay in her bar in peace, with a beer in front of her, chatting to her friends. Anywhere really, except on the verge of this adventure, which is too weird, too strange, too dangerous.

She asks, looking around, "Shall we go and have a beer? There wasn't a trolley on the train, I'm parched."

But he takes her hand and pulls her along.

"Not here, I hate stations."

"You're scared there might be a bomb?"

In fact, he's scared of being recognized and approached. She realizes that's the case within a few meters. While she's trying to think of something to say, how to behave, she is suddenly aware that half the people in the station concourse are staring at him. It's a kind of tide, discreet but perceptible, of faces turning toward him. She can feel behind them the tenfold attention of people who are pointing. He's used to it and walks fast without looking left or right. He doesn't allow the slightest eye contact that might let a passerby accost him. It seems to Gloria that all the women they pass, just after they recognize him, shift their gaze toward her and look her up and down with a total lack of sympathy. She's too old to stick out her tongue at them, and if she were to rush up and grab them by the hair and wrestle them to the ground yelling, she'd look like some mad criminal. She contents herself with scratching the back of her neck and pulling funny faces. She feels she's being exhibited, publicly humiliated. So she concentrates on her feet, restricting her field of vision.

As soon as she knew she was coming to Paris, she'd announced it to her pals at the Royal. Their reactions bordered on the insulting: "What does he want? I'd be suspicious if I were you." "Look out for yourself," with a hint of pity, or that's how she took it. At the time, it had irritated her. Why were all these people worried for her, just because something unexpected was happening to her? They hadn't shown any concern before, when she'd spent her life riveted to the same bar, telling the same stories and downing liters of beer. So why get alarmed now when she's off to see a bit of the world? *What the hell do they think*, she'd wondered, *that because he's on TV, the greater will be my fall?* If something comes to an end, it's always painful. But that's not a reason to advise people to stay home and not talk to anyone.

But now that she's here, holding hands with him, trying to keep up with him, she understands their awkward expressions, she sees what they meant, the people who advised her not to go. This story is too unbalanced, she is totally needy, and he needs nothing. It freaks her out to be some kind of whim on his part. A two-euro fairy tale, the fatal mistake that she's going to regret. Happiness doesn't just fall on your head like that, out of the blue, without your having asked for it, deserved it, discovered it. Why didn't she think of this before? Instead of jumping on the train the very next day, prize candidate for disaster.

Eric holds the taxi door open long enough for her to slip into the backseat. As soon as they're in, his phone goes off, imitating an old-fashioned telephone. He apologizes, says he has to answer it. His voice changes when he's talking work, more authoritarian, sharper, his replies are rapid, edgy, and irritable. Gloria watches Paris go past the windows. Eric's hand feels for hers. A few rays of sunshine, the first of the year, light up the scene as if by magic. The Parisian women are engaged in a ferocious competition, shoes with built-up heels, colored trousers with tops and jackets to match, pretty handbags with motifs. Four rappers are waiting at the lights, black giants dressed in white and pale pink, like gigantic Haribo Chamallows. They're laughing and joking, look like they're in slow motion. They cross the road, followed by two Japanese guys with a head-to-foot rockabilly look, mirror Ray-Bans and gelled hair. *This is super sexy*, Gloria thinks appreciatively. As she looks at these people, she forgets to worry or regret she's come. She's suddenly grabbed by the rhythm of Paris all around them, the noise, the bustle, the clamor.

A woman sitting on the pavement, clutching a baby, rocking to-and-fro, holding out her hand, chanting something. There are people driving tiny Smart cars, caricatures of the year 2000 like they'd imagined it back in the 1970s. A delivery boy on a scooter overtakes them without indicating, the taxi driver hoots at him. A woman veiled from head to foot comes face to face with a black girl in a miniskirt. A little dark man, well past forty, black high-top Converse and Diesel jeans, turns around to look at first one then the other, and goes on his way, laughing to himself.

"And yet seen from Beijing, we're all Europeans," says Gloria, almost to herself. She opens her eyes wide, happy to be there, feels full of energy and comfortable. Another homeless man, this one is lying full-length on the pavement. He's not begging, he's fast asleep. She has a sudden dizzy spell: How long would it take someone like her, with no family, to end up like that? As long as she stays in Nancy, the risk is lower because whatever she says about it, there's always someone who will take her in. But here, without a credit card, a checkbook—she's been banned from having a bank account since she was eighteen, with an occasional fortnight's grace every year—it could happen in a couple of days. The element of risk puts her on the alert, it's electric, not entirely unpleasant. She snaps out of a kind of reverie. Her mood has swung around too fast and too much, she's wearing herself out without any help.

She asks Eric as he ends his call, "Your father, when did he die? How did he die?"

"With my mother, a car crash, they hit someone head-on one night. I thought you knew."

"No, I just knew you'd lost your parents like me. But didn't your mother have cancer?"

"Yeah, but she'd got better, when she died it was three years later. I'd just taken some university exams."

"I'm sorry. And your sister? Does she live in Paris?"

"Yes. We don't see each other much though. She's married this complete prick."

"What does she do?"

"She's got three kids. Work you mean? She doesn't need to, the guy has shitloads of dough."

"Pity not to see your sister. When my parents died, I'd have been glad all the same to have a brother or sister."

"You're right, I should go and see her someday. You have no idea how much she *hates* you. And you'd scare her jerk of a husband to death, that would be fun . . ."

His phone rings again. Gloria tugs on her bra straps, which have slipped down. Her own parents had died within two years of each other, leukemia and a heart attack, when she was around twenty. Another unfair blow of fate that she couldn't share with anyone, because all the people she knew still had their parents and couldn't understand. How strange it felt to have no ties to the world. Only a few of her friends whose parents had divorced could imagine something of what it felt like. She often thinks of her parents, she wishes she could have known them better once she'd grown up. At the same time, she hasn't done anything that would make them proud of her. Eric is trying to finish his conversation. She feels she's about to cry and decides to change the subject.

"Sometimes I wonder whether I was given the wrong soul. Perhaps I was meant to be a fighter, man or woman, doesn't matter, anything that would let me go and fight. Really fight, beat people up, smash their faces in, knock out their teeth and get massacred myself. Let's suppose there was some crossed wires in the 1960s and something went wrong and I got a bloodthirsty maniac's soul in the body of a poor girl on benefits. Do you get what I'm saying?"

He blinks his eyelids to say yes. Gloria, when she starts telling her theories to people who haven't heard them, can be totally exhausting, and they don't even try to understand, but Eric doesn't let himself be impressed.

"The way things are going, your aggressive superpowers could be useful. But yes, it's possible, I've thought that way too, people who are useless and a total pain in the ass in peacetime can become heroes when war breaks out."

"Hey, steady on, I didn't say I was useless or a pain in the ass!"

"Yeah I know, but I'm trying to develop your idea."

"Leave my idea be, and don't call me a pain in the ass, please."

Eric puts up a finger saying to listen while he develops his theory about war heroes, but his phone goes off again, and although heaving a big sigh, he answers it and launches into a conversation. She moves closer to him and finds a way of snuggling under his arm. When a relationship is still okay, when she thinks this time's going to be different, this time she'll be able to keep her mouth shut, it could always go wrong. It's as if she's holding a ball of transparent crystal in both hands.

The taxi driver, a young crew-cut kid with a closed face and rings around his eyes, a Hand of Fatima dangling from the rear mirror, is talking aloud into his radiophone. His loud comments in a language she can't understand make it a futuristic scene, like something out of Philip K. Dick.

Eric strokes her wrist. "I'm glad you're here. Makes a change."

"From what?"

"Everything."

Gloria tries to look like a girl who understands what he means.

HIS PLACE IS so clean and white that she can scarcely believe anyone lives there. Below in the street, cars glide by, a string of lights. When she leans her forehead against the window, she feels the cold burn into her a little. She's intimidated. All her excitement has drained away, she feels worn-out above all. She slowly drinks her glass of vodka on the rocks. After one more of the same, her mood lifts.

He's taken three whole days off to be with her. Gloria whistles appreciatively when she finds out. "Kind of like a sabbatical year, is it?" When the exaggerated ringtone of Eric's phone goes off, he presses silent automatically and says, "I've never done that since I've had a phone, right?"

"Poor you!"

Mornings last till afternoon, making tea and listening to the radio. She likes it when Eric tells her what else he'd like to do with his life, or imagines the trips they could go on together. By turns intrigued, irritated, and seduced, they're examining each other and coming face to face. He's alarmed at the hostile bad faith with which Gloria accuses him of being rich while she's poor.

Systematically, she keeps returning to that, it's her excuse for everything, her open sesame to, "Leave me alone, I'm just a poor working-class girl, I've got nothing, you've got too much of everything, it's your fault, go fuck yourself." Her painful neurotic worrisome credo, sometimes bordering on the obscene.

"Tell me, Gloria, you keep complaining, but your father ended up with a good job as a manager, didn't he?"

"Leave my dad out of it. Do you think one generation's enough to wipe out a whole load of ancestors grubbing away in the lumpenproletariat? Anyone can see you don't come from there, right? If you don't believe me, look how I live. I'm on minimum benefits, it's not like I'm living a bohemian life. There's a *big* difference. If you're capable of understanding it."

"You could have made things turn out differently."

"Anyone ever tell you Zorro doesn't exist in real life?'"

He stretches his legs and clasps his hands behind his head with a smile.

"You're going to tell me *the world's not fair* and I'm a privileged moneybags? Do me a favor, Blondie, lay off, you're spoiling my digestion."

When she tries to find out how much he earns at his job, the sums he mentions leave her flabbergasted. He gets over €20,000 a month. Not to mention various perks. If he ever gets fired, his severance has been calculated in some clever complicated way but it'll come to something like €200,000. She contemplates these figures in her head for a few moments before concluding: "*Now* I understand why we don't understand each other!"

When Gloria listens to Eric outlining his arguments, part of her, the grown-up part, tries to understand how it works, while the other, the teenager, screams and shouts and wants to know why, why, why. Everything seems normal to him, the compromises he has to make every day to keep his job, not to have problems with the neighbors, to get on with his friends, and earn plenty of money. Everything he's prepared to tolerate in the way of stupidity, lies, bootlicking. At the same time, and for the first time, she is seeing at close quarters someone capable of making an effort without giving up immediately and saying, "Oh, I can't be bothered," someone who doesn't use pride as a way of avoiding difficult encounters.

They walk around Paris, she goes with him to buy a jacket. In shops that make her feel so out of place that it verges on panic. Even the bouncers and salesgirls look down their noses at her, as if they own the place. No one is creepier than rich people's hangers-on. It's not just the clothes, the prices, the customers, but something about the surroundings, the lights, the rhythms, and the sounds that all say the same thing: we're above that hoi polloi out there, we deserve the best.

The prices in the windows look to her like a bad joke. Everything here seems to say that she and all the people she knows are *nothing,* not just on their uppers, they don't even exist, because the wealthy can simply afford not to notice them. And here she is, with her minimum benefits, her grubby friends, the IKEA furniture they're only too glad to have because it means they've got a place to live, their petty scrimping and saving to survive. She feels her entire world is crushed by the arrogance of these shop windows, these price tags and these people—old ladies who've been face-lifted till they look like zombies. She'd like to be able to laugh at it all. The wealthy hold themselves very upright, convinced of their own importance.

She waits in front of the luxury delicatessen, Fauchon's, smoking a cigarette. She looks people up and down as they go in, actively detesting them. Elderly dyed-blonds, all twig-slim with ridiculous little dogs, hordes of frantic Japanese women, young anorexic girls with strained faces, old ladies with white hair and Hermès scarves. The clichés aren't misleading. Rich people are just like you'd imagine them: weird, ugly, and pleased with themselves. They can spot each other at a glance. Even when one of them dresses down, they keep something about them that says to their equals, "I'm one of us." She waits for him opposite Colette's, smoking another cigarette.

"Come in with me, don't be silly."

"I tell you I'll freak out."

"You look like a horse stamping its foot outside. You're scaring everyone."

She wants to run between the aisles waving her hands in the air and screaming, pushing people over into the displays. Breaking all the glass, the mirrors, the windows. Punching the old hags in the face, kicking the salesgirls, jumping up and down on the fashion victims, smashing the balls of the bouncers.

"These shops smell of death, they make me want to throw up."

"Just one more call and I'll take you around somewhere different, Barbès district in a taxi if you like."

"You're so droll, ha ha."

In fact, she does find him funny. She waits for him in front of Ladurée while he puts up with a long line at the counter.

She lights up and thinks aloud: "What a pathetic bunch of assholes, if you have to wait five minutes in the post office, you start moaning, but for a box of fancy biscuits at fifty euros a throw, you don't mind standing in line for half an hour. You are really so unbelievably *stupid*, down inside your souls you're poor, just poor sods, hear what I'm saying?"

From their astonished expressions, she understands that her insults have at least had the merit of surprise. Eric looks down as he comes out with an enormous shopping bag, he drags her away, hiding his smile.

"Now you've had your say, you won't be so worried how much they cost, you'll gobble them all up and say they're delicious."

"I won't eat one of them, hear me, not one! Never!"

She points at them and pounds her chest, she likes doing that, it resounds. She calms down quickly, because she knows quite well she'll wolf the lot. Eric sighs.

"Don't you ever give it a rest? Too much aggression kills aggression and you're exhausting in the end."

"Yes, but I'm the bomb in bed."

"You're the bomb, period, you freak everyone out."

"You love it, I bet. If you wanted someone nice and quiet, you wouldn't have come looking for me."

"So you feel obliged to carry on like that as much as possible?"

"That's my style."

And she sings him this Johnny Hallyday song, "Je suis né dans la rue," about forty times a day. As if it explains everything.

Eric grumbles: "Oh, it's all the street's fault, is it . . . ?"

The first days in Paris, the sex is just as bad as that first night. She doesn't care, she pretends it's fine and he seems to believe her. But gradually, almost without realizing it, she starts to concentrate, to open up, to reach for him. She allows arousing images to come into her head, she murmurs words she likes to hear, she starts to show what she wants, how fast or slow. He's considerate, good at it, sensual, and he loves her. In the end, she joins in the game. The first time she actually comes, it's a few seconds before him. And it makes her go into a long swoon. Because this time it works, it opened up, the dam broke and she can fill herself with him without reserve, no safety net, she lets him have what he wants. She's not afraid anymore.

HE GOES OFF to work every day at about ten, and doesn't get back until they've recorded the show, about nine at night. She watches him and talks to him when he's on their TV. She starts to get interested in the stories, the questions, what he's wearing, his guests, the audience, the editing . . . she gets fascinated by the whole show. She gradually realizes why people who make TV shows have such a different perspective from the people who watch them. Two populations, quite different. The upper classes in Paris are obsessed with television, the only thing that interests them. Making TV shows, *being* on TV, knowing how it works. The power of the small screen, its secrets, the money that's poured into it, the power struggles. Ordinary people simply watch it, with less interest than the ones who make it, and less credulity than the rich like to think.

When she phones the Royal for something to do, out of boredom, nostalgia, and also out of a sense of loyalty, she feels as if she's won the lottery. From Jérémy's delighted tone, she gathers with brutal clarity just how much everyone had thought until now that she was a hopeless case. She's shocked, because she hadn't realized that. The people she thought were her friends, now that she's so far away, it becomes clear they felt sorry for her, as if she were a homeless waif. Even Véronique, whom at first she'd been phoning regularly, is "so happy for her": "From your voice, I can tell you're having a marvelous time now." Gloria doesn't know what to say, it's crazy the way these provincials are reassured that she's back in the land of the living.

Regretfully, she realizes she must avoid her Nancy friends as long as she stays with him. The trap of congratulations, the bittersweet taste of envy. She starts telling lies, spontaneously, keeps quiet about some events, tries to downplay her pleasure at being with him, as vengeance for everything else, for the years of her systematic downhill slide. She's afraid of their jealousy, that they'll make her pay for it when she gets back, and also that they'll steal what she has. By telling them about it, she'll give herself away, it'll become distorted and she won't enjoy it.

And yet, it lasts, this fragile, magic moment when they have nothing to blame each other for. Neither of them has shown the other their worst side. For now, they've just been playing and making up, with their respective pasts.

He likes it just as much as when he was a teenager, watching her get into a rage, climb up the curtains, confront people, without being willing to let go or understand. He likes fighting with her. They're like a couple of Italians, always ready to scream and shout, then hug each other and make completely different sounds.

Then he takes her in his arms, even as she pulls away,

rocks her, and she starts to laugh and grumble, "I don't want to be in love with you, leave me alone."

It's a warm bath of affection, tenderness, caresses, and sex, everything she's been missing so much. She's beginning to trust him, to believe in him differently. Then it starts again, on the slightest pretext.

"Stop being such a hippie, it's so tiring."

"You talking to me? You sick or something?"

"Listen to yourself, Blondie. You're NOT in a remake of *Scarface*, or *Taxi Driver*, or the *Godfather*, or *Goodfellas*. You're not a man, you're not in the Mafia, you're not Cuban or Sicilian, you're nearly thirty-five, you still talk like some kid who watches too much TV."

If they'd been in a bullring and he'd waved a red rag under her nose, she couldn't have been more furious.

"So sorry I grew up where I did, you poor mama's boy! How d'you think *you* talk, you wimp? Normally? You and your bourgeois friends, you can't pronounce a syllable without thinking you're king of the fucking with-it world and you tell *me* off when I get cross. You're joking? Tell me you're joking, you can't mean it."

"Blondie, I've had enough of the class struggle every day at home."

"YOU started it. You're the one who doesn't understand the way you are, NOBODY wants to be like you, I'm sorry, people imitate Tony Montana, not people out of Desplechin movies. Guess why! NOBODY wants to be like you. Everyone would like your money, yeah, but not your pathetic style, get it?"

And she goes out for a walk. Or the contrary. Other weeks, they stay calm. She likes walking in Paris, it quickly disarms her. She likes the statues of winged lions, gilded eagles, sphinxes, she likes the houses built around the edge of parks, the courtyards, the little round turrets, the roof gardens and the great glass studios. She likes going from a working-class district to an arty one, and then into the really rich parts of town, wide and well lit, where there are no shops anywhere near. She likes the fountains, the Concorde obelisk, the old churches, the angels with swords that turn up unexpectedly, the whole improbable catalog, illogically juxtaposed, with nothing predictable.

She doesn't always understand the role she's playing alongside Eric. And yet, she seems to be indispensable to him, as time confirms. He clings to her, bombards her with text messages and phone calls when he's out. She thinks she must be his guiding thread, his beacon. He needs a girlfriend, like a kid who's been left alone, abandoned. He needed her at this particular moment, because he'd been suffering from some kind of massive panic, perhaps because of his success. If she grumbles and flies into a rage over nothing, her tempestuous brutality reassures him, paradoxically it seems to protect him—from ennui, from death, from apathy. He likes it when she yanks girls away from him when they come up too close, he likes it that she pulls funny faces at the dinner parties he drags her to, when she hears the stupid things people say. He likes it when she jumps five feet in the air in shops when she sees the prices of things. She's an element of the human race he wants to hang on to, his bit of wildness in the world, she feels like an endangered species being protected by this wealthy patron who's in love with her. She trusts him. She loves it that he manages to live in this big city and get by, talks to people without flying off the handle. That he insists on going to see films that aren't funny—worthy documentaries—that he believes in the virtues of effort and work done well. Even when it's to tease him to death, she likes it that he's like this. That he reads boring, long, books, always trying to find out more stuff, understand better. She loves it that he's fond of her, that he's tender toward her when he shouldn't be, when she's being super annoying. She loves it that he loves her, and that he contradicts her all the time, opens her eyes to the depressing complexities of life, that he calls her a hippie and a nutty leftist. Both of them have the feeling that they're looking down on the teenagers they used to be in a benevolent way, catching up for lost time, repairing what was damaged.

Eric shuts himself up with her at home whenever he can. They lock the doors, touch, have sex, explore each other's bodies in all sorts of ways, with variations more or less disturbing. It's lasted a few months. Their epidermises have had time to learn each other, become acquainted, discover each other in every way, desire each other, identify the other's pleasure, become an extension of each other, mingle, melt, know all the doors that open so willingly now. They've had time to unlock each other's secrets, to roll up and unroll each other.

It weaves their bodies ever closer. He cradles her, caresses her inside, makes her float, become more beautiful. She feels she was made for this. She wriggles and pulls up her knees so that he can fuck her deeper, so she can feel him inside her, opening the door to her womb and helping her take off.

He often brings her presents. He likes going to shops or ordering via the Internet. He likes *things*, just like a kid with toys. Gloria finds it exciting to be treated like a girl from his milieu. It's such forbidden fruit in her universe, as disturbing as finding yourself being fucked from behind by strangers, with a blindfold on—and discovering you like it. Nobody wants to find out that kind of thing about themselves. She likes having private access to his perversion, his weaknesses, and his dark side. He knows this, he brings out the gift, laughing, "You're not going to throw this in my face, are you? It's jewelry, it's heavy. I'm on air tomorrow, I don't want to have a scar on my face, okay?"

She senses that she gives value to his wealth. Added value. For reasons she can't fathom, he feels guilty, and yet he was brought up with this idea of getting on in the world, upward social mobility, domination. Guilty about conforming, possibly.

She often can't sleep at night, gets out of bed at about three in the morning. From their kitchen window, you can see the Eiffel Tower in the distance, and it lights up and flashes several times a night. Gloria rolls herself a joint, takes her Walkman, and dances around the apartment, looking at everything and wondering, *If tomorrow I decide I've had enough of you, would I ever have the courage to walk out and go back home?* She starts to understand the women she meets when out with Eric, who are married to repulsive pigs, but who stay and don't complain. You wouldn't want to be kicked out when you live in luxury like this. You don't want to go backward, back to your underprivileged town. So Gloria cultivates her hostility to these people, to their luxury, as if she were grooming her wings. Keeping her faculty of being able to piss off all the same. If ever . . .

"Come on, suck me off again."

Every morning he jumps on her when he wakes up. Although she explained to him firmly the first days that she's not a morning person. But he pretends not to hear and she ends up pretending she never said it. There seems to be no limit to their sex getting better and better. If for four days running it isn't terrific, she starts to conclude it's over. Then every time, the fifth day, something new happens, an orgasm so stupefying, pleasure coming from some outer space, or simply a torrent of love enveloping them both. She thought she knew all about physical love and he thought he was a stud. They're like two beginners, amazed at what's happening to them. He likes it that she's always ready. In fact, he's astonished.

"You know, I can tell you, other women don't like sex. Maybe for a couple of months and then bingo, it's over. Don't believe me? They're all like that, I'm telling you."

"That's because you've only ever fucked bourgeois girls, they're not brought up with the idea of freedom."

"Can't you give it a rest?"

AS LONG AS they're inside their bubble with the door shut against the outside world, things go well. She touches the palms of his hands, feels the softness of his lips, all distress is left outside.

But regularly they have to go out. Then the fear returns, metal wheels riding along and slicing her flesh down to the bone.

In the corridors of the metro, the atmosphere's about as joyful as a waiting room in a slaughterhouse. Discouragement, anxiety, poverty can be read on all the faces, a dark unhappy mass covering everything. Extinguishing their bright gazes, making their mouths turn down at the corners. Ashes and bitterness, burning cinders tended by undertakers, mouths of death thrilled with the smell of fear. The palpable and mystical expectation of an anonymous punishment, because in Paris, more than in the rest of France, people fear bomb attacks. Or some other kind of explosion. The imminent menace is almost tangible, in their bodies. And yet people's eyes resist, they try to remain calm.

Because at the same time there's a real kind of gaiety, energy. Kids laughing, girls dolled up to the nines, drunks guffawing in corners, tramps of the holiest kind. Gloria reads the graffiti scrawled on the billboards with spray cans, anonymous hands that deform the messages, so that for once the posters become interesting. Tell you something different. You never know quite what's coming.

In January 2004 poor people of a new kind had started appearing underground in Paris. People you'd never have expected to be there, and who are holding out their hands for the first time. An elegant woman, heavy makeup, in her forties, expressing herself in perfect French, but with a choking voice, standing in the carriage, explaining how many children she has, and what her situation is.

She's hawking some magazine produced for the homeless. People turn around to look at her quickly, surprised to hear that kind of accent. She can't keep her composure, goes on talking in the corridors, the words pour out unstoppably. Her hands are impeccable, she holds herself very erect. The kind of lady you expect to be teaching catechism classes in the vestry, not begging in the metro. Nobody gives her a centime. Farther along, on the steps up to the street, a girl of about twenty, all in black, nice hair, nice shoes, holds out her hand. She looks more like a student than a homeless teenager. Surely she must have a little place somewhere, a room, a wardrobe, a university degree? Sitting on the stairs, leaning against the wall, avoiding people's eyes, she is begging for charity. An entire slice of the population, educated, brought up to think they would have jobs, has collapsed suddenly, the ground giving way underneath them. They're not completely resigned, but they're not exactly on their feet either. Gloria thinks of Paris in the eighties, when she used to beg for money too. Those years seem very far away, and strangely festive, in retrospect.

BUT GLORIA THESE days only meets people who are not directly concerned with the problems of poverty. She hates going out to dinner parties.

Every time, she sets off in a good mood, but once over the threshold, disillusion hits. It's like a friend of hers once who developed a fear of flying. Overnight, she found she couldn't go near an airport without starting to sweat, panicking and trembling all over. Gloria feels the same kind of thing with these rich people's dinners and their stupid parties. And yet she shouldn't be complaining—the food's pretty good, the people don't smell bad, and there are some choice wines. Anyway, nobody ever speaks to her. She tries in vain to tell herself all this over and over—before, during, and after—but it doesn't change anything. She has this psychological reaction, like some people have allergies. It's uncontrollable and involuntary. Physically oppressive. A deep desire to lash out at the infuriating types she sees at these soirees: such a lot of crass stupidity dressed up in such expensive clothes.

That particular night Eric wants to go out, she wants them to cancel and stay home eating chocolate almonds and watching DVDs—Hong Kong movies or American soaps. But he refuses to make an excuse or to go without her, he follows her into the kitchen arguing.

"We're together, we're a couple. If you beat someone up in the street, I'm there for you. And if I take you out to a party, you should be there for me. It's depressing otherwise, you give me the impression that my whole life is so disgusting that you don't even want to look at it."

"It's not that, it's the company."

"But I like you to be there, do you understand? You make me laugh, with your funny face and rolling eyes, as if you were a virgin who's chanced on an orgy, and I like talking about the people afterward in the taxi. I want to know what you think about them, it's important to me, because you're very good at putting your finger on things."

Since she adores being flattered, she protests a little less strongly. He continues to persuade her, filling the kettle.

"Anyway it's not really a dinner party. It's just a little gathering, mainly people who make films. I've got to go, Gloria, otherwise when we invite them to come on the show they'll pull all sorts of excuses, do you understand? Come with me, we'll be home before midnight, I promise. And my sister will be there, you're always asking me about her."

Gloria pretends still to be hesitating, but the final argument was the clincher. She really wants to know what

Amandine is like nowadays. Although Eric claims they're not close now, they call each other every week. It's the only conversation he holds in private, he shuts himself in the bedroom or goes into the kitchen. Gloria would like to see the brother and sister together, out of simple curiosity. She opens the oven door to see how the cake's doing and a cloud of acrid white smoke comes out. She jumps back, swearing, bats at the air with her hand, and opens the window, while Eric leaves the kitchen laughing, a cup of tea in each hand.

An hour later, they're in a taxi heading for the west end of Paris, the Eiffel Tower flashing in the background.

This is a soiree "with buffet supper," hosted by a film producer. In the hierarchy of show business, cinema people come at the top. They're way above people who work in records (currently distraught by the crisis of the CD) or in TV (less prestige, and threatened by the Internet). Anyone employed by the big screen can boast that they have the sexiest stars, the ones who really sell advertising, and a flourishing DVD market. The producer in question lives in a huge Parisian apartment (two hundred square meters). You can tell at a glance that his lady wife doesn't need to work, all she has to do is leaf through the interior decorating magazines and choose curtains to match the season of the year.

Their salon is full of disconcerting furniture—a lot of it built from junk: a table with a lopsided leg, a bookshelf that's asymmetrical, a stool like the Leaning Tower of Pisa.

Gloria leans toward Eric and whispers, "Why on earth do they buy stuff like that? They're already unbalanced anyway. They should try and keep their feet on the ground."

Continuing to smile right and left, imperturbably, he links fingers with her, and winks his complicity. At this kind of evening gathering, he's an icon—a TV presenter. By comparison, the people back at the Royal in Nancy were quite restrained in their enthusiasm. A big red-faced man, sweating like a pig, virtually throws himself on Eric with a yelp, giving him a bear hug. Probably someone he hardly knows: the more effusive the demonstration, the weaker the connection. Gloria, of whom no one is taking any notice, leaves them and moves over to the buffet. A man in tails has been hired to serve and she asks him for a glass of champagne, which she downs in one gulp. Then holds out her glass, with a tight smile, doing the same again, turning her back on the rest of the company. Only after her third glass does she step aside, lean against the wall, and take a look around. If anyone had come up to her at that very minute, she could perfectly well have scratched their eyes out.

A woman in a pink ensemble that doesn't suit her has planted herself at the buffet, cornering a younger woman: "I just don't have the time, between my Reiki classes and tennis lessons, and I'm learning Hebrew as well."

"You're learning Hebrew?"

"Yes, you see I want to be able to read the Bible."

This is delivered in a very serious and considered tone. The younger woman, evidently lost, replies in surprise, "But it's been translated into French, you know!"

The older woman looks shocked. It's hard to show off to someone as dumb as this.

Gloria feels stifled, she has palpitations, she has a sense she's choking and is angry with herself for it. She wishes she could just laugh at this kind of idiocy among the rich, she'd like to get used to it, be able to treat it lightly, not give a damn. She'd like to be trivial-minded, get excited over some fancy top, put her hair in a chignon, take a lot of care with her eye shadow. Then act like everyone else: fake it, enthusiastically.

She looks around for Eric. The crowd in this huge room is very mixed, but at a glance she can tell it's a hetero gathering. The girls are young, ravishing, and numerous. As for the men, this evening, they haven't been selected for their looks.

Eric spots her and crosses the room toward her, but gets waylaid en route by a tall gangling man with spectacles, wearing a beautiful designer suit—wasted on his ungainly body. Finally he gets away and joins her at the buffet. Sympathetically, she offers him her half-full glass and he drains it off.

"I thought he'd never let me go. He hates our show, and he had to tell me in detail everything he dislikes about it, but it's classic—he knows more about the damn show than I do."

"The less they like it, the more they obsess over it, I've noticed."

Eric smiles. "You must be getting acclimated. I've never seen you look so relaxed on a night out."

"Yeah, it's cool. Shall we go home?"

She likes this precise moment when they're alone, a little apart from the others, and can talk about everyone else. He's amused by everything she says.

When it's like this, just the two of them, of course she thinks about the time when she won't be able to make him laugh, when he won't stay all evening at her side, and she feels her heart contract, and every fiber of her being begs that this won't happen. That it won't be like the shit that usually happens.

A woman approaches them, a little spliff in hand, wafting a strong scent of pot around her. She has perfected the look of a classy tart: perched on sublime high heels, wearing a torn figure-hugging T-shirt signed DOLCE & GABBANA, very long hair, shiny and blond. Killer class, but with a sense of humor. She looks tough and hard, but as she comes up to them she's all smiles. Eric whispers, "She's a friend, a real one, not in quotes." He rarely says anything nice about the people they meet at soirees. Gloria pays attention and holds out her hand, keeping a wary eye on this lady, abandoning for a couple of seconds her usual psychotic reactions. She's looking protectively at Eric, more maternal than sexy. And then, wow, sensational event, she actually turns to Gloria after greeting the famous man, and does the unlikely thing of talking to her when they've been introduced.

"So you're the lucky girl. I've heard lots about you."

A nice husky voice, just a touch of vulgarity, enough to give it some edge. Gloria mutters back: "Only nice things, I hope?"

"Of course. It's unheard of, meeting him several times with the same woman . . ."

Because she really wants to be aggressive, and the champagne has also removed her inhibitions, Gloria looks at both of them and asks without any particular animosity, "You two've slept together, haven't you?"

Eric whistles, impressed. If he's embarrassed, he hides it very well.

"Well spotted, *before*, yes, quite often. But no one ever guessed."

He exchanges a smile with the lady, who confirms this

with a movement of her head, amused. She takes a good look at Gloria. She must have the same sense of humor as Eric because she seems to like the direct approach. She passes her joint across to Gloria, who makes the mistake of taking a long pull on it before blowing it away to her right. It goes straight to the top of her skull, and she loses a frightening number of neurons right away. She has to put her hand out to the wall, as inside her brain is turning somersaults. And at this very moment Amandine, Eric's sister, chooses to come over to join their little group. He points them out to each other.

"You've already met, I think."

A little too much bravado and apparent ease to be entirely sincere. They shake hands. Gloria concentrates on keeping her mouth shut, she's so high and feeling weird. Her eyes are goggling, it's impossible to hold the gaze of the woman now scrutinizing her.

She's beautiful. Well, on the surface. Tall, dark, with regular and symmetrical features. A tilted chin, elegant, chic, upper class. Thin straps, a black dress that's both discreet and remarkable. She holds herself leaning slightly back, a slim body, slow gestures, full of confidence. She then determinedly turns her back on Gloria. Banished to limbo, Gloria couldn't care less. She notes that brother and sister don't look alike physically, but they both have the same air of amused arrogance. Eric whispers, "I'll be back," before accompanying Amandine away. The lady with the spliff doesn't move off at once to talk to important people. She introduces herself, she's called Claire.

Gloria warns her: "I'm so high I don't know whether I'm coming or going."

"Me too. Nice though, don't you think?"

"No, just peculiar."

A well-known actress goes past, considered to be good, but she's very disappointing: all the charisma of a coffee table. Erect and well-dressed, but seething with rancor and frustration. Everyone in this room is hooked on appearances, because only the facade is on their side: beauty, wealth, recognition. But the inner secrets are screaming another message underneath these shells: vanity, loneliness, miserable ambition . . .

They're a gang of whisperers, dropping hints, nothing is ever said out straight or direct. They nudge and wink, lie, conceal, spin. These people are weighed down by their secrets, more than in other milieus, hence the feeling of imminent danger, as if a volcano were bubbling beneath their feet. Fear and shame are gurgling inside them, but they walk head held high, convinced of their own importance.

"So, have you known Eric a long time?"

The lady in the very expensive shoes rouses her from her dream. She is certainly charming, with her upturned nose, her amused smile, her lively brown eyes, her delicate hands, and her air of being a cheeky little girl, which lights up her mature woman's face.

Gloria manages to say, "Since we were in our teens. But I'm too stoned to talk about it."

"A little pick-me-up, then?"

Gloria can't see Eric. She follows Claire into the kitchen, where a whole lot of people are gathered, having a little pick-me-up with straws up their noses. Once they've let themselves go, lost their inhibitions, they look even more ghastly. Claire is joking with a young independent film producer, left wing, prematurely bald. She sets her lines up alongside his on the same silver tray. Her wrist makes delicate movements, she's asking him questions about a project, will he be shooting this summer, and his answer takes forever. He's as depressing as a rainy fortnight. A throwback to the eighties, false candor, totally artificial. Quite sexy with it, if you like men who aren't too bright. Cheaply dressed, tending to go red in the face, can't hold his drink, innocently making his pitch, like a fluffy little chicken opening its beak, asking for its share. Convinced he's got an absolute right to it all. Gloria leans over and takes a long hard snort, "Thanks, that's so cool," and feels terrific. If you don't take it often, the effect is immediate and beneficial.

Okay, too bad, it doesn't matter really, all these squares. She wants to lose her prejudices. She reasons with herself, she's stoned, contented, and quite lucid. *Just try not to get worked up, go with the flow. You've never seen this kind of stuff before, stop being so annoying. Go out on the balcony, admire the view, have a laugh with Eric, stop being on your guard the whole time.*

She tells herself to get a grip, listening to a Tupac track—"Come with me / Hail Mary nigga, run quick see / What do we have here now"—on loud in the next room. She dances on the spot a bit, imagines she's boxing with all these frauds, like a raging Minnie Tyson. *Wham*, *bam* at their heads, everyone. Claire takes out a pouch and starts to roll another joint.

"The key is to take it in turns."

Gloria's starting to warm to her, this decadent bourgeois woman. The penniless producer goes off in search of his girlfriend, who'll be getting jealous, he tells them with a little self-satisfied giggle. Gloria, afraid that Claire might move off too, with her grass and coke, grits her teeth and launches into a hurried monologue.

"You know Eric well, do you? Have you known him long? I hadn't seen him for twenty years, it feels really weird to be here, you can't imagine."

The other woman listens to her attentively and passes her the joint. Nobody has ever acted so considerately in the months that Gloria's been here in Paris. And it matters to her more than her pride will let her admit. To compensate, and considerably helped by the generous lines of coke her new friend lays out every ten minutes, she puts on a real show for her, telling her a mass of things about herself, more or less fascinating or indiscreet.

Finally, Eric reappears, apologizing: "I was with Amandine, trying to cheer her up. Okay, shall we go?"

For once he's the one who wants to leave first. Gloria thanks Claire, a bit too loudly, but the other woman seems to take it well. On the way to the door, they meet the sister. She takes advantage of Eric promising some actor he'll call him during the week to grab Gloria's wrist, look her in the eye, and snarl quietly: "I warn you, this time if you hurt him, I'll kill you, understand?"

Buoyed up by all the coke, Gloria whispers in her ear with a smile: "Taken over your mama's job, have you? So if we stay together, you'll lock him up again? Family tradition?"

The two of them shoot murderous glances at each other, briefly and inconspicuously.

A TAXI'S WAITING downstairs. Eric has a contract with some company or other. Inside the car, it smells of unhygienic old man. Gloria opens the window and gets told off at once: the heater's on. She immediately explains to the driver, "I have to open it or I'll be sick, I'm pregnant, second month, terrible sickness."

The man grumbles but lets it pass. Eric hasn't been following their exchange, usually her tricks make him smile, but he's sunk in thought. Gloria keeps quiet for two minutes, her brain racing with the coke, then scratches her nose and asks, "Your sister, was she moody like that before?"

"And *you're* asking *me* that?"

"Well, she doesn't like me, come on. At least it's out in the open. But I couldn't really care less. About her. I find I'm easygoing . . ."

"Do you realize how high you are? You could be sitting next to the minister of the interior and the editor of *Le Figaro* and you'd be laughing your head off . . ."

"Your pal Claire, on the other hand, she likes me. Dunno why, but she's fascinated by everything I tell her, or it makes her laugh. It's not complicated chatting with her. Do you think it's a trick so she can sleep with you?"

"It would be a very roundabout trick, but why not? Was I dreaming or were you telling her about our past, how we met?"

"How we met, how we broke up. Or, sorry, how you dumped me and broke my heart, how I went through hell on earth, etc. Well, I had plenty of time, you'd vanished for an hour at least. She introduced me to the guy whose place it was, the producer. Know him? A phony, that guy, and she works for him?"

"She has for ages. She develops projects for him."

"Why isn't she the boss? Anyone can see he's clueless. Whereas her, I really like. She told me I ought to write up our story, she said it'd make a super film. And the little producer, he was the same, all over me, he was nodding away, 'Yeah, yeah, could be, could be.' You could put him on the rear dash of the car, he'd nod his head off."

"He's bulletproof, he only makes blockbusters, has for years. For him there's no crisis. What crisis? On the contrary, there are just people who want to be entertained. He makes the kind of films the kids keep going back to see seven times. Not to hurt your feelings, but I don't see how the story would interest him. Not enough Chinese psychopaths bursting in and smashing everything up."

"You haven't heard my new version. I do kickboxing all the way through."

"Still, good idea, though, to write the story. If you feel you can. It *is* a good idea, isn't it?"

"If you say so. But don't get too keen, you don't know how much it might piss you off."

"It would be a change for you. You might be getting bored here with nothing to do."

"Me, bored? Seen the size of your TV set? I never get bored, I leave that to people who are stressed out. But I wouldn't mind making a bit of money. Do people pay you for writing stuff?"

"Don't be childish, of course they do."

"Eric, what's the matter? You're not your usual self. I don't like this, not at all."

He looks surprised. But he knows she's right. They've reached the house, there's a silence while Eric pays the taxi driver, bending down. He gives a big enough tip to placate the old guy who stinks. It's freezing cold, the air is fresh and invigorating. For once it's a pleasure to breathe in Paris.

ERIC'S ENTOURAGE IS getting concerned, taking him to one side, with anxious looks, embarrassed at having to talk to him. They're giving him words of warning, trying to protect him, whispering in his ear. The whole group reacts as one, in a desire to expel the foreign body.

Because what the fuck is he doing with this strange blond woman? She isn't even all that pretty. In eastern Paris there are plenty who are better looking, if he really wants to take up with some working-class girl. She doesn't talk to anyone, and worse, she looks a bit shopworn. Why not go for someone younger? Who'd suit him better? Spontaneously, the group takes the place of his dead parents and tries to fix him up more suitably. It would be in everyone's interests, obviously. They find her vulgar, provincial, absolutely lacking in charm. Not very cultured either! Gloria sees what they are up to, after a fashion. She doesn't tackle any of them aggressively. If people try to talk to her, she barely turns her head toward them. She can feel, and almost see, the fear among Eric's friends when they see her installed like this. In the eyes of the women, especially, she sees immediate revulsion. She sticks out like a sore thumb, so much herself, everything they're afraid of being. Awkward, shy, ill at ease, putting on weight, with a glowering expression. If she wasn't with him, of course she'd feel the pain of their attitude. But he's always at her side, his lovestruck preference protects her, he's with her against the rest of the world. So it becomes a fun game, something between the two of them. He's delighted to see the way she gets on people's nerves. Spontaneously everyone wants to be friends with Eric. So he thinks it's great that one can annoy so many people.

THREE WEEKS LATER, she arrives at the Champs-Élysées half an hour early. She goes for a walk while she waits. A Japanese woman asks her in halting French if she can help her find the way to the Louis Vuitton store. Gloria doesn't even understand what she means, but shakes her head and hurries on. Some kids are in a group around the George V metro station. All boys and mostly black. They're making a huge din and chasing each other around. Apart from being about six feet tall and weighing about a hundred kilos each, they're acting like little children. The windows of the Disney Store are full of fluffy toys in bright colors. Some Saudi women, draped in rich fabrics, only their eyes visible, are waiting to cross the road, their arms full of Chanel, Armani, and Dior bags, and heading for Cartier. Outside the Virgin Megastore, two employees in red uniforms are smoking a quick cigarette on the pavement. In front of all the boutiques, black bouncers in suits watch the passersby.

Gloria ended up emailing her screenplay to Claire a week ago. She started writing it "just to see," for want of something to do. She spent ten days sitting in bars, writing in school exercise books. When she'd got a final version, she spent three sleepless nights typing it all out on the computer. Which made Eric laugh.

"It's all or nothing with you, isn't it? You bugger about doing nothing, then you throw yourself at it full time.

Don't you have a medium-speed switch?"

"I'm not going to spend a year on it, am I? Got to get a move on."

When he came home, he'd sit by the computer, surprised that she didn't want to do anything else. Gloria had kept saying, "I've nearly finished, almost done." And when he pressed her to go out to dinner or a party, she knew how to calm him down.

"Want me to read you the bit where the heroine is looking for her boyfriend all over Paris, and he hasn't even written her a letter to explain?"

"Why the hell did I take you to that party, eh?"

"'Cause you can't stop doing stupid things."

He jumps from one idea to another, frowning.

"Did you ever talk to your parents about the psychiatric ward?"

"Never had time."

After that, there were very few things that she had kept to herself, saying she'd think about them later.

When she's finally finished it and typed it up and printed it out, she asks Eric to read it. Without thinking, happy to have done it, more exhausted than she would have imagined, drained but not relieved. Eric reads the screenplay in one sitting. Then he acts a bit strangely. More loving, but sadder. He says several times that it's very good. Something has come between them like a thin veil. She's no longer a total savage with nothing in common with his world. He's torn between a delighted admiration, "So that's it, all you have to do is want it enough, and you can write!" and a general sense of unease at the problems this is going to cause. Gloria persuades herself that this is just temporary, that he's too preoccupied. But it's their whole world that starts to slip and needs to be rebalanced, detail by detail, raised voice by raised voice. Every quarrel ends with them clinging to each other, and she desperately wants to believe that their embraces will be enough to wipe the slate clean.

Since the party at the producer's house, Amandine has telephoned every evening, and every evening Eric has cloistered himself in the bedroom for hours, murmuring softly to her, making her laugh, or listening to her. It certainly helped Gloria to get on with writing her story. She had to find something to do during those long conversations. One night when she was working away, Eric was pacing around the apartment wondering how to tell her or wondering if he should lie.

"I'm going out to dinner this evening."

"And you're not going to bother me for hours making me go with you?"

"I can see you're working."

"So you're off to see your old flames?"

"I'm going to see my sister."

"Ah. I'd have preferred it if it was your exes. Then I wouldn't have anything to complain about."

She's already checked his telephone, like a suspicious nagging wife, to see that it was indeed Amandine's number that called every night. She felt angry with herself doing this, despised herself for doing it, and thought it was ridiculous after that to be unhappy that brother and sister should find something they shared, needing each other.

A certain distance, almost imperceptible, has sprung up between them. Like the proverbial grain of sand: almost nothing. And all this time, whether scribbling in her notebooks or crouched over the computer, Gloria has convinced herself she's worrying about nothing.

In physical terms, though, they've been getting on better than ever, every week has brought them closer together. One morning when she came at the same time as him, she started to weep, just like the girls in books she had always thought so pathetic—she had felt the tears, enormous, full tears, roll silently down her cheeks. And sensed an emotional weight she had always dragged around with her fly upward, like a moth. Something inside her had come out, a star that should have been there always, but now it could shine and twinkle in her own heaven. A light in an ink-black sky.

During the ten days she spent writing, she persevered, correcting as she went, driven onward by the urge to get it finished, without really thinking about what she was doing. At first she thought it would do her good to look back on her past, to impose some kind of order on it, and to shed light on the wanderings of her damaged self. But it's simply her vulnerability that's expanding and taking control. She feels weighed down by the same lies that only yesterday had protected her. The lighting has changed a little, and everything's different. She'd like to be a girl to whom these things hadn't happened. She'd like to be someone who hadn't run away from home out of distrust. She'd like to be herself, but cleansed of all that. She'd like not to know a whole lot of things she does know, things she is deeply acquainted with in her flesh, and above all, she'd like not to have opened all those trapdoors under her feet.

She'd finally emailed the script off to Claire without really expecting a reply. Gloria had missed an interview about her benefits, she needed to go back to Nancy, and it was slightly depressing to have to move heaven and earth to get them to send her less than €200 a month. Not even the price of a sweater in Eric's world.

Gloria was sitting watching the Disney Channel, entranced by *The Lion King*. She heard Claire come in on the voice mail, and got up to reply. The husky tones congratulated her enthusiastically, said they must meet and have a chat about it. After putting down the telephone, before telling anyone, Gloria put on a disc of the Clash, drew the double curtains, and allowed herself a little dance session in the dark, arms in the air, drunk on this strange triumph, heavy with both promises and threats.

When Eric had come home that night, Gloria was worn-out from having danced so long and with such persistence.

"She called me, she's flabbergasted, it's so great, it's a fantastic story, she cried, she laughed, I've got to go and see her, isn't it brilliant?"

And he lifted her up and swung her around, congratulating her, even more thrilled than she was. But he warned her not to get too excited: "Film people, they're famous for it: they keep stringing you along for months, then at the last minute they cancel, they're cockteasers, you've got to protect yourself." Actually he was getting more excited than she was, and Gloria was proud to have impressed him. But their happy evening was brought to a halt around midnight when Amandine left a voice mail in tears, appealing for help. Eric, spreading his hands in a gesture of powerlessness, sincerely sorry, disappeared into the bedroom for the next two hours.

Gloria's blood was boiling.

"Are you fucking her or what, your bitch of a sister?"

"Don't be stupid. She's really in a bad way."

"Pity it has to happen just when we've got together."

"I don't think she timed it on purpose."

"So it's a new development, is it, that her man's become a total shit?"

"Gloria, for God's sake put a sock in it for two minutes, try and understand."

"Are you looking at me? Do I look like someone who wants to understand or do I look like a chick who's just had some fantastically good news and wants to pass a happy evening celebrating?"

"What am I supposed to do, hang up on her?"

"Yes! I want you to tell her you've got your own life to live, and that she can sort out her problems herself. Can't she leave him, don't they have any doors, so she could just walk out?"

"She's got kids, it's not so simple."

"Oh, of course you're right. There's the big house, the sports car, the family château for holidays, and she might miss all that. But I won't call her a tart in front of you, in your family there's a different word for it." She gets up, bursting with fury, she's angry at herself for it, she's losing her mind, and in all this the only clear and tangible thing is her anger.

"Just call her back, your tart of a sister. Call her back and tell her that thanks to her we have a fight every night, she'll be thrilled to bits, the bitch. It will give her the feeling that she exists."

Until that night Gloria had managed never to lose her temper on this subject, avoiding it as scrupulously as possible and never saying anything disobliging about Amandine. But once she'd stepped over the mark, she was going to bring it up every night from now on.

THE PRODUCTION OFFICES are on a street off the Champs-Élysées, and the staircase leading to them is so huge a herd of cows could easily stampede up it. The banisters are highly polished, there's a thick red carpet, the stair rods are gilded. Ridiculously fancy.

The secretary is a pretty smiling blond with a slightly impertinent air, just fresh and chirpy enough to be this side of charming. Gloria sits and waits, hardly daring to look around at the posters of successful films. She leafs through *Gala* magazine, all about stars and their pregnancies, and the *Officiel du cinéma*, full of obscure articles, fantastic budgets, and unnatural couplings. People walk through the anteroom, papers in their hands, they make unfunny jokes to the secretary who shrieks with laughter. You can tell that they're putting it on, forcing themselves to be in a good mood, but there isn't much relaxation about it. They particularly like to make gags about sex, so that everyone can tell they're cool with that. In fact, it spreads the unease, because the whole place stinks of false cleanliness and true frustration, which grips you by the throat and reduces the amount of pure air.

Claire arrives in the hall, a good half hour late, big smile, outstretched hand. She's wearing a sky-blue outfit today with white boots, replicas of a 1970s model. Classy. She shakes Gloria's hand and takes her into her office.

A room that's way too big, with a sheet of glass at least two meters long perched on a black metal structure. The shelves are full of books, screenplays. And there are posters of films and photos taken with "friends" at Cannes. A huge portrait of Pasolini covers all of one wall.

"For crying out loud," Gloria says to herself, "is that really at home here?"

"Your script's terrific, very filmic, very rhythmic, the dialogue's funny and the characters are attractive."

Gloria wonders how a screenplay can be anything other than filmic. She's heard all this already on the phone. She presumes that if she's been called here, it's because her script really is okay. They must love it. Drowning under these vague compliments, she sinks into a little black armchair and the conversation carries on before slowing down. "I haven't sweated so much over something since I was in school," Gloria says, concluding it. Luckily, Claire suggests they have a beer, then another. Followed by vodka.

The boss arrives, the little man with the hypocritical smile, the school geek with the timidity of a weasel, the inhibitions of someone who doesn't have the courage to act on his aggressive feelings, but bides his time until he can strike, when, for instance, your back is turned. Gloria gets his number at once. He comes in, holding a screenplay across which he's written BULLSHIT in big red letters. He holds it out to his colleague with a weary expression. "It's just one damn thing after another, call him and tell him no way can I take it." Gloria keeps quiet and looks somewhere else, sipping her beer. Then he starts to gripe about some "woman who came for a night out with us" and then complained she hadn't enjoyed the evening. Evidently, this isn't done, and he'll never forget this faux pas, sooner or later she'll pay for that. Gloria wonders whether in all this performance something is going on subtly, directed at her— she's not sure about this—or whether the little producer genuinely hasn't noticed her sitting there in the middle of the room, with an appointment to see him.

In the end, he condescends to become aware of her presence and for the first time in her life, Gloria finds herself facing someone who has such power over her that she doesn't listen to her instincts. Which would have told her to drink up her beer, pat him on the shoulder, and say good luck, sort it out, and take herself off home. Not get mixed up with them. Not to ask herself why Claire, sitting beside him, is looking at him as if he's Baby Jesus. The power of power. Not to ask what the silences in this room are hiding, not to hang around. Only, she wants to know if she's going to be paid. It's like when you've sat down to play for money and started winning, and you want to see how far your luck will hold. So she pretends to be interested, simulates politeness, and already she's telling herself off for plastering a smile on top of the nausea she spontaneously feels, as she listens to the siren voices. After the compliments, the little producer is listening to his own voice as he drones on, gets mixed up, contradicts himself, spills out platitudes. Gloria listens to this meaningless speech for so long that it really feels like hard work, then she takes advantage of a pause to ask timidly: "How much?"

The little producer gives a start. That seems to excite him, so after another half hour of platitudes, she plucks up the courage to ask him if he wants to buy her script, and for how much. She's mentioned money. Madness. He goes bright red, he's delighted, he's in a real-life situation, dealing with this girl from *working-class* France, a girl who asks *how much* when she's been told they like her script.

Ah, but it's not so simple, she's told. People don't just

buy a screenplay "like that," it has to be "polished." Gloria looks around, holds back from making any comment, but doesn't see what the point is of showing off how rich you are if you're going to throw a tantrum at the first request for money. Or perhaps that's just the point? So that she can sense that she'll get some, but first of all she'll have to crawl, that it's within reach but she'll have to do everything they ask her.

Claire passes her a fifth beer, and Gloria asks again: "So when *do* you pay?"

"When we sign the contract."

"And when do we draw up a contract?"

"Once the screenplay has been perfected and we're convinced it's worth investing in."

"So until then, I have to work for nothing?"

The little man smiles, that means yes, she's got it. The secretary pops her head around the door and whispers he's wanted on the phone. He gets up and goes off to his office. Gloria doesn't realize this, but at least she's had the good fortune to be in his presence for more than thirty minutes.

THEY'RE SMOKING PIPES of pure hash on their balcony. She watches the streetwalkers coming and going on the pavement below. Eric is looking up at the moon, where the stars are shining.

"He's a shit, isn't he? Comes on like some captain of industry, I-rule-the-world. Typical left-wing bastard. When he's talking to me, I feel like he's a missionary who'll explain how to pray to God, so my soul can go to heaven."

She's groaning, but trying not to make too much noise, and follows Eric back to sit down in their living room, unable to concentrate on anything except her project. Either it'll get made, any minute, or it will vanish without a trace. For her, that means a difference of several thousand euros. She forbids herself to get excited, while holding herself like a machine gun, full metal jacket, ready to blast the opposition to smithereens. Eric flips through a few foreign TV stations and stays in front of the set till four in the morning. His show is in a rut, he'd like to find a good idea to suggest for next year. He's patient, casual even.

"He's supposed to be left wing, I thought you'd have some fellow feeling with him."

"Yeah, sure he's left wing, the prick. He knows he's no Einstein. He feels depressed that he's not cool enough for the circles he runs in, so he wants to get down there with the proles, and he thinks that someone like *me*, being a poor scrounger, will be so thrilled he's deigning to consider my case that I'm going to lick his boots forever and ever, amen. Well, he won't be disappointed when we meet, pathetic, incompetent cocksucker."

"Can't you just calm down for a couple of minutes?"

"No, dammit, it's war, and you ask me to calm down! Is he giving you bribes behind my back or something?"

"You should be *glad* that you know you've written a good story and found someone to sell it to."

"Not my style. Don't mistake me for some poor dumb hippie."

"No chance of that."

He pulls her to him, they lie down on the couch side by side and watch presenters of every nationality strutting their stuff on TV.

And lo and behold, it's easy, it's magical again, just the two of them. They recover their good mood, find the right words, and their gestures are comforting. She makes a real effort to control herself regarding Amandine. Eric is once more considerate, attentive, and funny. It's a kind of remission, the idyll is back, they want it to seem like convalescence. He advises her to use his lawyer, but they'd had lunch with him, and Gloria thought she'd pass out before they reached the coffee. Too unpleasant, too full of himself, and arrogant. Another guy who took three hours to express a simple idea. She'd rather be cheated than turn to someone like him.

"YOU KNOW, MY dear Gloria, if this film doesn't get made, I won't be the one losing sleep over it. It's not me that will wake up in despair tomorrow morning. It doesn't matter to me. Think about it."

Once more, her instinct tells her that the right thing to do at this point is say, "No, me neither," get up, take her bottle of beer, and exit.

The little producer sighs, exasperated, then leaves his office. Gloria stays sitting there, looking at her contracts. Claire comes in after a while, drinking coffee from a plastic goblet. She looks drawn.

"Is it true you don't want to sign? We can't start on anything without a contract you know."

"My lawyer screamed bloody murder when she saw these papers. She told me I shouldn't sign. I don't know what to do. The boss, he just went out and said if it wasn't signed by tomorrow the whole deal's off."

She'd like Claire to tell her he'd never dare do such a thing, but from her expression she realizes he absolutely would. Someone who takes weekends off from midday Thursday to Tuesday morning is surely capable of canceling plenty of things.

Before she leaves, she picks up a big black felt pen and signs all the documents. Everybody has warned her this is just what not to do.

She's opened a kind of door inside herself. She's got something to lose now, for the first time in many years. Having this screenplay, being dependent on that stupid little man, who says every week that he's going to put it into production, so he'll buy it, and enable her for the first time in her life to earn some serious money. She went into this as if she'd just carried out a stickup, tossing something off in a fortnight that would make her enough to buy a new car. But it's not so simple. For weeks now, he's been stringing her along, calling her in, making her wait outside his office, making her accept all kinds of unpalatable things, swallow covert insults. And yet she keeps going back. Because she *wants* this film to be made. She keeps her smile fixed in place, the first lesson in hypocrisy, never stop smiling at this stupid fucker. She doesn't realize in fact how much it's costing her.

SHE DOESN'T REGRET it right away, on the contrary. For several weeks she's regularly congratulated, invited, made much of. They sign her first check, she's sorry she's not back in Nancy now, to be able to roll into the Royal yelling, arms in the air, fist clenched, "Here I am folks, let's celebrate and drink to the producers." Eric shares her excitement, genuinely. But the sum of money means nothing to him. Five thousand euros, that's pretty much peanuts for him. She calls Michel but, as usual, it's Vanessa who answers and you have to put up with her for ten minutes before she passes it over to her man. Yes, he's glad for her. But Gloria doesn't dare show as much enthusiasm as she'd like. They haven't seen each other for months, he sounds washed-out, no doubt high on dope since this morning, doesn't seem to be paying much attention, he's probably reading his emails while he chats. In the end, Gloria tells him her story, pretending it makes a good anecdote. And Michel congratulates her, kindly, but without seeming that involved.

When she arrives at the offices now, the secretary jokes with her, people offer her the odd joint or a glass of bubbly. She's the coming thing, the surprise hit, she's written the screenplay of the month, the thing the boss is currently keen on. He calls her in every five minutes, gives her some demo tapes to choose the good one, the best. He listens to her opinion, he finds her impressive, spot on. She isn't fooled, she's not going to amuse him for long.

What she underestimates, dangerously, and what Eric can't guess, is that by spending hours retyping a line of dialogue here, a description there, reediting the scene from the hospital or the location of a party, adding depth to one character or another, this screenplay, taken on as a lark in the first two weeks, has become transformed into something else. She's becoming attached to her baby. But it's just a mass of words printed on paper, nothing more. She goes back to it regularly, goes plunging back into those past days, looking for more material. It waltzes inside her flesh, she feels off-kilter. She's feeding this screenplay with herself, she's stripping herself bare in it. Without realizing, without knowing that it counts, she spends all her time absorbed in this and doesn't protect herself from anything.

One day the producer wants her to come and meet this director, "just to see."

"I don't need to see," Gloria tells him. "He's a total zero, it's common knowledge, there's no need to go and have a meal with him. I'm not going to change my mind about his lousy films by watching him chew his lunch."

"You *are* going to go along, he *loves* your story, he wants to meet you, and I want him to make this film."

"So where do I come in?"

"You have to finish writing the screenplay with him."

"But the screenplay *is* all finished. We're NOT going to introduce aliens with big boobs, that wouldn't fit with the story, I'm sorry. That clueless director with his tiny prick will just mess up my script. If he were any good at making movies, we'd all know about it. But no, a string of flops. Is he someone's son or something?"

"I really don't see . . ."

"He's not *even* anyone's son, and this is the third film he's going to be allowed to ruin? Do you think I'm an idiot?"

"But I make the decisions around here."

"Yeah, but it's my work."

"And it's my money."

She pretends not to have heard. A little voice inside is telling her, *See, you are an idiot, joke's over.* She pretends not to have heard, because of what she should reply. She carries on, calmly and brutally loquacious.

"I turn up here, you tell me this kid's read the screenplay, without anyone telling me—I think I should point out I'm not the cleaning lady, I'm the woman who *wrote* the fucking screenplay. So if this loser says he'd like to 'cut out a couple of clichés,' you'd be happy to pass that on to me. That's either stupid or it's mean, either way it's not surprising if it really makes me mad."

"Listen, your story's fine, but the public's getting a bit blasé about reality shows now, you need to put it into the hands of a pro."

She simply swallows her wrath this time, while fixing him with a glare.

The little producer hates it when she throws a tantrum. He likes to humiliate her, make her wait around, make his shitty little observations. He likes the idea of putting her into a harness with this young director on her back, just for the fun of seeing her struggle and get beaten. But he doesn't like her losing her temper in his office.

Gloria looks out of the window as she listens to him. His dry little voice goes up a couple of notches when he's crossed. He's acting as if he knows how to keep his cool, but he's getting antsy on his soft leather couch. What she'd really like to do is bite his ears off. His delicate shell-like ears. She'd like to grab his head, hold it in both hands, and bite the ears off. But she stays calm, says nothing. All she's suppressing is festering away in the pit of her stomach, turning her whole life moldy. And it's herself that she's learning to hate the most.

She goes to see Claire, who offers her a little pick-me-up and a good joint. And talks nonstop so that Gloria can't get a word in to complain or ask for help. Claire's embarrassed and annoyed. But quite used to this.

EVERY NIGHT, SHE waits for Eric to come home. She's stopped drinking. She's full of energy. She's given up drink, cocaine, and weed. She doesn't want to have anything in common with the production people, directors, actors, screenwriters. Taking dope gives them all too easily the impression that they're cool dudes, in their sulfurous lives. Whereas they're a lot of cowards, with reduced neuronal circuits. As if they need to make themselves more stupid. Since they like their dope so much, she decides to leave them to it. No more familiarity. She's noticed in their discussions that she's gotten too relaxed. With the alcohol, the spliffs, the coke. She mustn't let them colonize her, she must keep her distance. Now that it's far too late, she finally thinks of protecting herself.

Eric selects a disc by Funkadelic, she wanders around for a few minutes, makes a pot of tea. She wants to give him time to decompress, but she wants to tell him everything as well.

"Today, what I did was I headbutted this director. You know the one I mean, the kid. We were in the Japanese restaurant. And before we left, I couldn't take it anymore. He stood up, he must have thought I was going to kiss him. I was so furious, I took a deep breath and gave him the headbutt of my life. He fell over backward onto these two posh old women. Like in a film, in fact. Just like that."

"And the producer, after that?"

"He's stopped answering the phone. It's been days now. I'm not in his good books anymore. Him, Claire, they're not talking to me. I daren't go back. Of course, I've thought about it."

"You didn't tell me all this before."

"It was so predictable that this would happen. I'm a bit ashamed, I admit."

"And now you're depressed."

"No, I'm going to pull out of the project. I'm going to see if it interests someone else, and if not, I'll get, oh I don't know, some friends to read it."

"Gloria, you can't take your screenplay back just like that. You signed a contract, you got paid."

"Yes, I can, it's my story, and just because of €5,000 I'm not . . ."

As she says this, Gloria realizes it's not true. There are some moments like that when everything teeters on a knife-edge, they stick in your memory, intact forever. The red double curtain in the apartment, blazing with color because of the setting sun, the sound of George Clinton, the croc-skin shoes Eric wears when he's on TV, although you never see his feet. The sachet of Earl Grey tea, the green cups.

It's what she has never been willing to admit, but it's been lying in wait for her, pulling faces, ready to fall on her at this very moment. She's been fired, like a stupid little idiot. From her own story.

She had thought they wouldn't make the film at all, she was ready for that. What she hadn't thought of was that they would make it, but without *her*. She didn't have enough faith in her own screenplay for that. It was a strange feeling, and, above all, what she didn't realize was how strongly you can get attached to something you've made, produced, brought out from inside yourself. It was the first time she'd felt she owned something. And now she was dispossessed. Let them give her back her story and leave it at that.

The first night, she thought she'd be able to get over it. The first week, she made a real effort. Shrugging her shoulders, laughing that, anyway, she's had her €5,000, so let's wait for another check if they make the film, and don't think about it anymore. Give up, move on. Just some words strung together, don't go breaking your heart over that.

To console her that night, Eric says things she thought she'd never hear. Silly, loving things that strike to her soul, breathe softly on the pain, and make it go away. She promises to rediscover her sense of humor and devil-may-care attitude and not throw a tantrum. When he says these sweet things, the pain melts, it's beaten. All that's left is this fantastic love that Eric wraps around her. The way he kisses her collarbone, the hollows of her elbows, under her navel. Gloria delights in it, lying on her back, and she sings in a low voice the words of old songs she thought she'd forgotten.

ONE DAY, LYING in the bath, reading a magazine, she turns a page and comes across a photo shoot of the company making the film. It feels like being punched in the jaw, takes her breath away. She'd like to be able not to react, to feel less pathetic. She gasps for air. She has the feeling of having awakened old ghosts, presences around her, amplified. Two arms are feeling for her in the dark— two skinny, outstretched arms—wanting to grip her, draw her in.

With every outburst of rage, she calls the little producer on his phone. She insults him, screams at him, invents words to call him everything under the sun. He doesn't change his number. He threatens to complain to the police.

She doesn't exist. In his mental universe, she simply doesn't exist and has no right to anything. He's paid her. He's surprised that she got back in touch, exactly as he would be if the two little Chinese girls who sewed his slippers were to ring his doorbell and ask to see how well they fit. A string of people wiped out from his consciousness, appropriation with violence, and the refusal to see that there's someone else at the other end.

He's perfectly at ease in his impunity, genuinely astonished that anyone could question it. His conscience is clear, he's come to an agreement with it, so that he doesn't need to understand. Understand or see.

He sometimes picks up when she phones. He takes a mournful tone to remind her that there are worse things in this world, much worse things, than having her story stolen. She screams in return, screams into his voice mail too: "Liar, filthy liar, I'll never stop bothering you . . ." She's obsessed. Ever since she was a child, guys like him have been comfortably lounging around on other people's backs, jerking off while they bust someone else's guts. She's obsessed—he'll pay for this, the little she can do to try and ruin his stupid life, whatever it takes, she'll do it. Return to sender, she wants him to feel something of what he's done to her. The terrible contempt for what she is. Return to sender.

WHEN SHE LOSES control in front of him, which happens more and more often, Eric avoids face-to-face confrontations as long as possible. Then, when it breaks out, he takes it. After every outburst he's there to cheer her up. She's like a boxer on the ropes and he's pouring combative advice in her ears.

"Don't have a nervous breakdown just because this guy behaved like a shit. I feel bad now about having ever taken you to his place. But just don't let it get to you! You're not going to let yourself collapse and stay down over a little setback like that. Come on, where's your pride, your strength, otherwise you'll spend all your life crawling on your knees . . . I don't know what to say . . ."

"It's eating me up. It's like voodoo. I'm trying to get over it—give up my rights and not lose my head—because I can't do a thing about it. But I can't help it. It's driving me mad."

"Do you think you're going to have to kill him?"

"Are you sick or what? No way. I don't want to have to remember him every day of my life, rotting away in prison for twenty years. No, I'm going to forget him, digest him, eat him, spit him out, shit him on the ground, I'm going to forget this guy. Completely. Utterly."

"And how long will that take?"

"Could be a lifetime."

She laughs. Herself, she finds it hard to believe how this has choked her. And then she calms down. Till the next time.

Furious, full of venom. But at the same time caught up by a giant hand looming over her, blocking out the light. One day that hand will grab her.

It's become a ritual, she locks herself in the bathroom, squealing with rage, stifling cries so as not to be overheard. She looks once more like the madwoman in the attic. She stares at herself in the mirror, red-faced, deformed, eyes bright with tears. The calm interval was short, and when it all comes back, it's a hundred times worse than before. She scratches her face, her chest, her stomach, hits herself. Her body has become a map of bruises. She bangs her head, then takes a shower and covers up the wounds.

She'd thought she was over it, she'd thought like a fool that love would save her from everything, but her demons have returned full throttle. And this time they're determined to completely destroy her.

It's worst of all when she's outside. She falls into a rage at the baker's when some old granny looks at her (she thinks) in a funny way, or in the street when a bus driver honks at her for crossing the road just in front of him, or in the post office when some woman or other starts making a fuss in a loud voice. The slightest thing and she's off. Crazy with aggression, she goes right up to people. Because she's tall she can loom over them and shower them with insults. And she reads in their eyes their mixed feelings: panic with a large measure of contempt.

Then, calming down, she swears to herself she won't do it again. But there's some kind of internal short circuit, it's beyond her consciousness. There's a button that gets pressed by the slightest little frustration, and suddenly she's screaming her head off. She is a spectator, helplessly watching her own destruction. Paris, an electric city, just accentuates her problems, amplifying her madness.

Eric can see this from the outside and he can predict what's going to happen. He doesn't laugh about it anymore because of the seriousness of her outbursts these days. While she doesn't realize it, he can predict hours ahead that she's going to explode and make a huge scene. He sees her boiling up for it, starting to shake, turning on herself. He's tired, tense, anxious the whole time and keeping watch. Even when she's calm for a few days in a row, he's waiting for it to start up again.

THE SUN'S SHINING. She's wearing some new shoes, fantastic ones, that make her look quite different. Beige, thin straps, high heels but not too high. Gloria looks at her silhouette in the shop windows. She can't recognize herself. She bought these shoes just after getting her second check for the screenplay—because they're shooting the film now. It's fine, nice to be out of doors. People look at her differently, it's the shoes that make all the difference, she looks good in them.

She's forgotten to take her Deroxat pill before leaving the apartment. She has flashes of vertigo, strange ones, nonexistent vertigo. She feels as if she's falling, astonishingly, with the sound of synthetic cymbals clashing. Percussion and zoom, it's not nice at all, she feels sensitive all over. Weird drug. The rest of the time it's been quite good, for the last few weeks she's been taking it, a sort of chemical feeling. It makes her want to talk compulsively, her nerves are both calmed down and alert. A precise, futurist kind of tension. She's been to see a psychiatrist who, according to Eric, has helped Amandine a lot. The sister is now so completely freaked out on antidepressants that she's been to dine with them several times. No hostility or distrust anymore in her attitude, she goes through life openmouthed, looks around at the furniture, smiling vaguely. Gloria feels somehow cheated: you can't feel angry at someone in that state. According to her brother though, this grotesque apathy is an improvement.

The psychiatrist is a young man, charming manner, his office is light and full of reproductions of art. The high window looks out onto a park, his bookshelves go up to the ceiling, bulging with old books. He had listened to her, absentmindedly, looking at his highly polished shoes, and diagnosed "overactive inhibition." Gloria made him repeat this, with a frown: extra-inhibited? She likes paradoxes but this is beyond anything. The guy was quite sure of himself: "You need a little treatment." She paid €120, and almost threw the prescription away, not wanting to have anything to do with this medicine.

But the week after that, she'd ended up rolling on the ground in public. She was approaching the Champs-Élysées from Place de la Concorde, going through the gardens, where there are a lot of embassies, plenty of armed police, and old trees in blossom. And like acid reflux, without warning, her fury had stirred again. She called the little producer. "Hello, you bastard, I'm calling to say the future lasts a long time and you'd better drop this film, because if not, I swear to God you'll pay me what you owe me, hear me, you filthy millionaire, or do you have too much coke up your nose that you can't understand what I'm saying? Bad news, you scumbag, I'm going to be your personal Bin Laden till the end of your days. CAN YOU HEAR ME?" Then she had gone on her way, and the silly man had called her back, with the regretful tone of someone who has nothing to be ashamed of. "Gloria, really, I'm *so* sorry it didn't work out," as if they had been lovers. That was the point at which she started to scream, there in the sunshine, with the crowds of people passing by, spitting into her phone, which she finally hurled onto the ground, smashing it, yelling bloody murder. Then she'd rolled on the ground. A real crisis. When she was little, she didn't do this kind of thing, but she's certainly made up for it after thirty. On the ground, among the passersby, she lay sobbing with hate and impotence, calling out for vengeance and reparation.

When she got home, she looked for the prescription.

ERIC IS KEEPING her at arm's length, he's exhausted. You can see it in his face when he's on TV, his features are looking drawn, he's less amiable with his guests. Amandine's threat—"I warn you, don't hurt him"—ridiculously goes round and round in her head, with intolerable clairvoyance. She swears this isn't going to last, she'll turn back into the girl he came looking for back in Nancy, the one who helped him to be happy.

The first month on Deroxat had come as a long liberation. It's so effective and soothing that she sleeps ten hours a night and another two in the afternoon, and she's dropping with tiredness by midnight. She's steadily losing concentration, that's obvious. Whatever the subject, she can't feel interest in it for more than five minutes. The outbursts of anger and the unhealthy obsessions have gone, everything is sliding away. She's not really there at all, she feels heavy. In no mood to crack jokes. *So this way*, she thinks regretfully, *I'm not going to find my GSOH again.* She's sure that before all this she really had a sense of humor. She wonders what's become of it.

IN MONTMARTRE, THE police are patrolling and there are armed soldiers in the streets, because of the terrorist threat. In a bar where for once there's a mixture of classes, races, and ages, she's waiting for Michel, who's in Paris for two days. He's staying at a friend's apartment with his beloved, up on the hill. The January sales are on, everyone's wearing nice new clothes. A woman is leaning over her buggy, sweet as sugar to her baby, but bitching away at her man. A guy with a felt-tip in hand is looking through the small ads in *Le Figaro*, spread on the table in front of him. A teenager in a pink Puffa jacket is chattering into her phone. Gloria tries to control the paranoid attack she feels rising. No, it isn't the typical calm before a big storm, but she smoked a joint before coming out, already in the metro she was feeling on edge.

He arrives at last. She's glad to see Michel. To come face to face with him again in a bar, in a working-class district, playing with the cardboard beer coaster, is a source of comfort to Gloria. He hasn't changed too much. A little neater and tidier perhaps. His clothes have had nodding acquaintance with an iron. He looks in better form, more lively.

As soon as he joins her at the table, he says cheerfully: "Paris suits you. You've changed, know that? Even over the phone I could tell, your intonation has changed, and the way you move. If anyone had told me . . ."

And yes, she has noticed by the way people look at her that she's changed. She'd been treated as a snob the other day by some tramps, three of them drinking on a bench. She hadn't replied when they'd asked her for money, so they'd laughed at her: "Oh, perhaps the duchess has better things to do!" She'd turned around, genuinely puzzled, to answer back, but the biggest of them had said, "On your way, rich bitch," in exactly the tone she might have used to say it herself. She'd gone on her way, in some distress.

Michel watches the passing girls over her shoulder. He says, "I've always adored Paris."

"So, what's it like in Lyon?"

"More concerts than in Nancy. More pretty girls."

"Things okay between you and madame?"

"She wants to be a mother."

"Ah, well, normal . . ."

"Yeah, I'm in favor. Not going to spend my whole life ducking out of responsibility. But sure, it freaks me out a bit. Mainly because of getting some work. We're living off money from her parents at the moment, so, having a kid . . ."

Gloria says nothing. She can see in advance that the new mother's not going to stay with him. He's too hardcore, too irreparable. A year goes by and it's one too many, then it's like you've got a tattoo—no way back. And Michel has collected plenty of these years that are one too many. *Too late, my boy, we've been playing away too long, and now we've had it.*

It's been months since she sat for hours drinking in an old-fashioned bar. She's missed it. She warms up, feels herself reviving.

Once she's had plenty to drink, she tries to explain to Michel why it's complicated being with Eric, but out of context, it's hard work making herself understood.

"He loves money to the point . . . well almost of veneration."

"Isn't that pretty normal? Otherwise it's hard to live in the city, especially Paris. Since he makes plenty. What's the problem? He doesn't make you do the same as him," Michel replies expansively. Adding: "And you never wondered why you don't admire him for that?"

"No, never. Everything's difficult with him. Going out in the streets, a big deal, everyone recognizes him. It wears me out in the end. Like a bad joke."

"Well, watch out this time, don't spoil it."

"I want it to work out. But I'm not getting there. I can't stand his sister, although I can see she's classy and she needs him, that's normal too . . . but I don't have anyone here. I'm like a kite that's lost its string. It's scary."

She drops her head, tears in her eyes. Michel grips her hand in his, comes to sit alongside her, and puts an arm around her shoulders. He remarks: "You're a bit of a ball-breaker, you know. And it's like you really dig putting yourself through it, don't you?"

"I'm not doing it on purpose. I just don't fit in. I can't manage to fit into their world."

"Even in Nancy you were like that."

"Yeah, you're right, I'm not happy anywhere. I'd probably do well to end it right now, but I don't want to die. I just want to kill everyone else, it's different."

"I know, I've known you a long time. With most people, it just passes in the end. You get older, you've got less energy to destroy yourself. So you calm down and there you are, but in your case . . . Why don't you write another screenplay, since you sold the first one?"

She bursts into tears, he's embarrassed. So much so that it gets to be funny and she laughs out loud. She doesn't explain to him why his remark has touched on her sorest point. It would be a waste of time. She knows that to anyone from the outside, it's incomprehensible. She orders her fifth beer. The Deroxat allows her to drink more alcohol without collapsing. As for her liver . . . They discuss antidepressants, amphetamines, and codeine. The bar's closing, and they stagger along the pavement. She feels absolutely great. Michel waits with her till a taxi deigns to stop, and his presence is familiar, reassuring.

She thanks him effusively: "It's been a long time since I had such a good evening, a normal one, like that. It really did me good to see you."

Finally a taxi pulls over and picks her up, and she waves her hand to him as it moves off.

She winds down the window and puts her head out, letting the air blow her hair as they drive. Sighing. What the fuck is she doing in a city like this, returning to an apartment that isn't home, has nothing to do with her? In a life that isn't like hers, but now that she's in it, she knows that what went before doesn't suit her either.

She's lost her links to her old world, but she has never felt close to the one she's in now. She's torn in different directions, at a loss.

HARDLY IS SHE back home—determined that things will be fine, that she isn't going to go crazy again—than she hears herself begin to scream. She rolls on the floor in front of him, she starts hitting herself. He's used to it, takes her in his arms, calms her down. There isn't any sign of love in his gestures now, just a resigned habit. It's as if he's wounded. She doesn't want to make him feel like that. So she screams even louder.

Later, deep into the night, she wakes up bursting with rage. Against him, against the world he's in, against the people he sees, against all that money, against herself, against Michel, against the little producer, against Amandine. But essentially, against herself. She gets up and starts to hurl plates against the wall. One by one, she breaks a whole pile of plates, making a racket. Sobbing. Eric doesn't even get up. She goes across the floor, barefoot, thinking she'll walk on them. But at the last minute she sees herself and realizes it's just to punish him for not coming to console her. So she calms down. Once more, shame, regret, the feeling of everything getting away from her. She goes to fetch a dustpan and brush and sweeps up the fragments of the plates. Without cutting herself. She's tired enough to go back to bed and drop off to sleep.

Eric's starting to crack up more and more often, and yells back at her. That's like a trigger: shout louder too! And then it degenerates. One February afternoon, when the sun is shining, he punches her full in the face, in a fit of desperation. She falls over backward, still surprised and outraged that men can pack so much energy into bodies that don't look so big. Then she screams, hoping to make him feel guilty, as he shrugs his shoulders: "Can't you see what a total asshole you are?"

The honeymoon's over. The last remark leads straight to the same old recriminations.

"Listen, Blondie, thirty times a day you shout at me for having money and giving it to you. *Thirty times a day*. If it's so horrible, why don't you just get out? I can't stand being yelled at anymore."

Exactly the words she's been waiting to hear, all this time: *get out*. Hearing them, she throws herself on her back, and bangs her head repeatedly on the floor. Eric leaves the room, and puts on the loudspeakers next door.

He pays extra attention, these days, to everything he says. It has gradually come over him. He chooses his words, his arguments. To try and avoid starting her off again. He doesn't insist now on her coming out with him to dinners or soirees. He's too afraid she'll make a real scene, a scandal that'll turn out badly. Or kill herself in the middle of a dinner party. He hardly goes anywhere himself, she's gradually extinguishing him. She knows that people are gossiping about this, in his circle, saying that he's finished. Because of her. The crazy woman. They did warn him. Everyone feels sorry for them. It makes her mad with rage to hear echoes of this. Because it is only too fucking true.

She doesn't have the courage to walk out. She says she doesn't know where she could go. And it's hard for him too to give up the lovely dream they had. So he waits. Perhaps he's still hoping it can get back to "the way it was." As with any addicts, they kid themselves that it's possible to start over. Just like junkies who keep searching in vain for the kick they got from their first hit, but now can only experience the exorbitant demands of their habit.

THAT EVENING, IT'S cold outside, absolutely freezing. It's the beginning of the weekend, Eric has come home, and she is shouting at him before he's closed the door. He says nothing for a moment, then goes to open the windows wide, spreads his arms, and it's his turn to start yelling at the top of his voice.

"Look at all the good you've done me. You never stop moaning, you're a burden, the only fucking thing I've done wrong is to fall for you and to love going to bed with you, the only fucking thing, do you hear me, bitch? You're scared of everything, all the time, the only thing you've got any energy for is to get on my back, and apart from that, you're a deadly, toxic ball-breaker. So what exactly do you want?"

His arms outstretched, he's yelling like a lost soul. She replies nastily, through gritted teeth, in a trial of strength, to show she's not impressed.

"So sorry to be unhappy, I see that it isn't the fashion among the pricks who make TV shows to have feelings. You're obviously not the sort to let emotions enter into anything."

He's crouched down beside her, head in hands and groaning. She remains hard and full of hate, but seeing him so destroyed, so battered, and his eyes in torment because, after giving all his love to a woman, he can't make her happy, she is wounded to the core at having done this to him. In return. Giving all her love to a man and only managing to make him end up groaning and rolling on the floor. And it had been such a great love story only a little while ago. She attacks again, she knows she should stop, but she attacks.

"Would it suit you better if I did the same as your sister? Lobotomize myself, to stop you thinking? Is that your idea of how life should really be? Run away and bury yourself alive so as not to disturb anyone else?"

"Gloria, stop it, I can't stand anymore of this."

She doesn't like his tone or the new calm expression with which he says this. Now that she knows it's imminent, she's terrified that he's going to leave her and yet that doesn't calm her down. On the contrary.

He stands up, every one of his movements is slow, as if premeditated and heavy. "*Your* pain, the only thing that counts around here, you've got a monopoly on it, *you're* the only one who's really suffering, is that it? I don't know why anyone would feel sorry for you, since you never try to escape from it. From *your* identity, *your* pain. That's all there is. If you didn't have it, you'd be lost, you'd have nothing at all."

She has been trying to lose all his esteem, his affection, his love, and when it happens, it hits her so hard in the pit of her stomach—it's agony. If she had any sense of humor left, she'd make herself laugh. But she's punctured, empty, and her cloud is vanishing inside the hole.

Some magical instinct makes her think she should get up, even while she's still sulking, get up to change the disc. And it's because she's standing upright beside the shelf with the CDs, which is next to the window, that she's able to grab his sweater when Eric makes a dash to jump out. In extremis. Gloria reacts before she even understands what's happening, she only realizes when she's hanging on to him with both hands, and he's hanging out over the void, seven floors up.

She's managed to stop him from falling, but is now clinging on to him, she still can't believe he did it. She's holding both his hands, they're like acrobats. That's the first thing she says, in fact, the situation is enough to stop her fighting, she turns herself immediately into some kind of professional, a nurse, a fireman, lying expertly through her teeth.

"I've got you, I've got you, don't be frightened, okay? We're like acrobats, no problem. Can you find a foothold? No? If you could, you'd have done it already. Don't worry, I'm holding you, okay."

Like in a Hitchcock film, except that he's heavy and very real, and her hands feel slippery. She holds firm.

He looks at her, straight in the eye, suspended over the chasm. Without any reproach, fixedly, he's given up on everything. She looks down at her feet, mustn't slip, helps herself by pushing her knees against the wall underneath the window. She pulls with all her strength, her hands threaten to slip along his wrists, but that doesn't make him blink.

His eyes remain fixed on hers, at the time she had other things to think about, but afterward that gaze would haunt her. He doesn't want to die, but he no longer has the strength to fight and get himself back up the slope. He doesn't hate her. He doesn't blame her. He's like a child who's been tortured by his mother. No reproach and no guilt in his gaze. Just a wound. Wounded tenderness. Just the refusal of someone who's been wiped out. Something worse than hate, indifference, or reproach. At that moment, just deeply injured tenderness.

Cautiously, she allows her feet to slide along till they are against the wall, takes the strain on her thighs, leaning back, draws strength up out of her heels, up into her shoulders, and gives another heave. The last one. Eric is now high enough up to get his elbows onto the windowsill and to haul himself up painfully. The first centimeters are agonizingly conquered, seconds last for hours. Then they both collapse heavily back inside the apartment.

They lie there, out of breath on the floor of the sitting room. They're not yet in the grip of terror. It takes a few minutes before they can realize what has happened and feel frightened to death in retrospect.

Gloria looks up at the ceiling, it's slightly cracked in the center. A voice inside says, *Right, everybody out now, it's over, it's finished, that's it.*

She'd like to be able to apologize, but she has apologized so often these last days, she's sworn so many times, held in his arms, sworn she won't do it again. She turns her head sideways, sees him in profile, his eyes are shut, a few tears are running down his cheek. She realizes that he's waiting for her to go, and she stands up slowly.

She sits up, then gets to her legs. The fear has ravaged her whole body, she feels stiffer than after a week's hard training. A deep calm has overtaken her, as usual after a crisis. A frozen despair.

SHE GOES DOWN into the nearest metro station. Because it's warm, because there are plenty of people, she can sit down without spending any money and nobody will ask her what she's doing. She takes line three, the first train that arrives. A young lad, rather pudgy, circles under his eyes, wearing a hoodie, looking more like a poor dingbat than a hip-hop type, stares insistently at her. She gazes out of the window so as not to meet his eye. She doesn't know where to get off. She has nowhere to go, nowhere, nobody.

This kid keeps on staring at her. He ends up giving

Gloria the weird impression that her new life has already come to look for her, making friends in the metro, people more or less as lost as herself. They'll end up hanging around together for a few days, long enough to be separated by the police or someone else, keeping each other company, wandering souls. Getting picked up forcibly when the weather's too cold, being hosed down in some refuge, having their things stolen. Then carrying on again next day. It reminds her vaguely of something, but she's no longer so young, times are different and the "fun and freedom" side of that kind of life doesn't strike her that strongly today.

So the worst has happened and here she is. Right in it. No point fretting now about being on her own, without any money, a homeless person. This is it, she's reached rock bottom.

She remembers that OTH song, "Euthanasie pour les rockers." But even that doesn't exist. A place where people like her can have an injection to put an end to it all.

Gambetta metro station, three-quarters of an hour later. She gets out. The hooded kid follows her, he still hasn't taken his eyes off her. Going up to her, he addresses her feverishly but confidently, "Love your tits, wanna go to bed with you."

Gloria stiffens and expects to explode as usual, making a scene and alarming the security people in the metro before getting chucked out like a nutcase. But for once, she remains quite calm: "I haven't got time for this, just fuck off, why don't you."

From close-up the kid smells of sweat, his skin is awful,

his face is covered with spots with white centers. But underneath the acne, his features are actually quite good, and he doesn't look as unpleasant as all that. Off his rocker perhaps, a bit mad, but there are traces of intelligence in his face. He insists: "I just wanted to go to bed with you."

She frowns, indicating bewilderment: "Hey kid, didn't you hear me the first time? I'm a girl, not an animal, and I said something. What don't you understand about fuck off?"

She speaks quite close to him, she's gabbling a bit but not getting really angry. Too tired. Or perhaps her demons are having a rest, thinking they've put in some overtime today—now that she's alone and feels like crying.

The kid looks at her then mutters that she's a nutcase before moving off, talking to himself, hands in his pockets. She smiles and follows him with her eyes, wretched waif, and now she really is alone and in the dark. The demon of anger has left her, having drunk its fill, and is off in search of more exciting prey.

The cafés in Place Gambetta are all off-putting modern places. Gloria doesn't have the strength to go any farther, she just goes into the first bar she finds. She orders a beer at the counter, then goes downstairs to phone Michel.

She wants to tell someone that she's out on the street and unhappy. She's relieved when he answers in person.

"I'm not bothering you, am I? I'm in this bar, hardly any money left."

"Say, Gloria, great to hear from you. It's been a while."

"I'm not in a good place. I don't want to ruin your evening."

"Oh, so am I. So don't worry about disturbing my mental state. I'm back in the shit. She's left me. She's gone to her mother in London. And I'm back in Nancy."

"What?"

"She got fed up. Well, actually, she met someone else. She didn't tell me, I found out. On the pretext I was doing heroin again—come on, it was just three or four shots! *You* can understand how pissed off I was getting, I needed a bit to make something happen, you know. Next day, she gave the landlord notice on the apartment, packed her bags, ran back to mama, and next thing I know she's engaged to some square. Rock was fun for a few minutes, but she couldn't take too much of it."

"And you're not heartbroken."

"Yeah, yeah I am."

"You don't sound it to me."

"You want the truth? When she said, 'Game over, take your stuff and get out of here,' I thought I'd die, that she was the love of my life, I wanted to have a kid with her . . . And then once I was on the train, instead of crying my eyes out, I felt relieved, I have to admit it. I don't want to live in Lyon, don't want a job, don't want to be a daddy, and my fiancée was starting to get on my ass. So I should really be quite grateful to her. But that's enough about me, what about you?"

"Shit, I'm really sad for you. But it's lovely to hear your voice. Something tells me we'll soon be seeing each other back at the Royal."

"Have you been having scenes with your man again? Punched him in the face?"

"No, in the balls and really, really badly like I usually do, but this time, I absolutely thought I was more in love than usual. Well, that's life, my life anyway, that's the way it is."

"Gloria, don't be stupid. Go and see the guy, tell him you love him and stay with him. You know it, I know it, everyone knows it: he and you are meant for each other."

She's standing up at the phone. Behind her people come and go to the washrooms, there's the regular sound of the swing door which bangs a few times before closing. She can see the big phone directories, yellow and white, fat, torn, with writing all over them, they date back to the last century. The telephone's an old-fashioned coin-op one. The light's yellow. Listening to Michel telling her she and Eric are a sensational couple has a weird effect. He carries on.

"Listen, I know when you saw me with Vanessa you realized right away it wasn't going to work. I could see from your face. I didn't want to hear that, but I knew what you were thinking. But with you it isn't the same. You've got to go through with it, change your life course, do you see what I mean? At our age, we have to take the right fork in the road."

"Oh, stop making me feel bad by going on about it. It's over, it's too late. I'm outside, he doesn't want me anymore, don't know how to tell you."

"So you'll wait another twenty years before you guys get it together again?" Michel's voice is super calm.

Gloria sighs: "Don't exaggerate—are you cross with me . . . ?"

"No, but I'd like to get inside your head and let off a few rockets in there."

She goes back upstairs, feels in her pockets to check she has enough to pay. Some jerk at the end of the counter begins to stare at her. Gloria turns her head and looks determinedly in the other direction.

The guy, far from being discouraged, comes over to her.

Very tall and extremely ugly. That doesn't prevent him trying to pick her up.

"Can I get you a drink?"

"No."

"So you don't want to chat."

"No."

"So tell me what's the matter."

"I've just beaten up my boyfriend. I left him on the ground, drenched in blood. I didn't feel like cleaning up right away, so I came out for a drink."

She thinks she's doing quite well, cheerful in the midst of her tragedy. The guy rolls his eyes and moves off. So it even worked. She drinks off her glass to her own health.

Two hands land on her shoulders and Gloria finds herself facing the café owner, who could have been a rugby forward, a giant, and not nice about it. "Outside, you. We don't want you making a scene here." She doesn't have time or a chance to justify herself, or to shout that this isn't fair. She's out on the pavement, stumbling to regain her balance and not fall on her face. She manages to stagger upright a few paces farther on, near a bench on which is sitting none other than the kid from the metro, the one who wanted to sleep with her. He looks at her, pulling a face. Gloria shakes her head.

"Don't look at me like that. I didn't do a thing. Did you see how that guy pushed me out?"

He agrees with his chin, and gives his big smile again.

"Pity they didn't have any tar and feathers. Were you nasty to them or something? You can't help it, eh?"

She looks at the bar, incredulously, then at the kid who holds out his can of 8.6, good of him really. She drinks a mouthful, sits on the back of the bench, and looks sideways at him. She's heard people say how sometimes, when you've reached rock bottom, you see God or an angel, an apparition in the sky, some kind of life-changing meeting, i.e., when other people have bad things happen, something like a miracle occurs. But when she's down on her luck, providence sends her a useless spotty teenager who's obsessed with sex. Gloria scratches her neck and looks up at the sky.

She says, "You can see the stars for once. Usually in Paris, can't see a thing."

"Can you lend me one or two euros? I'm thirsty."

"Same here. Come to the corner shop with me."

The kid gets up.

"Haven't you got a home to go to, lady?"

"No, I did something stupid, I got kicked out."

"You must be a real pain in the neck if everyone kicks you out. Can you pay for a hotel room for us afterward?"

"Oh, give it a rest, Lost Boy."

The corner shop's run by a Moroccan, it's narrow and poorly lit. She wants classic beer but the kid wants 8.6 and argues about it.

"It does my head in faster."

"Exactly, it does my head in, that's why I don't want it."

The shop owner's not listening, his eyes are riveted to the TV screen, watching a football match.

They sit on a bench on the rue des Pyrénées. Gloria kicks her foot into empty space.

She says, "I can't believe this, that I'm here."

"Cry if you like, won't bother me."

"Very kind, I'm sure."

Then they have nothing to say to each other. On the

other side of the road, a very beautiful Chinese girl, slender figure, leather coat, and steel-capped Docs, is striding up the street. They follow her with their eyes in silence. The streetlamps shed an orange light, it's cold. A big white car glides silently past like a dolphin. A van slows down alongside them. Two men get out and are changing the billboard in the bus shelter. She watches them at work, more for something to do than out of curiosity.

When they leave, she reads the title of a film on a dark blue background, *Bye Bye Blondie* in big white letters. In the foreground there's this daffy girl with jet-black hair. Pretty: small nose, pouting lips, high cheekbones—a total airhead. Behind her, in the background, her boyfriend, with a silly haircut: a trashy sort of male bimbo, but cute as well. Sexy. And of no interest.

Gloria goes nearer and looks at the poster more closely. With her fingertips, she explores the holed lining of her coat. She's expecting to go into shock and have violent convulsions, but no, nothing.

At the top of the poster, under the title, they've written: *WHEN LOVE IS THE CRAZIEST THING . . .*

She murmurs, almost amused, "So they couldn't think of anything more stupid than that. How can anyone be so pathetic . . . ?" The kid looks at the poster. He gets out a Posca marker from his pocket and scrawls in big letters under the title, *UP YOURS*, and bursts out laughing, screwing up his nose and shrugging his shoulders.

ALONE AT HOME, Eric's sitting in an armchair. Quietly. *Let her go.* It's the only possible solution, he's tired. His head's swimming, he's felt stifled now for weeks.

Too much yelling, too much pain he can't deal with. He's breathing freely, without the straitjacket he's felt around him these last weeks. He's full of a clear kind of exaltation, but devastated as well as liberated. There had been something so promising in this story, a saga that he'd loved, sincerely, that went beyond him and had haunted him since his adolescence. When he'd found her again, it had brought him back to life, sure of what he wanted and what he should do. But then it had all turned so complicated, he doesn't want to be destroyed by it. He doesn't know how to deal with it. He thinks about his sister, whom he'll tell tomorrow. She never believed in it. Yet she's used to it by now and has let him go ahead. Still, pragmatically, she has always taken the view that a girl you meet in a psychiatric ward isn't going to make you happy. He wanted to play against the rest of the world, to be right in the face of the evidence, he'd thought this was love. He wanted to take the risk with her and then they'd arrive on the far side, safe and sound. But they'd only managed to drag each other down. It's time to give up. To give in to the damned evidence. After all this time struggling, letting go will be like a holiday. He knows the months to come will be painful, like a hangover. Returning to a reality that he was running away from when he went back to find her. Their story's not romantic anymore, it's just pathetic and sordid. It's terrible, he tells himself, to feel relieved because the woman you loved has left you at last. But that's life, he clears his throat, and thinks about it magnanimously. It happens all the time, and it happens to everyone. It was stupid pride to expect that it would somehow be different for them. He gets up and smokes some grass at the window. Down below, the poster on the Morris column has changed. *Bye Bye Blondie*. His heart contracts. These little blows of chance. What seemed obvious a moment before suddenly trembles and seems to be no more than a mirage.

THE KID SHAKES his can of beer over his open mouth to catch the last drops. He nudges her with his elbow.

"You better go home, lady, it's time for the last metro."

Then he does up his jacket, waves goodbye, still grumbling, and wanders off. Even this clueless idiot has dropped her. Yes, she must be a total pain in the neck.

She doesn't have a centime in her pocket. She looks again at the poster, all that fuss about—well, what? Now she's amazed that she found the energy to get so worked up about it, about the screenplay that got away. The little producer, his pals, his milieu—each as lamentable, disagreeable, and toxic as the other. Acting astonished if chickens sometimes come home to roost. "Oh really, people get angry when they're constantly humiliated? But what else can you do?" Amazed that anyone dares answer them back. "They've got it in for us? But why? And who would give these losers a living if we weren't here?"

Everyone's kindly neighborhood bosses, cheerful owners of everything. Sincerely surprised that anyone could want to get compensation from them. The hell with them all, she doesn't give a damn.

She's full of a new exaltation—and it's certainly paradoxical. She doesn't get angry. She's ready to leave. Let it go. She feels old. She wants to go back to her local bar, find her friends. It's over, this adventure, the scandal, the fuss she made, and all this self-harming, just because she was cheated. She feels older, wiser, ready to set off.

THE DOORBELL WAKES him. He'd dropped off to sleep on the couch, a dead sleep. The window's wide open, outside it's pouring rain. The Taxi Girl vinyl he'd put on before going to sleep is crackling on the song he kept playing over and over when he was a kid: "*Et son regard si triste / une croix tracée dans la chair sur son front*" ("And her eyes are so sad / A cross scratched in the flesh of her brow"). It's three thirty-three, he knows it's got to be her. She's soaked through, standing at the door.

"I didn't mean to come back. But I didn't know where else to go."

"Come in."

He lets her go past, for once she's not attacking him.

"I don't want to ruin your life. I just didn't have anywhere to sleep."

"You saved my life, guess I can put you up . . ."

"Cool, I see you've got your sense of humor back. I'll take off tomorrow."

She'd like it if he objected, say he wants her to stay. But he just goes over to the fridge, helps himself to orange juice, and offers her some. They sit down in the kitchen, he switches on the radio, classical music.

"See the poster down there?"

"I've come all the way here from Gambetta on foot. I've seen every poster in Paris. Honestly, it's like in a sitcom. If God really wanted to stick it to me, he would have done exactly that. Mind if I get a dry towel for my hair?"

"Go ahead, this is your home."

"Don't overdo it, please."

She comes back from the bathroom, rubbing her hair energetically.

"But it's so weird. When I do something stupid, I pay a price a thousand times higher than anyone else, don't I? They could have not managed to make the film, they could have not done a big promotion for when it came out, or they could have advertised it when I wasn't around. But no, it's just the night when I walk all the way across Paris. And, you might say, I've never walked that far before in my life."

"Well . . . and you didn't smash all the glass fronts of the posters to tear them down?"

"Not even. Surprised myself."

"You seem quite calm."

"I walked a lot. And now I've stopped making such a fuss, now that it's totally fucked-up, because I went over the top."

By turns sad and exalted, relieved and torn to shreds, they are looking at each other in silence, hesitating between effusion and distance, between speaking and remaining silent. They're circling each other, without knowing quite what to do. She gets up and makes them tea, fetches the milk from the fridge. Gestures full of habit, her body knows where things are kept, where everything is. Eric watches her move around, his arms folded. Since she's come back, they haven't touched each other.

She avoids his eyes, then declares: "Don't look like that. As if you were responsible for something. Nobody can live with me. Even me. I don't find it easy to live with myself. But I can't leave myself. If I could, I'd run a mile."

"I'm not looking any particular way. I'm just tired. It's been a long day. And don't be so pretentious, I'm going to bed."

He gets up, leaving her alone in the kitchen.

Out loud, to nobody, she announces: "I'm going to have a shower."

Then scratches her head and mutters: "Why did you call me pretentious?"

Under the hot water she closes her eyes and wants to cry, but she must have done too much of it lately, her eyes sting and nothing much comes. She admits to herself finally, what her body already knows: she's at home here, she's in the right place, with him. What she doesn't know, on the other hand, is how the hell they are ever going to be able to make it work.

The bedroom's in half darkness. The moon's shining onto the sheets. He's already asleep on his side of the bed. Gloria lies down quietly beside him and goes to sleep quickly, her head pressed into his back.

The Feminist Press is a nonprofit educational organization founded to amplify feminist voices. FP publishes classic and new writing from around the world, creates cutting-edge programs, and elevates silenced and marginalized voices in order to support personal transformation and social justice for all people.

See our complete list of books at
feministpress.org

THE FEMINIST PRESS
AT THE CITY UNIVERSITY OF NEW YORK
FEMINISTPRESS.ORG